# STRAY CATS

by Guy Winters

# DEDICATION

This book would not be possible without the generosity of Joscelyn Hayes and David Schultz. I simply could not have completed this work without their attention to detail and dedicated support.

**A special note to the reader:**
This story is intended for a mature audience only. It contains adult situations and graphic language and is not intended, nor allowed to be read by individuals under the age of 18.

## What others have said about this book:

"This story had me halfway down the page. Great character development, solid plot and storyline. Absolutely loved it! Very well done!"

"I've loved your character development and how you carefully walked them into a believable relationship. There is so much potential in your characters."

"This is, without a doubt, the best Trans/CD story I've read this past year. Maybe even these past two years. Wonderfully written, the interaction between the characters feels genuine, and it's long enough for you to appreciate it fully."

"I love the feelings I come away with reading this story."

"Three people finding love, acceptance and refuge from a judgmental world around them. I'm touched, and inspired."

"It takes talent to interweave so many characters with their own stories in a story that is so believable."

# =ONE=

Alex Wells walked out of his bathroom wearing a well-worn t-shirt and boxers. He glanced out the window at the street in front of the house as he brushed his teeth silently. It was a chilly and rainy day outside. The streets were slick with rain and a mist hung in the air from all the traffic that whizzed by the house.

Even though it was chilly outside it was rather cozy inside his tiny apartment. Living on the third floor in this ancient Victorian mansion meant that heat in the wintertime was never an issue. Some days he even had to open his window when his neighbors on the floors below decided to really crank up the thermostat. The creaky old relic that housed his apartment and a dozen more had been cut up into mostly small efficiency apartments during Wilmington's urban expansion period in the nineteen-seventies.

Alex walked back into his bathroom and spit into the sink. He looked up into the mirror and felt his beard. He hadn't shaved today but from the looks of things he wouldn't have to. He noticed that his beard was getting thinner and a little finer. It seemed to coincide with the rest of the transformations that have been happening to his body. They all started about three years ago. Alex studied his face a moment. His features were becoming softer and actually looking a bit androgynous. His hips have grown wider and his skin softer, his slender frame, which at one time looked boyish, was noticeably feminine.

Damn it, why couldn't he be just like everybody else? Why couldn't he be just a normal guy?

Alex pushed back his light brown wavy hair and sighed, a gift from his mother he mused with a wry smile. His hair was getting finer and softer too. He brushed the tangles out of his damp hair and pulled the long strands into a ponytail then wrapped it with an elastic hair tie.

He took off his t-shirt and checked the ace bandages wrapped tightly around his chest. None of them had slipped so everything was fine. Well as fine as things could be wrapped up like a mummy so no one would notice his secret. He sighed once again and pulled on a clean t-shirt. He added a flannel shirt over that and then some well-worn jeans. He had to dress in layers, even on hot summer days just to keep his secret well hidden.

Alex sat down at a thrift store desk and looked at his computer screen. The cursor was flashing near the end of a story he was assigned to write. It was for a graduate seminar course and it was due this coming Saturday. He sighed and hit the save key. Maybe he would have time to finish it tomorrow. He was tired of staring at it. Besides, he had to go to class and if he didn't hurry he was going to be late…again.

Five minutes later Alex closed his apartment door and glanced both ways down the hall. There were three other apartments on this floor and he knew from the landlord that two of them had been filled recently. Yet in the three months that he had lived there, he rarely saw any of them and never the person who lived across from him. Alex considered that a moment then he shrugged his shoulders and wandered down the stairs at the end of the hallway.

On the way out of the apartment house Tom Reilly, the landlord, poked his head out of his apartment door. A towel partially covered a head full of auburn hair, still dripping wet from a recent shower. It looked like he hadn't shaved in a couple of days but that didn't seem to matter. Reilly changed his facial hair the way women changed their nail color. It helped that he had a thick beard to match his unruly hair.

Tom was shorter than Alex. But what he lacked in height he made up for it in personality. "Hey Wells, I got a little pot-luck thingy happening this weekend in the backyard. You coming?" Tom winked a watery blue eye at Alex.

"That depends, what time is it?"

"It starts at six so you should be able to make it for a while before you have to work."

"What should I bring?"

"Beer would be nice and maybe some chips." Reilly's words became garbled as he shoved a toothbrush back into his mouth and began to scrub.

"Okay, I'll see what I can do."

Tom shrugged and walked back into his apartment.

"Hey, Tom."

"Yeah?"

"Can I borrow your bicycle? I'm out of gas money and I'm going to be late for class."

"Sure, it's around back."

Alex turned and walked out the back door of the building. Leaning up against the porch railing was Tom's bike. It was a rickety old thing, a throwback to the sixties with wide tires and no gears. Even though it wasn't much to look at it sure beat walking. He rolled the bike around the house and pushed off pedaling down the street. No matter how he looked at it he was going to be late again.

He hadn't traveled more than five blocks when he approached a busy street corner. The light turned green as he came up to the intersection and he kept pedaling to pass through it quickly. Suddenly a car sped up to the intersection and did a soft stop on the red light. It turned and clipped his rear tire sending him flying across the street narrowly missing the back end of a parked car. He landed on his back and skidded several more feet tearing the back of his coat and shirt to shreds on the rough asphalt.

The ace bandage on his back managed to save him from getting any serious road rash but his jacket and the shirt and undershirt were completely ruined. The bicycle, twisted into a pretzel, lay across the intersection, its front wheel still spinning. After his head stopped spinning he sat up yelling. "What the hell! Son of a bitch! Did you even look asshole! Damn it!"

Alex felt the cool damp air against his back then he felt the bandages loosen their grip on his chest. Suddenly he knew everyone would see him, naked and exposed. The thought frightened him. "Fuck!"

Alex started to get up when a middle-aged woman came out of her car shouting for him to lie still as she ran towards him.

"Don't move! You could have hurt your spine! I've called an ambulance, they'll be here any minute." The woman was kneeling in the street nearly beside herself in tears.

"Are you hurt? I don't see any bleeding."

"I'm late for class lady." He tried to get up again but her hands held his shoulders and pushed him back down again.

"Please, just wait for the ambulance, they'll be here any second."

Alex clutched his tattered coat and shirt around his body trying to keep his secret hidden. The ace bandages hung loose across his chest and he pulled at the fabric in a futile attempt to protect his chest.

His mind began to reel with the thought that people would see him, that they would know his secret. He imagined that they would all point and laugh. A freak, a pervert, something to see on the six-o'clock news, his mind was spinning with fear. He couldn't stand them looking at him, this was a nightmare, his worst nightmare. He had to keep his chest covered no matter what.

The woman ran back to her car and pulled a coat from the back seat. While she was gone Alex managed to stand up. He started to walk away but his legs were still a bit wobbly and his head continued to spin so he stumbled over to the curb and sat down. The woman returned and wrapped her coat around his shoulders.

"I said you shouldn't move young man. What if

you broke your back or something?"

Alex just glared at her then he shook his head and looked away.

The ambulance arrived a moment later. They pulled off her coat and wrapped him in a blanket then they loaded him into the ambulance as a police car pulled into the intersection and switched on their flashing lights.

All this time Alex was still clutching his coat and shirt to protect his chest.

"Hey lady, I can't pay for this!"

"Don't worry. It was my fault, I'll handle everything." She handed him her business card. Then she handed her card to the ambulance driver as well. It read Margaret Cummings of 'Dresher, Cummings, and Sanford – Investments and Securities'. "All my contact information is on the card. Just give it to the ER nurse."

Alex stuffed it in the pocket of his jeans. A police officer asked him a few questions, mostly routine, about what had happened and was he hurt, then they released him to the EMT's to take him to the hospital.

In route, one of the medical technicians checked his blood pressure and used a penlight to see if there were signs of a concussion or shock.

The technician wanted to make him more comfortable but Alex refused to let go of his shirt and the remnants of his coat. Instead he pulled the blanket around him like a life jacket.

Once in the receiving area of the hospital he was wheeled into area cordoned off from other beds by a privacy curtain. Several nurses came in and attempted to remove his garments but he refused to let them. Eventually a doctor arrived and seeing the frantic look on Alex's face he asked the rest of the medical team to leave. Alex looked at the name badge on the doctor's coat. It read Dr. Alan Phillips, M.D.

Once they were alone, the doctor wore a stern expression. "What's going on?"

"Look Doctor Phillips, I don't have insurance, okay? Some lady hit me while I was on my bike and knocked me across the street. I'm okay, all right? I just need to get to class. I can't afford to be late again."

"Don't worry about that, the duty nurse will call your college and tell them what happened. In the meantime let me do a routine examination."

Alex sat patiently waiting for Dr. Phillips to complete his checkup.

"Why won't you let them remove your clothes?"

"I just don't want them to, okay?"

"Whatever, aside from a couple of scrapes and bruises, I don't see any signs of trauma. But I would like to keep you here for observation for at least twenty-four hours to..."

Alex interrupted. "Sorry doctor, no can do. I've got to get to class, and then I have to go to my part-time job. You can treat the scrapes on my arm and the cut on my forehead but I'll keep my clothes on, okay?"

The doctor threw up his hands and scowled at Alex then he turned and left the room. A moment later a nurse came in and dressed the scrapes and bruises on his arms and forehead.

About then Margaret Cummings arrived at the emergency room. She was ushered back to see Alex who was still sitting on his gurney wrapped in a blanket along with his tattered shirt and coat. The nurse finished bandaging his wounds and scrapes as Margaret Cummings entered the room.

"Why are you refusing treatment? I pay a handsome fee each month to make sure that my insurance will cover everything."

"I'm fine, look I'm as good as new. See?" He waved a free hand, "No broken bones. I just need to go. I'll be fine."

"At least let me drive you someplace."

Alex lowered his head and sighed. Then he glanced up at the clock on the wall. "Okay, it's too late to go to class so you can drive me home."

Alex followed her out of the emergency room and got into the passenger seat of her car.

"Which way?"

"Turn left at the light, I live on Park Street near 18th"

They sat in silence for most of the way to the apartment house.

She slowed down for a stoplight "What are you going to school for?"

"I'm working on a graduate degree in writing."

"Have you published anything?"

"Mostly small stuff, a few short stories. Nothing much. Here it is. That's where I live. This will be fine. Thank you. I'll be all right."

"Please, call me tomorrow, my cell number is written on the back. I'm so sorry this had to happen."

"Rainy days, Mrs. Cummings. Shitty things happen on rainy days."

Alex climbed the three flights of stairs to his

third floor apartment.  He walked into the bathroom and slowly removed the shirt and coat that he's been clutching against his chest this whole time.

The elastic bandages fell away.  He looked at his chest and sighed.

"Shitty things happen on rainy days."

## =TWO=

It was well known in the neighborhood that Tom Reilly liked to party. That became apparent when Alex attended his first 'full house back yard bash' as Reilly liked to call them. Only the tenants were invited, and one or two of their friends, begrudgingly. The beer flowed freely and the usual fare of burgers and dogs were welcome on Alex's meager salary.

Oddly enough, the one person who didn't attend these little backyard gatherings was the person who lived in the apartment directly across from Alex. Reilly told him it was a girl. Her name was Rachel Thompson.

Reilly nudged Alex in the ribcage and winked at him when he told Alex that his neighbor was a real hottie. Alex grinned sheepishly and nodded. He decided he would judge that for himself. He was never quite sure of Reilly's taste or his intentions, however friendly.

Later that evening, in a moment of sobriety, Reilly went on to say that Alex's neighbor often worked late hours, was quiet, and wasn't much of a party person.

"Which was too bad, if you know what I mean." Reilly nudged him with a bleary-eyed wink. The alcohol was beginning to have an effect on his landlord again.

Alex shrugged his shoulders and chalked it up to fate. If they were going to meet it would happen regardless of any desire on his part. Not that desire had anything to do with it. Perhaps curiosity was more to the point. Rachel Thompson was the one person who lived in the apartment house that he hadn't met. It made him curious, but only to a point. If people wanted to be left alone he understood that more than anyone.

Alex turned around and nearly ran into Amanda Simpson, a girl who had an apartment on the first floor near the back of the house. Her cute face was framed with silky dark brown hair that fell straight down to her waist. She had a cute nose and eyes that sparkled delightfully.

Alex glanced down at her hand as it braced against his arm. Her skin glowed with that soft creamy tan quality that so many girls envied. She laughed brightly as she tried to keep her balance. "Hey Alex, you almost ran me over."

Alex fell back against a tree to keep from knocking her down. "Oh, sorry, I didn't see you behind me. Hey, I haven't seen you in a while. Have you settled into your apartment?"

"I'm okay but you look a little banged up. What happened?" She held onto his arm, now more for the contact than the need for support.

"A car decided to share the ride on the back of Reilly's bicycle the other day. I took a nosedive, did a mid-air pirouette and pancaked in the middle of the intersection. Bet you didn't know I was such a gymnast. The bystanders gave me 2.5 points with a 5% degree of difficulty."

"Ha!" She laughed out loud; it was a delightful laugh that made Alex smile. "No broken bones?"

"None that have shown up yet. So how's work?"

"The market has been going haywire lately so it's kept me really busy."

Amanda told Alex a week ago that she worked part-time as a stock analyst for a brokerage house downtown. She told him that she like the fast paced craziness of it all.

She wore a mischievous grin. "How about you? Still doing the graduate student shuffle?"

"Yeah, pretty much the same, classes, work, sleep, and more classes."

The small talked continued for a while. Alex always liked to talk to Amanda. She was bright and bubbly with a beautiful smile and dazzling eyes. It didn't hurt that she was down right gorgeous either. She obviously worked out from time to time which kept her slim and shapely.

A couple of other tenants stumbled across some tree roots as they walked by talking. They fell against Amanda and she leaned against Alex to keep from falling. Alex smiled sheepishly as he wrapped his arm around her waist and kept her balanced.

He thought about how much he enjoyed her company. He remembered the first day he met her. She was standing in the front yard of the apartment house staring at a large pile of boxes and furniture that were unceremoniously dumped on Reilly's front lawn. He was walking up the front steps of the apartment house as she stood there with a perplexed look on her face.

"Hi, you look a little troubled." He scratched his head with a wry grin.

"They just dumped my stuff on the lawn without even as much as a sorry, or an offer to help me carry it inside," Amanda growled contemptuously.

He offered to lend her a hand and she's been thanking him ever since.

The partygoers lingered in Reilly's back yard for the rest of the evening. By nine o'clock, when Alex had to go to work, things had finally quieted down. He said good night to Amanda and headed off to work.

As for his neighbor across the hall, fate finally dealt Alex the right cards two nights later. Rachel Thompson, the mysterious reclusive neighbor from across the hall, was climbing the stairs ahead of him. He was coming home from his part-time gig at a nearby convenience store. It was nearly two in the morning and he was exhausted. He had spent most of the night restocking the back room.

Rachel Thompson was tall, maybe five-foot ten in stocking feet. As Alex gazed up at her the first thing he noticed were her beautiful legs. They were slender, nicely shaped, and they finished in a cute round butt that sashayed nicely in a tiny skirt as she climbed the stairs ahead of him. He was slowly trudging up the stairs when he turned a corner on the landing and noticed her. He stopped a moment to admire her beauty. Half way up the last flight of steps she paused and glanced back at him. Her long hair had amber streaks running through it as it fell in gentle curls down her back.

From where he stood it looked to Alex like she had a runner's body, tall and graceful without being skinny or awkward. But even taking in all those other features the part of her that captivated Alex's attention the most was her beautiful green eyes. They shimmered in the soft light that illuminated the hallway. There was a sparkle in them that was totally mesmerizing.

She smiled subtly and then turned to finish the last steps on that flight of stairs when she suddenly broke a heel. Alex climbed the stairs quickly and caught her as she started to fall. They both managed to stay upright and when she took a step towards her apartment it became apparent that she had twisted her ankle.

He wrapped her arm around his shoulder and helped her into her apartment. Then he walked across the hall and retrieved some ice in a bag for her ankle. It was a bit swollen but fortunately it didn't look too bad.

Once he got her settled in on her couch he decided that it was late and he really needed to get some sleep so he offered her his cell number if she needed anything. She smiled shyly and thanked him before he closed her apartment door.

The next day after classes, Amanda saw Alex walking up the front steps holding a bag of Chinese carry out as she was coming out of the front door with a shopping bag in her hand.

She offered an impish grin. "Hey, your turn to cook tonight?"

"Sort of. My hallway neighbor sprained her

ankle last night when she was climbing the stairs in heels that are dangerous enough on level ground. I thought I'd help her out with a 'meals on wheels' for the night."

Amanda smiled as she touched his arm. "That's really sweet of you Alex. I'll be sure to ring your delivery service when I get sick too." She added a couple of fake coughs and a big grin for good measure. Then she skipped down the front steps, waved and was off down the sidewalk with a, "See you," and a smile.

What started out that evening to be a bit awkward between Alex and Rachel eventually turned into a lovely dinner. They talked clear past midnight. She had a marvelous smile and a delightful laugh.

Alex didn't see her again for almost a week after that. He remembered that she mentioned once that she worked part time at a bar downtown. Tuesday was one of his nights off so he thought he'd check it out.

Moulin Rouge is a bar on the east side of downtown, and he realized, after he got there, that it was mostly a gay bar. That didn't bother him but still, it did come as a surprise.

Rachel spotted him the moment he sat down at the bar and suggested that he sit at a table near the back. He followed her to the table, which as it turned out, was part of her section. They flirted a bit for the better part of the evening. It wasn't too busy that night so they spent a lot of time talking, mostly about her work at the accounting firm downtown and his classes at the university.

Just after one in the morning she told him that

she was going to get off work soon and she wondered if Alex could give her a lift back to the apartment house. She told him the other day that riding the bus home late at night can sometimes be dangerous and waiting for a cab can take hours once all the bars close.

They got back to the house a half hour later and he walked her to her door. She turned and looked at him a moment. Alex didn't know if she expected him to try something or not so he just stood there, his cheeks flushed and feeling awkward.

He broke the awkward silence with a simple "Good night." Then he turned to cross the hallway to his door.

"Good night." She paused as she watched him fiddle with his lock. "Hey, I just want you to know that I'm not exactly what I seem to be."

Alex shrugged his shoulders and looked at her with a puzzled expression. "Okay."

"I wanted you to know that before anything might happen between us, that's all."

"That's cool. I wasn't expecting anything. Except perhaps that it would be nice if we could get together over coffee sometime."

Rachel tilted her head slightly and smiled. "I'd like that." Then she opened her apartment door. She stood silently watching as he opened his door and went inside. Then she closed her door and the third floor hallway fell silent once again.

The following Saturday afternoon Alex walked into the house laden with plastic bags filled with groceries. The way they hung off of him he looked like an over-eager delivery boy. As he closed the front door he saw Amanda walk quickly from her apartment towards the back door of the building. From what he could see it looked like she was crying.

Alex dashed quickly upstairs and dropped of his groceries in his apartment. He grabbed a couple of sodas from the fridge and bounded down the stairs quickly heading for the backyard. He walked out onto the porch and saw her sitting alone in a tree swing under an old oak tree that shaded most of the backyard. It was clear from her posture that she was upset.

Alex stood quietly a moment and watched her shift back and forth in the swing. She held her cellphone in one hand and wiped her eyes with the palm of her other hand. He came off the back porch and walked across the yard to lean against the tree.

Amanda looked up after a moment and smiled meekly. Alex waited silently.

"Hi," she said softly looking back down at the ground.

"You okay?" He handed her a soda.

"Thanks. My mom just called. My cousin Susan is getting married next month."

Alex walked over and sat in a chair near the firepit. Amanda continued to sway in the swing. Her eyes glistened and her cheeks were still moist.

"That's a good thing isn't it?"

"It is." She wiped her eyes again. "Susan was the one bright spot in my otherwise fucked up childhood in Vancouver. These are happy tears." Her tears continued to trail down her cheeks. "Well, maybe happy mixed with a little melancholy."

"Why?"

"Because my life continues to be fucked up."

For the first time since he sat down, she finally looked at him. "Part of me is incredibly happy for her but the other part of me is a little sad that my life has turned out the way it has. Kicked out of town with a one-way ticket to no-where's-ville."

Alex sat silent for a moment and watched her sway gently in the swing. He figured that something or someone was behind the rough way she was treated, landing like she did on Reilly's doorstep. But he didn't believe in chance or coincidence. Everything happens for a reason. The interesting part is discovering the secret to the puzzle.

He smiled and leaned forward to look her in the eyes. "I think you live a very charmed life, Amanda Simpson. " He wore a big grin as he stood up and opened his arms wide.

She looked up skeptically.

"You got a 'do-over'," he announced broadly.

"A what?"

"A 'do-over'." He dropped his hands to his hips. "It's what happens when the universe deals you a hand that is so terribly wrong that in one fell swoop things are reset and you get to start again fresh. You are truly blessed Amanda Simpson, and that is nothing to be sad about." He finished his announcement with a flourish and a bow. Then he looked up to see her reaction.

Amanda paused a moment and considered his words. Suddenly a smile began to grow on her face. She looked up at him and grinned. Then she rushed over and kissed him on the cheek.

"Alex, you're wonderful! Thank you so much! Of course I'm blessed. I just needed you to point that out to me!" She squealed with delight as she wrapped her arms around him and gave him a big hug.

"No problem Amanda." Alex returned her hug. "Tell your cousin 'best of luck' from me and call me if you need anything."

She gave him one more squeeze and kissed him on the cheek then she released him. "I will, thanks."

He walked over and stood on the porch a moment as he watched her flip open her cellphone and dial a number with flair. Her cousin must have answered because it seemed like she was quickly back to her bubbly self. Alex smiled and walked back into the house.

The next day Alex saw Rachel coming out of her apartment. They chatted for a moment in the hallway. It wasn't much, just small talk. The sort of 'how's your day' sort of stuff that often passes between two people who live in the same apartment house.

Then out of the blue Rachel leaned over and kissed him on the cheek. Alex blinked a moment and stood motionless, looking a bit stunned. He thought he must have a 'kiss me' button on his shirt.

When Rachel opened her eyes she blushed. "I'm so sorry."

"What for? That was very nice. Unexpected, but nice."

"I don't know what came over me. I just had this sudden urge to kiss you. Maybe it was a thank you for the time when you helped me after I turned my ankle."

"You're welcome, anytime."

Alex turned towards his apartment and pulled

out his keys.

"Hey." She glanced down the hallway from side to side. "Can we talk?"

Alex looked at her quizzically.

"I mean in private. I have something I want to share with you but I don't want others to," she shrugged her shoulders, "you know."

"Of course."

Rachel opened her door and led him into her apartment. It was much bigger than his, perhaps twice the size. She had a small kitchen with an island counter off to one side and a living room area to the other side of the room. Next to that was a door that led to a separate bedroom with a small bathroom attached.

Alex walked over to the two windows that looked out onto the back yard of the house. He could see the firepit and the old swings that Reilly built for the last 'back yard bash' down below. Then he turned to survey her apartment.

"Wow, this is really nice." There were pictures on the dresser and a couple of nice paintings on the wall. "Who's this in the photo?" Alex pointed to a man and a woman. They looked like husband and wife, maybe her parents.

"That's my uncle Fred and his wife Abby. They let me stay with them one summer after my father kicked me out of his house when I was seventeen."

"Shit, why?"

"Because of who I was at the time and what I was becoming."

"Huh?"

Rachel walked over to the couch and sat down.

"Sit here Alex. Please. I want to tell you a little

about me. But first you have to promise that you'll not share this with anyone."

"Of course. If you ask me I'll keep whatever you tell me a secret forever."

"Thank you."

She paused a moment, as if gathering the courage to start with her story.

"When I was little, I was always frail as a child. I didn't develop physically like other kids my age. I always felt that there was something different about me, like I was not normal. At least not normal according to what I saw around me, the way normal boys and girls were growing up. When I was ten I had this crush on a boy. His name was Johnny. He was one of the kids in the neighborhood. We went to school together, we were in different classrooms but we saw each other a lot. We often played together when all of the kids in the neighborhood gathered outside for a game or something."

"One night we were playing hide and seek. It was getting dark and Johnny and I were hiding in a bunch of bushes near my house. It was old man Spangler's house. He was widowed and lived alone. I think he worked at the car plant or something because he left early each day and didn't come home sometimes until after dark."

"Anyway, we were hiding in some bushes in his front yard. I guess I couldn't resist my urges any longer and I reached over and kissed Johnny hard on the lips. Johnny pulled away in shock but that wasn't the worst of it. Old man Spangler was standing right behind us and he shouted, 'Get the hell out of my yard you little faggots!'"

Rachel lowered her eyes and glanced away for a

moment. She turned back and looked Alex in the eyes.

"You see, Alex, I was born a boy."

"Huh? You're so beautiful," Alex whispered. "I never would have guessed." Alex's voice trailed off as he watched her reaction.

Rachel looked down at her hands folded in her lap. Her eyes began to tear up. She drew a big breath and shuddered as she let her breath out slowly. She dabbed her eyes gently then continued.

"I hid the fact that I was different from my parents for a long time, but eventually my mother found out. She caught me going through her underwear drawer one day when I pretended to be sick from school."

"I skipped school a lot after that night with Johnny in front of old man Spangler's house. The boys at school were merciless, especially Johnny. That made the whole thing so much harder to take. They would punch me or trip me or push me against a wall and try to choke me. I tried my best to stay away from them but middle school is a difficult place to hide."

"After my mother found out about me she tried her best to 'cure me' as she put it. I went to a bunch of child psychologists who poked and prodded and scratched their heads. They were all a bunch of pill pushing quacks."

"Finally my mother took me to this one family physician and he and I had a long chat. Apparently he had a niece who was born the same way as me so he understood the struggle I was dealing with. He told me that there was really nothing wrong with me. I was shocked that someone actually said that."

"He said that there are people who are born genetically with one gender and psychologically identify with another gender. He talked to my mother and told her that he thought she should support my situation any way she could. After that I started hormone therapy. I began it on my twelfth birthday."

"From then on, I started to identify with being a girl and things went from bad to worse at school. It wasn't the boys that were the worst. It was the girls. Boys can be mean but girls are vicious. They saw me as competition because I dressed nice and looked pretty. Even though I continued to dress like a boy. I guess they saw it as a challenge and took it the wrong way. I was just trying to figure out who I was at the time. I barely had time to think about chasing boys."

"And not all the boys rejected me. There was this one boy who transferred in during the tenth grade. His family had just moved to the city and he was new to the area. He was also very cute and all the girls set their sights on him. It wasn't my fault that he liked me but there was no explaining that to the girls. I can't begin to explain the wicked things they did to me."

"Finally, after the fifth time I came home from high school with bruises and a black eye, my mother pulled me out of the school. I was too ashamed to admit that I had been beaten by a bunch of girls. She home-schooled me until I was seventeen. I got my GED and went on to community college to study accounting."

"When I was still going to high school I always dressed as a boy. When I was at home I loved to dress up in girls clothes, I bought all sorts of frilly things, the softer the better."

"But I had to be careful how I dressed when my dad was around. He wouldn't stand for any of it. One day he caught me dressed in a frilly dress and an apron. I was baking some cookies for my mom and he came home early from work. I had to think fast. I explained to him that I was practicing for a school play. He bought it that time but when he caught me dressed in a nightgown and panties one night it was everything my mother could do to keeping him from beating me and throwing me out of the house that very moment. I left the next day and never looked back. I was seventeen and homeless."

She paused with a sigh. "My father was a brute of a man. I never understood what my mother saw in him. She told me one day that the only gift she was ever grateful for from my father was 'me' and that made me cry." Rachel dabbed her eyes again. "I guess it still does."

"My mom finally got fed up with the bastard because a year after he kicked me out of his house she left him. She lives in Springfield now and I see her from time to time. She's much happier and she has a new boyfriend. I've met him and he's really nice."

"I see why you like to keep to yourself," Alex said softly.

"It's not that I want to hide from anybody, Alex. I'm no longer ashamed of who or what I am. I just find it difficult to open up to people I live around because of everything that's happened in my past. I've had a lot of experience with people judging me and I prefer not to put myself in those kinds of situations again if I can help it. Besides, most people don't understand who I am and prefer not to get involved." She glanced sideways at Alex briefly. "But somehow I felt you would be someone who would accept me and could be my friend."

Alex sat for a moment and looked at Rachel. His eyes began to tear up. Could he tell her? Could he share his secret? What would she think? That he's some sort of freak? Then he realized that she had just shared something incredibly intimate with him.

Rachel reached over and took his hand to gently squeeze it. "Hey, what's wrong? Why are you crying? I said that I'm okay with who I am." She handed him a tissue. "When I think back on all of it I like to believe that it's made me a better person. They say whatever doesn't kill you will make you stronger," she added with a cheery smile.

Alex wiped his eyes with the tissue she gave him then drew a big breath and blew it out quickly. He knew he had to tell her; he just wasn't sure how to start.

He slowly began to unbutton his shirt as he whispered softly. "I want to show you something."

Rachel watched him closely. She had no idea what could be so upsetting to cause such a reaction in him.

As the last button was undone, Alex pulled his shirttails from his pants to reveal an elastic bandage wrapped tightly around his chest. Beneath the bandage she could clearly see two sizable bumps. Did he have breasts? She looked up into Alex's eyes. He has breasts? Was he a girl trying to be a boy?

Her voice quavered. "I don't understand." She reached forward and gently touched the bandage. Beneath it she could feel the firmness of a full breast.

She could see that Alex was trembling.

"The term is 'intersex'." His voice shuddered nervously. "You can look it up on the internet. It's apparently a medical condition. It doesn't always manifest early in life. They began to develop about when I was twenty. At first they were very sensitive and then they began to swell and grow. I went from a flat chest to a "C" cup in eighteen months. They haven't grown much since then. I suppose if I went on hormone therapy like you did my body would grow even more feminine. I'm still a fully functioning male," he added sheepishly, "everything still seems to work. But I have no idea who I am up here anymore." He pointed to his forehead.

Rachel pulled Alex into a hug. She took a big breath and squeezed him tightly. "Oh my God, thank you." There were tears in her eyes. "You can not imagine how scared I was to tell you all of this. Somehow deep inside I knew that you would understand me. I had no idea that you were like me!"

"I'm nowhere near as brave as you are Rachel," he replied as she continued to hold him tightly. "This all came on much later in my life. I never had to endure the kind of crap that you did when you were in high school. I don't think I could have done it. You're so much stronger than I am."

"Maybe," she said releasing him and gently rubbing his back, "but I'm so glad I said something today."

"Why?"

"Because not only do I have a new friend," she leaned back with a huge grin, "I have a new girl friend!" She hugged him again and Alex groaned as she held him tightly.

"Does anybody else know about you?"

"Nobody, you're the first one I've ever told, outside of a few specialists in Colorado and my mom, of course."

"Not even Amanda?"

"No, why would Amanda know anything?"

"I'm sorry," Rachel suddenly changed her tone. She moved to sit beside Alex and looked down and away from him. "I just thought." Her voice trailed off.

Alex smiled at her. "We're friends, Rachel, that's all. I only just met her a month ago. I helped her bring some of her boxes into her apartment when she moved in. We talk in the hallway from time to time but that's about it."

"I saw you both yesterday in the backyard." Rachel was embarrassed to admit that she watched them out her window. "You looked like you were very close so I guess I assumed."

"I saw her go out to the backyard yesterday when I came home from school. She looked a little upset. Her cousin is getting married next month; apparently they're very close. She was feeling a little homesick, that's all. I tried to cheer her up."

"I'm sorry. I guess I misread everything. I was a little jealous. You two always seemed so happy together. It made me want to open up to you because, well, I wanted you as a friend too."

"Well, I'm flattered, and I'm glad you were a little jealous because if you weren't we would never have made this connection. You can imagine how much of a burden this has been for me." He placed his hands on his chest.

Her tears began to trail down her cheeks.

"Hey, don't cry." He wiped away her tears.

"Thanks, they're happy tears not sad ones."

"Good. But you really should get to know Amanda." He turned and settled back on her couch. "She's bright and cheery and I think she's really smart too. I think you might really like her."

"Alex, girls frighten the hell out of me. I know on the outside they appear all soft and frilly but inside they can be monsters."

"Those high school girls really did a number on you didn't they?"

"I guess." She sighed. "I still have the jitters when I'm around a bunch of them at my day job."

They both sat in silence on the couch for a few minutes, lost in their own thoughts. Rachel glanced sideways at Alex then she closed her eyes and willed her mouth to open.

"Alex?"

"Huh?"

"Are you sure you're okay with who I am? You're not freaked out or anything?"

"After what I just showed you I should ask you the same thing," he said.

"Would you, ah, would you show them to me?"

"You mean without the bandage?"

"Yeah."

"Oh, okay." He sat up and took off his shirt then he pulled off the hooks that bound the bandages in place and slowly unwrapped the elastic bands. A moment later his breasts were released and they swelled to their true form. There were red marks where the bandages pulled tightly across his chest and a few stray hairs that interrupted his otherwise smooth and creamy chest. His aureoles were modest in size and his nipples stood out prominently from each breast. He started to cover himself with his hands but Rachel placed her hands on his wrists and gently moved them away from his body.

"Oh, they look lovely."

Alex watched in amazement as Rachel lowered her mouth to one of his breasts and, using her tongue, she lightly touched his nipple. He closed his eyes and relished the velvet touch of her tongue on his breast. It sent chills down his spine.

Rachel closed her mouth over his breast and began to suck. She drew in a breath and savored his smell as she sucked and nibbled at his breast. Then she moved to the other breast and did the same thing while she brought up her hand and pinched the first nipple, pulling it out between her thumb and forefinger.

"Oh."

It shocked her a moment and she pulled away abruptly. "God, I'm so sorry." Her face flushed with crimson. "I don't know what's come over me." Rachel's heart was pounding as she buried her face in her hands.

"Hey," Alex murmured as he took her hands from her face and kissed her on the forehead, "it felt lovely." He reached up and put his hands besides her face and drew her face down between his breasts.

She kissed Alex there lightly as she nuzzled his breasts then she moved up his body trailing kisses up his neck until she kissed him on the lips.

"Thank you." She wrapped her arms around his neck and gazed into his eyes.

Alex smiled shyly as Rachel released him then moved over and leaned back against the couch. She reached across and took his hand then kissed it and gave it a gentle squeeze.

"They really are beautiful, Alex. I wish mine were that soft." Her heart was still racing but it was beginning to slow down a little.

Alex sighed a little and looked over at Rachel. "You have no reason to be envious Rachel, you are simply stunning. If I wasn't so awkward around women I would have been stalking you a long time ago." He grinned sheepishly and then blushed bright crimson.

"Wouldn't that have been a surprise," she added with a chuckle.

"All the way around."

They both laughed a bit then settled back into the couch with a smile and a sigh.

Rachel looked at the bulge that was growing in the front of his pants. She reached over and with a tender touch she placed her hand on him. Rachel rubbed her hand against his jeans and looked over to watch his reaction.

He closed his eyes to savor her touch.

Then she got bolder and opened up the zipper on his jeans.

Alex simply smiled and kept his eyes closed.

Rachel pulled out his cock, leaned across, and began to lick it. Alex moaned in response to the velvet touch of her tongue. His pants were tight so he reached down and unbuckled his belt to remove them. Rachel helped him slide them down and out of the way. She paused a moment to admire him lying there while she stroked him gently. His beautiful breasts heaved with each breath he took. His cock became rigid in her hand and pre-cum was forming at the tip.

Alex looked up at her with a blissful smile then he closed his eyes again.

Rachel brought her face towards his cock and began to draw him into her mouth.

"My God you're amazing," he whispered to her as his body arched off the sofa. She slipped her hand beneath him and let her fingers play with his ass. A moment later her thumb began to press against his rosebud. He moaned again and she brought her thumb up to her face. She released his cock a moment and licked her thumb. Then she took him back into her mouth and brought her thumb back to his ass. She pressed again, still with gentle pressure and her thumb slipped inside.

"Oh," he cried as she entered him.

"Did I hurt you?"

"No, I guess it was more of a surprise than anything else. Your mouth is amazing. I've never had this happen before."

"This can happen as often as you want from now on," she said with a wicked grin. Then she took him back inside her mouth and continued to swirl her tongue around his shaft. Her thumb continued to move in and out of his ass slowly loosening his muscle.

"My God you're tight."

"You've entered virgin territory."

Alex's breathing became more erratic and he started to buck and grind his pelvis into her face. Rachel knew he was close. She started to suck harder as she rammed her thumb into his rectum several more times. She was reaching for his prostate. Her movements were massaging him there. Suddenly he sucked in his breath and the first shot of his cum hit the back of her mouth. It was followed by several more. She continued to suck and swirl her tongue around the head as he shot another stream of his seed into her eager mouth.

As the waves of his orgasm subsided he relaxed against the sofa and Rachel pulled her thumb from his ass. She moved up his body towards his face planting kisses along the way until she found his mouth. Her tongue dove into his mouth exploring every part of him passionately.

He could taste his seed on her lips.

Finally, Rachel relaxed and resting her head on his chest she nuzzled his breast and kissed him there again.

"Wow, thank you."

"You're welcome, and believe me when I tell you that I enjoyed that as much as you did."

They stayed there a moment holding each other in a lover's embrace.

Alex closed his eyes and hugged her tightly.

That was truly amazing. He wondered what she looked like? How would he react when he saw her naked? Would he be able to take her into his mouth and suck her like she just did now? He'd never had this happen before and he worried that he might do it wrong.

"Rachel, I'm completely out of my depth here. I don't know how to act and I don't want to hurt you but…"

"Shush." She placed a finger across his lips. "Don't worry about it. Just follow your instincts and you'll be fine."

"Okay."

She looked at her watch. "Hey, you want to go out for dinner before work? It'll be my treat."

"Sure but we can go 'Dutch' if you want, I just got paid."

"I'm asking you out, okay? I just got paid too so don't argue with me." She leaned over and kissed him on the lips. "You can buy next time."

Alex grinned sheepishly and nodded. "Okay." Then he pulled up his pants and began to put on his shirt.

"I need to change before I go to work." She picked up her coat and walked towards her bedroom then she paused and turned at her bedroom door to watch him dress.

He picked up his bandage and rolled it into a tiny bundle.

"What about your bandage?"

"I just don't have the will to put it back on right now. I breathe so much better without it. Besides it's cold out so my coat will cover me up until I get to work. I'll put it on when I get there."

"Okay." She walked into her bedroom. "I'll be out in a couple of minutes."

"No problem. I'm going across the hall to use my bathroom. I'll wait for you by the stairs."

"I'll be there in just a sec," she said from behind her bedroom door.

Alex took a minute or two longer to finish buttoning his shirt then he opened Rachel's apartment door and crossed the hallway to his place. As he was opening his door Amanda appeared on the stair landing below. "Hey Alex, there you are. You want to go eat somewhere before you have to work?"

"I'd love to but I already promised to go with Rachel." Alex quickly covered up his chest with his coat.

"Oh. Ah. Er, can I go too?"

At that moment Rachel opened her apartment door and stepped out into the hallway. Alex turned to her and smiled.

"Amanda wants to know if she can join us. Is that okay with you?"

"Huh?" Rachel glanced at Alex and then at Amanda. She studied her face a moment then she smiled meekly and nodded. "Oh, okay, sure." She looked down a moment and blushed slightly.

Amanda grinned broadly. "I just need to grab my wallet and I'll be ready. I'll meet you both in the foyer." She dashed down the stairs towards her apartment.

Alex ducked into his place quickly, went to the bathroom, and then grabbed his coat, stuffed the elastic bandage in his pocket and joined Rachel at the top of the stairs.

"She's not a monster, Rachel." Alex gave her hand a gentle squeeze.

She wore a worried frown. "If you say so. But old wounds heal slowly."

They meet Amanda in the foyer and headed out the front door of the house. Down the street, a couple of blocks away, were several small mom and pop restaurants that catered to the locals in this part of town. They settled on a little Chinese place near Twentieth Street.

Amanda dropped her napkin onto her plate. "Oh, that hit the spot, good pick Rachel." She grinned broadly and downed the rest of her wine in one gulp. "So when do you have to go to work, Alex?"

"I'm on at nine tonight."

Rachel dropped her napkin on her plate. "Me too."

"I thought Alex mentioned that you worked at an accounting firm downtown Rachel."

"It's only part-time so I need to supplement it. I wait tables at Moulin Rouge a couple of nights a week."

"Oh, that's cool. I've been in there a couple of times, that place is fantastic."

Alex looked at her skeptically. "You do know about their clientele don't you?"

"What? You mean it's a gay bar? Sure," Amanda added with a smirk, "I got that the first night I was there. It's sort of hard to miss. But that doesn't matter. It's just a fun place and I like the atmosphere."

"Are you, ah…?" asked Alex softly.

Rachel darted a quick glance at him.

"What, into girls? Nah, I'm just into people. I'm not hung up on labels. If they're cool, I'm cool."

Rachel smiled at her and snuck a sideways glance at Alex.

Alex set his chopsticks down and looked at Amanda with renewed curiosity. "Where are you from Amanda?"

"Uh-oh, life story time, huh?" She quipped with a sarcastic grin. Then she raised her hands and replied. "Okay, okay. I'll go first then it'll be your turn." Alex filled her glass up half full from the bottle of wine and then replaced the cork.

"Thanks," she said with a wry smile. "I'm originally from Seattle by way of Vancouver. Then I got sidetracked in Salt Lake City and eventually I landed here. My ex-boyfriend/lover/husband dumped me on a bus in Salt Lake with a one-way ticket for the east coast. He told me that I'd find more like-minded people out here than I would out west and he was probably right. I met you guys after the first month I was here. Life is already much better here than it ever was in Utah."

Alex glanced quickly to Rachel and then to Amanda. "Husband? Are you still married?"

"Nope. After a month of playing the role of the blushing bride he decided that the liberal side of me in the bedroom was too much for him to handle and he had the whole thing annulled. He was a dyed in the wool Baptist and his ideas about bedroom behavior didn't coincide with mine."

"No smoking, drinking or Rock'n'Roll?"

"Yup, you got it," she added with an ironic smile.

Rachel sipped from her water glass then set it down. "So how do you pay the bills?"

"Mostly with a trust fund that my grandmother left me. But I do like to keep busy so I work downtown as a stock analyst in a brokerage house part time. I'm pretty good at it and it keeps me out of trouble. What about you Alex?"

Amanda looked back over to Alex and in doing so she gestured with her wine glass a little too quickly and spilled several drops on his jacket.

"Oh shit, I'm sorry." She dipped a cloth napkin in her water glass and started to dab his chest where the wine was soaking in. "Here let me. If you don't do it quickly the stain will set." Her voice trailed off as she continued to dab the wine spots and felt something she hadn't expected.

Alex sat there stunned, unable to move as he glanced across to Rachel with a frightened look on his face. He quickly tried to brush Amanda's hands away but it was too late. From the blank expression on her face it was clear that his secret was out.

Amanda blushed brightly and turned away briefly. Then she turned back with a meek smile on her face.

"I'm sorry, that was way too forward of me. I should have asked first."

"It's okay. It's an old jacket anyway. I got it months ago at the Salvation Army. Between the pasta sauce and ketchup stains, a few wine spots will never be noticed." He grinned sheepishly and moved his hand to touch her arm gently.

Trying to recover a sense of balance between everyone, Rachel pushed back from the table. "We should probably be going. I have to take the bus across town and it takes forever."

"Yeah, my shift starts in less than an hour so I need to head out too."

Amanda smiled sweetly. "Rachel, thanks so much for taking me out for dinner. I know I sort of barged in on you guys."

"Don't worry about it," Rachel replied. "Life's too short to be hung up on formalities."

"Hey, don't forget your fortune cookie." Alex handed each of them a cookie and took one himself. He cracked the cookie and pulled the slip of paper out.

"Sudden love takes the longest time to be cured." Alex read his fortune out loud then he looked up at

Rachel and Amanda with an awkward smile.

Rachel pulled her fortune slip out and read it out loud.

"Your future is found in your past." She nodded her head with a chuckle. "Sounds appropriate."

Amanda read hers. "Mine is 'of the three things that last: faith, hope, and love. Love is the strongest.' I like that."

They got up from the table and Amanda followed Rachel and Alex out of the restaurant. Once outside Rachel parted from them with a wave. She walked down the block towards the bus stop and Alex walked with Amanda back towards their apartment house.

She avoided his eyes as they walked along the sidewalk. "I'm so sorry Alex."

"Don't be." He shrugged his shoulders. "You were probably going to find out sooner or later anyway. It's hard to hide things like that from your friends."

Amanda looked up and beamed at Alex. "Thanks, that means a lot."

"You're welcome."

"Care to explain?" She gestured towards his chest.

"I can't now, I've got to go to work." He walked up to his car parked on the street. "Maybe tomorrow if you're not freaked out about it."

Amanda stood a moment and looked at Alex. A huge smile grew on her face. She ran over, wrapped her arms around him and gave him a big hug.

"Actually I'm a little jealous," she whispered in his ear. "I think they're bigger than mine." Then she kissed him on the cheek and let him go. She ran towards the apartment house and turned back towards him once she reached the steps. She smiled impishly and gave him a little wave.

Alex smiled and waved back then walked around his car, got in and drove off.

Later that night, or actually early the following morning, Alex trudged slowly up the stairs towards his apartment. He was exhausted and although he faced a mountain of homework due later that day, he was clearly uncertain if he was ever going to get through it the way he felt at the moment.

At the top of the stairs he met Rachel standing outside of her apartment, waiting.

"Hey, did you just get back?" He leaned against the wall for support.

"Yeah."

"This climb is bad enough in the daytime let alone at two in the morning."

"And in heels," Rachel replied with a wry smile.

"I haven't tried that yet."

"Don't, it's not for the faint of heart."

Alex paused a moment and stood by his door. He shook his head gently and smiled at Rachel. My god, she's beautiful, he thought. She stood there in a tight mini skirt and sequined blouse under her long coat. At the moment, her spiked heels made her taller than Alex.

"So, what happened after I left? Did she figure it out?"

"Pretty much, I mean come on, they're sort of hard to miss when I'm not wrapped up like a package." Rachel broke into a broad grin. Her eyes began to sparkle. But before she could open her mouth Alex gave her 'the look.'

"Don't even go there Rachel, I know what you're thinking."

Rachel covered her mouth in a feeble attempt to fight back a snicker. "Okay, sorry. Did she ask you how it happened?"

"Sort of, yes." He turned his key in the lock on his door. "I had to go to work so I told her I would tell her tomorrow. I mean today if I see her."

"What are you going to say?"

"What else, I'll tell her the truth. If you can't be honest with your friends what can you be?"

"Cool." Rachel nodded with a wry smile as she turned back to open her door.

"I think she'll be okay with it Rachel. I know you have big issues with women but really; they're not all monsters. Some of them are as beautiful on the inside as they are on the outside."

"I hope you right. Maybe I'll find that out someday." She paused a moment as she watched Alex open his door. "Good night."

"Good night." Alex shut his door softly.

Amanda heard Alex come in the back door from work. She rubbed the sleep out of her eyes and looked at her alarm clock. It was two-fifteen in the morning. She must have dozed off waiting for him to return. She grabbed her robe and threw it over her shoulders as she dashed for her door.

She was anxious to talk to him even if it was late. She ran out of her apartment pulling her arms through the sleeves of her robe. If she hurried she might be able to catch him before he went into his apartment. She padded softly up the stairs but stopped suddenly when she heard voices.

It was Alex and Rachel. She didn't want to eavesdrop but she couldn't help but listen. Tears began to run down her cheeks and across a gentle smile. When they left she waited until she heard Alex's door click shut. Then she turned and tiptoed softly back down the stairs.

As she soon as she stood in front of her apartment door she paused a moment and wiped her eyes. Then she turned the key to open her door. She took in a big breath and let it out slowly.

"Today is going to be a really great day," she whispered softly to herself. She smiled sweetly as she walked into her apartment and quietly closed her door.

**=THREE=**

It was the middle of the afternoon before Alex walked back into the apartment house. He had just finished his last class for the day and he was truly beat. Between working at the convenience store and trying to carry a full graduate load things were beginning to pile up.

At least the weekend was coming up so maybe he could get caught up. He started to ascend the stairs. As he looked up he saw Amanda sitting alone on the top step.

"Hi." She smiled meekly. "You look tired."

"I am. Between work and school it seems that there's little time for sleep."

Alex continued to climb the stairs until he reached Amanda. He turned and joined her on the top step.

"What have you been up to?"

"Work, mostly. I just got back a half hour ago. The markets still have the jitters. It makes everybody downtown act like they just gulped down fifteen pots of coffee."

She leaned over and nudged his shoulder. "When I got home I thought I'd look and see if you were around."

Alex stood up and offered her his hand. "Come on, I'll put the kettle on for tea. But you have to climb all these stairs to get some."

"It's like daily aerobics isn't it?"

"Definitely. Can you imagine what life was like during the summers for the house servants when this house was built? Up and down these stairs a hundred times a day and if you don't know by now, mid-Atlantic summers can be brutal. Thank God for air conditioners."

Amanda followed him up the stairs and into his apartment. She flopped down on an old battered couch across from his desk and looked around his room. It was Spartan by comparison to hers even though she only moved in a month ago.

"You live like a monk up here don't you?"

"I suppose so." He plunked down two cups of tea on the table in front of her. "All my money goes to paying for classes at the university. I'm sort of living from hand to mouth and that doesn't offer a lot of wiggle room."

"I might have an old Grateful Dead poster laying around. If you want you can use it to cover up some of these cracks."

"Ha! I'll think about it." He shook his head as he chuckled.

"Where's your bed?"

He grinned. "You're sitting on it. It folds out when I'm not too tired to make it up properly."

"Oh," she said meekly, blushing.

Amanda sipped her tea a moment and they both

sat in silence. She glanced sideways at Alex a couple of times and looked up once when he cleared his throat but otherwise the atmosphere was rather awkward. Finally Alex decided to break the ice.

"So, here I am sitting in my apartment with a beautiful girl and all we can think about is what I've got under my shirt. Weird isn't it?"

"Not so much weird as it is awkward Alex. I mean the last thing I want to do is ruin a friendship by saying something stupid. But I have to admit, it was a bit of a shock yesterday."

Alex pulled out an iPad from his backpack and opened it up. He opened his browser and typed in the word 'intersex' in the search window. Then he clicked on the first link and the browser opened up a Wikipedia page.

"Here," he said handing Amanda his iPad, "maybe this will help."

Alex sat back and sipped his tea while Amanda quickly scanned the page.

"So, this is what you have?"

"It's not so much what I have as what I am."

"Sorry."

"Don't be, there's a lot of misunderstanding in general about things like this. Everybody likes to lump us all into one category and then call us all deviants and perverts. It's ignorant and convenient for them but horribly wrong for the rest of us."

Alex went on to tell Amanda most of what he told Rachel the day before. He added in the fact that up until three years ago he always thought of himself as an average guy. He wasn't much into sports but he didn't dislike them either. He'd dated women before and he would again if he could find a woman whose head wasn't filled with a twisted sense of morality or she wasn't hung up on gender identity issues.

He glanced out his window with a sigh. "But those girls can be hard to find."

Amanda glanced at Alex. "Are you and Rachel dating?"

"Not yet, but maybe." He turned back from the window to look at her.

"Oh," she almost whispered.

Alex watched a wave of emotions play across her face and as she began to tear up. He walked over and sat down next to her then reached out and took her hand.

He leaned in and kissed her on her cheek.

"Amanda, you're my friend. Nothing will ever change that." Tears continued to well up in her eyes. She wrapped her arms around him and buried her face on his shoulder.

"I know she hates girls and I'm afraid that once you two start dating that you'll stop talking to me and everything," she sniffled. "I don't know if I can take that right now."

Alex wrapped his arms around her and rubbed her back then he leaned down and kissed her on the top of her head.

"Not going to happen. I like you too much. Besides, who else is going to spill wine on me on a regular basis?"

Amanda choked back a laugh and hugged him tighter. She tilted her head up and kissed him on the cheek. "By the way, most people think I'm a bit twisted and I certainly don't have any gender hang ups," she added with an impish smile.

"I already figured that out from yesterday. But

hanging with me and Rachel could be a challenge for you."

"I'm up for it," she leaned back grinning at him. Her eyes twinkled with mischief.

"I figured you would be, but I had to say it."

She wiped her eyes. "Can I use your bathroom?"

"Sure." He pointed across the room. "It's over there."

Amanda got up and walked towards the bathroom as they heard a knock on the apartment door. Alex walked over and opened the door and Rachel walked in with a large pizza box.

"Breakfast," she sang as she struck a pose with a twinkle in her eye. But once she spotted Amanda she began to balk and she quickly changed her posture. "What?! Oh, I'm sorry. I didn't know. I - I." Rachel started to back out of the apartment.

"Rachel, wait," they both said simultaneously. Rachel stopped then glanced back and forth between them. She looked confused.

"Rachel, don't leave. I'm not trying to come between you and Alex." Amanda stood looking downcast. "I'm just his friend, that's all."

"I know, I'm sorry. I was just surprised and I didn't think before..." Her voice trailed off to a whisper. "I should have asked."

They all stood a moment in an awkward silence until Amanda broke the ice.

"Rachel, I get the impression that you don't like me and I'm sorry if that's true. I know you're close to Alex but I really want to be your friend too if you have room for one more in your life."

"I - I," Rachel stammered a moment then she stood motionless for several minutes studying

Amanda's face. The room was silent, even the clock seemed to stop ticking.

She remembered Alex's words. "She's not a monster." And his words continued to repeat inside her head as she stood watching Amanda closely. She figured that there was only one way to find out.

Rachel set the pizza box on the table in front of the couch and walked towards Amanda with a determined look on her face. Amanda stood near the bathroom looking a bit like a deer caught in the headlights as Rachel bore down on her.

Rachel took Amanda's face in her hands then she planted a passionate almost rough kiss on her lips. She took Amanda's hand and lowered it down to her crotch and pressed it between her legs. Amanda's eyes began to expand as she felt something she hadn't expected. Rachel nodded to her slowly then released her hand.

"Still want to be my friend?" She stared at her intently.

Now over the initial shock of Rachel's sudden revelation, Amanda's lips rose into a broad sweet smile and her eyes began to sparkle. She looked up into Rachel's face. "Yes, I do," she whispered back to Rachel and then she glanced at Alex beaming.

Alex broke the silence between them. "Hey, the pizza is getting cold. Looks like the rich girl bought again. You know one of these days you are going to have to let me buy."

Rachel paused a moment and considered Amanda's response then she turned towards Alex with a grin and wrapped her arm around Amanda's shoulders. Amanda stood blinking at the sudden turn of events. "Oh I'll let you buy all right. But you're not going to get off easy. I've got my eye on a nice little French restaurant downtown. You're going to take us both on a date tomorrow night."

"I am? Both of you?"

"Yup, it'll be just us girls. We're celebrating the fact that I have a new friend," she said hugging Amanda. "So wear something nice because we are." Then she gave Amanda another hug.

Amanda wrapped her arms around Rachel and squeezed.

Alex chuckled; it was a sight to see Amanda, dwarfed by Rachel's height, squeezing her tightly. "Careful Rachel, that one will squeeze the stuffing out of you."

"That's okay," Rachel replied sweetly, "I've come up short on hugs in my life. So I'll take all I can get." Amanda closed her eyes and hugged her again. Alex beamed and Rachel sighed.

Then she returned Amanda's hug.

## =FOUR=

The following night Amanda asked Rachel if she wanted to finish getting ready down in her apartment. Rachel thought that was a good idea and told Alex that he should meet them there at a quarter past seven.

Alex showed up in clean slacks and a slightly rumpled tie beneath his well-worn sports jacket that covered up his tightly bandaged chest. When he opened Amanda's door his jaw nearly dropped to the floor. Rachel and Amanda stood there with radiant smiles on their faces. They were both, in a word, stunning.

He stood there with a foolish grin on his face. "I can't believe it. I'm going out to dinner with two of the most beautiful women in the world."

Rachel and Amanda blushed a bit when they saw the look on Alex's face. Their eyes sparkled with delight as they slowly turned to give Alex the full effect. Rachel wore a soft pink silk dress that clung to her like an evening glove. It finished well above her knees and the neck swooped down daringly to reveal her ample breasts. Her makeup and hair was amazing and it looked like she even redid her nails to match her lipstick. Finally, she finished it all off with a pair of incredibly high stiletto heels.

Amanda was equally captivating. Her red gown flowed around her body to finish mid-calf. It gently hugged every curve. It was the first time Alex noticed makeup on her and it only enhanced her dazzling eyes. Her nails were painted to match her gown and her shoes were equally as high as Rachel's. Together they both looked amazing.

"I'm going to have to fight off every male in the restaurant tonight."

Rachel and Amanda smiled coyly. They blushed again and then said "thank you," as they walked out the back door of the apartment house arm in arm with Alex.

They headed for his car in the parking area around the side of the building. Alex, acting the gallant escort, opened the doors for them and helped them into his car.

Twenty minutes later they sat at an elegant table near the center of the restaurant and every male eye in the place was glued to their every move.

"I'm living every guy's fantasy right now, you both know that don't you?"

Rachel and Amanda smiled demurely. They buried their noses in their menus and giggled.

Rachel looked across the table at Alex and smiled. "That was simply lovely. And you don't really have to pay for this Alex; we both know how much it costs to go to school. I was just teasing you."

"No, no. I said I wanted to buy and I meant it.

Besides, the real treat for me is being able to spend the evening on a date with two beautiful women. In case you haven't noticed you two are the center of attention here tonight."

Amanda reached across and squeezed Alex's hand then smiled at Rachel.

Amanda had a thoughtful look on her face. "Alex, do you think you have a spare five hundred dollars laying around? I want to invest it for you."

Amanda winked at Rachel and squeezed Alex's hand again. "I don't have any insider information if that's what you're thinking but I am pretty good at what I do. I bet you I can turn that five hundred into a couple of thousand in six months if you're willing to let me play."

Alex dropped his mouth open and she gently moved her fingers over to close it for him. "Amanda, I know it's a risk and I know that there are no guarantees, but hell if you could even do half of that I could breathe a whole lot easier this fall when tuition is due."

"When are you planning to finish up?"

"Next spring if all goes well."

Rachel set down her fork and dabbed her mouth with a napkin. "Cool. Then what?"

"I have no idea. Full time at seven-eleven?"

Amanda had a slightly pained expression on her face but Alex just shrugged.

"Let's go," she whispered, "I'm not used to wearing heels this high and my feet are killing me." She grinned sheepishly and turned to Alex. "I suppose that I just spoiled the illusion, didn't I?"

He smirked a little at her candor. "Not in the least, I will admit that I find high heels incredibly sexy but you two would look good in anything, even bare feet."

The waiter brought the bill and Amanda offered to handle the tip, which Alex objected to at first. But he didn't put up much of a fight. Then they headed back to Alex's car for the return trip home.

A few minutes later Alex pulled his car into the apartment house parking lot.

"Oh, I don't want this night to end," Amanda lamented as she walked into the foyer of the apartment house arm in arm with Alex and Rachel. "Hey, I have a new bottle of pinot noir in my apartment. Let's grab some glasses and take this party to the back porch."

Rachel and Alex looked at each other then smiled. A couple of minutes later Alex managed to pull the cork out of the bottle and poured them each a glassful.

"Wine is like truth serum for me." Amanda sat holding her wine glass up and gazing at it in the moonlight. "Its beauty is irresistible."

"So are you, both of you." Alex murmured softly then he blushed. "That was corny wasn't it?"

"Sweet, but totally cornball," Rachel replied.

Amanda sighed and took their hands in hers. "I'm so glad I met you guys. I haven't had this much fun in forever. Leaving Salt Lake City was the best thing that ever happened to me even though I didn't think so at the time."

Alex glanced at Rachel then he turned to Amanda. "So what was the real reason why you were so upset about your cousin's wedding?"

"Uh-oh, truth or dare time is it?" Amanda looked

over at Alex and Rachel. Her smile faded into melancholy. Perhaps it was the wine or finally having friends that she felt she could really trust. Whatever it was, she decided to open up to them. She was glad to have friends that would accept her for who she was.

She told them that her stepfather abused her when she was younger. It started off with a pinch and a cuddle but it got progressively worse. She told them that her real father passed away when she was nine and when she was thirteen her mother remarried.

"It took a while for me to notice, I was still trying to adjust to a new family arrangement, but over the months that we were together my stepfather was gradually becoming more aggressive around me. I did some research and found out that he was actually a convicted pedophile although my mother never knew that little detail about him until much later."

"My stepfather was an informant for the FBI and while he was in the witness protection program he met my mother. They started dating. One thing led to another and they got married. My mom knew he was under some sort of protection by the feds but they never told her everything. That and a lot of other things were what probably fucked me up so badly when I was a kid."

"Did he?" asked Rachel.

"No, thank God, he never managed to rape me, but he came close one night. I was a senior in middle school at the time. My mother caught him in my room while I was sleeping. She finally worked out what kind of a bastard he was. The twisted little fucker couldn't keep his hands off of me."

"She clocked him with my field hockey stick. He never knew what hit him. My mom told me afterwards that the next thing he remembered was waking up in a hospital bed with restraints and a cop standing outside of his door. That was the last I saw of him."

"After that things settled down a bit but I never looked at life the same way again. I finished high school and went on to college," said Amanda draining her glass. "I dated a lot through those years with boys as well as girls. But I never felt really close to any of them. I was running with a rough crowd in those days. My rebellious youth I guess."

"I sort of held them all at arm's length, so to speak. I finally met this guy from Salt Lake City. I had just broken up with a girlfriend after six months of arguing and I was sort of on the rebound. He was nice and he had good manners, which was a refreshing change from the usual crowd I had been hanging with up until then."

"So as the story goes, one thing led to another," she said with a shrug.

"Did you know he was that uptight before you married him?" asked Alex.

"Kind of," Amanda replied. "I mean we weren't doing it but I just thought he respected me so I went along with it. Of course, this all culminated in quite a shock for him on our wedding night. I got a little drunk and started playing with his ass. He went ballistic; he started quoting the bible and everything. I tried to calm him down but he was beyond calm, he was nearly frothing at the mouth," she said with a chuckle.

Amanda stood up and walked to the end of the porch. She looked out at the back yard and sighed.

"He spent the rest of the night in the bathroom

behind a locked door," she added with a chuckle.

"I finally had to pee so bad I had to use the restroom in the hotel lobby.  After that, the whole 'barefoot and pregnant in the kitchen thing' reared its ugly head," she said sarcastically.

Then she turned and faced Alex and Rachel.

"So, less than a month later he had the marriage annulled and shoved me on a bus with a one-way ticket for here.  And that, was the best thing that ever happened to me."

Amanda walked over behind Alex and Rachel and wrapped her arms around them both.  Then she kissed each one of them on the cheek.

"Because that's when I met you two.  Believe me when I say this, you both are a wonderful breath of fresh air."  She walked around the table and emptied the rest of the bottle into her glass.  "Well, you've heard my story, what's yours Rachel?"

Rachel sat back and began to retell her story.  Alex decided to replenish the empty wine bottle on the table with a fresh one he had on reserve in his apartment.  He ducked back into the house and retrieved it along with a plate of cheese and some crackers.  By the time he returned Rachel was telling Amanda about the first part of her transformation into becoming a woman.

"It was painful I will admit it," Rachel continued softly.  "The mind plays tricks on you when you're in pain and alone.  There were times when I felt like I had done something terribly wrong to my body.  But I have never looked back with regret.  When it's complete I believe that I will finally have the body that God intended me to have."

Alex stopped behind her.  "So you're going to

complete the reassignment surgery?"

"Next spring, I hope."

"Well this time you won't have to do it alone," Amanda added with a warm smile.

"Absolutely," said Alex walking around and setting the wine and cheese on the table in front of them. "You can count on us to raid your refrigerator the whole time you're gone."

Rachel's eyes glistened as she looked at Amanda and Alex. "You're an asshole Alex." She smacked his butt lightly. "But I love you, babe. Amanda it will be your responsibility to make him behave while I'm gone."

"Absolutely.      Okay, no more waterworks. College boy is back with the wine.  Oh, and he brought snacks too.  You're just in time to fill us in on your life story, sweetheart."

"There's not much to tell."  Alex sat down across from Amanda and Rachel.  "I think that I had a normal life growing up, at least I always thought I did. We moved around a lot when I was little.  My dad had a hard time finding steady work until he passed away when I was fifteen.  He was a mechanic.  But from what my mother told me before she died, Dad wasn't a very good one."

"Most of my later years were spent growing up in Denver.  It was where my mom had most of her family.  I didn't play any sports and I sort of hung out with the nerd kids and surfed the web.  I used to write short stories and post them as real life experiences under a false name on Internet websites.  After a while I got bored with that and started to write longer stories.  An English teacher of mine in the eleventh grade saw one of my stories and encouraged me to submit it to a contest. I won that one and a few more. That, plus a few scholarships, helped me get through college. After college I ended up taking graduate classes here in Wilmington. And that's the end of the story."

"But what about those?" Amanda pointed to his breasts encased behind elastic bandages.

"There's not much I haven't told you already. Three years ago they started to grow. My body has slowly changed bit by bit, my hair and skin is softer and most of my body hair has disappeared. I went to a couple of specialists and eventually the family doctor. The conclusion was that all of this is a natural maturation of my body and I was categorized as intersex." Alex shrugged his shoulders and looked away from Rachel and Amanda, blushing slightly.

Rachel sliced a piece of cheese and she placed it on a cracker. "So, what now? Are you going to get breast reduction surgery or are you going to let things go and see what happens?"

"Well, I can't afford that even if I wanted it right now. Mostly, I'm not even sure what I want. I mean these are only the tip of the iceberg," he said as he pointed to his chest. He looked around then leaned forward to whisper.

"My gender identity concepts are all out of whack, my hormones are all over the place, and because of that and everything else, I have these urges and desires that completely fly in the face of all I ever thought was 'normal' in the world."

"Like what?" Amanda moved to the edge of her seat. She propped her elbows on the table in order to rest her chin in her hands and her eyes twinkled in the light.

"Like clothes and shoes and boys and girls and sex. Even what stories I want to write and how I want to write them." His voice had a hint of exasperation. "My head is a total mess right now."

Rachel looked at him quizzically. "I don't understand. Do you want to dress as a woman? I can help you with that, you know."

"I can too," chirped Amanda with a grin.

"Yes and no." He paused a moment and studied their faces. He took a big breath and let it out slowly. "I can't believe I'm telling you guys this. I've held this inside of me for such a long time."

Alex looked around again to make sure no one else was near enough to hear him. He turned to Rachel and Amanda and smiled sheepishly. "Okay, here goes," he said in a whisper.

"There are times when I want to be as frilly and sexy as any woman can be. I even bought a pair of high heels last month from a website on a whim."

Alex began to blush as Rachel and Amanda's eyes shone with excitement. The girls both wore an ironic smile and they each reached over to take one of his hands.

"Then, it's as if my mind rebels against all of that and I want to be totally macho. I feel like I need to kick or punch something. Sometimes I want to stand on a street corner and spit and scratch my balls or any other part of my body that needs scratching. And other times I want to curl into someone's arms just to snuggle up and feel safe."

"I feel like there are two different people living inside my head at any given moment and I don't know which one is coming out today. I'm not violent or anything so you don't need to worry, it's really just my own personal struggle. But there are days when I really feel like sitting on the floor and crying out of sheer frustration. But then I have to go to work or school or whatever. I put on my happy face and I try to stuff it all back down deep inside and hope I can deal with it later."

"Wow," murmured Amanda softly.

"You do know the solution to all of this, don't you?" Rachel asked as she rubbed his hand gently.

"What?" he asked glumly.

"Shopping," she said softly with a lilt in her voice.

"Huh?"

"Oh, yes, absolutely!" shouted Amanda then she quickly covered her mouth. She looked around a moment and then whispered "absolutely" again with a big grin.

"What you need is a complete makeover, dresses, shoes and underwear, makeup, the works."

"Victoria's Secret." Amanda cooed softly like it was some sort of magical incantation.

"Why?" Alex was feeling a bit uncomfortable.

"Because wearing a pretty dress and dangerously high heels won't solve everything, but it might at least let you understand on a deeper level who you are," replied Amanda. "When a girl feels pretty nothing else matters in the world."

"How will that solve anything?"

Rachel leaned forward and squeezed Alex's hand. "Because I know what it means to try and stuff things down inside you. I also know that it will come back to you a hundred fold if you don't learn to handle it now. At least exploring that side of you will get it out in the open so that you can learn to deal with it. You may decide that once is enough. You may never wear another bra or slip on another set of heels for the rest of your life but at least you've confronted it."

"I'm still not convinced."

"And you never will be until we're done," replied Amanda. "Thursday, after your last class, we three are going shopping. You have to let the inner goddess ascend sweetheart. Let life take you where you should go. This will totally be my treat. And Rachel is absolutely right, stuffing these feelings back down inside means that it'll all blow up someday and that can get ugly."

Amanda leaned in and kissed Alex on the cheek. "You were there for us, Alex," she added softly, "and we are here for you."

Amanda and Rachel hugged Alex together. Alex sat perplexed a moment with an awkward smile. He wrapped his arms around both women and sighed. "Isn't that just how fate likes to fuck with your life?"

"What do you mean?" Rachel leaned back to look at him quizzically.

"I spent the last ten years of my life looking for the perfect woman and now I find two. I don't want to hurt either one of you but I don't know what to do. I really like you both a lot." He sat for a moment and glanced sideways at Rachel and Amanda.

He closed his eyes for a moment and sighed. "Fuck. I need to go to sleep." He got up and walked into the house.

After Alex left Amanda sat looking confused. She turned to Rachel looking troubled. "What was all that about? Did I say something wrong?"

Rachel leaned back in her chair and folded her

arms. "No. I think the issue is that he likes both of us. And he doesn't want to hurt either of us or be hurt."

"What do you mean?" Amanda paused a moment. "Oh." She considered the situation further. "So, what are you going to do?"

"I don't know," Rachel leaned her elbows on the table and rested her chin in her hands. "We both really just met him. If we trip now we could screw up the whole thing. What do you think we should do?"

Amanda sat a moment longer and thought about everything he said. Then her eyes began to sparkle with a mischievous gleam. She stood up and leaned across the table to Rachel.

"I'm going to take your hand and we're both going to march up those stairs. Then we are both going to fuck his brains out." Amanda added with a wicked grin. "That's what I think we both should do."

Rachel's eyes gleamed with delight as Amanda grabbed her hand and tugged her through the back door. They took off their heels and scampered up three flights of stairs like it was a foot race. Amanda laughed and giggled all the way to the third floor.

"Shush." Rachel placed her hand over Amanda's mouth when they finally reached the third floor. "If we don't quiet down we'll have Reilly up her in a heartbeat." She reached over and gently knocked on Alex's door.

The door opened slowly and Alex poked his head out.

"What are you two up to?"

Amanda wiggled around Rachel and pushed Alex back as she entered his apartment. Rachel entered behind her and both girls grabbed Alex and pulled him across the hall towards Rachel's apartment.

"Wait, what are you doing?" Alex whispered urgently.

"What we should have done days ago," Rachel whispered in reply as she wrapped her hand across Alex's mouth.

"And what we're going to continue to do until you finally understand that we're all in this together," Amanda added as she helped Rachel pull Alex into her bedroom.

Rachel pushed Alex onto her bed as Amanda stepped behind her and unzipped her dress. Then Rachel did the same for Amanda. In a moment both girls were standing in front of Alex with nothing on but their panties.

"Wait a minute!" Amanda stood looking at Rachel's breasts then down at Alex's. "Why do I have to be the one with the smallest tits? That's totally unfair."

Rachel laughed. She grabbed Amanda and pushed her onto the bed next to Alex. She followed behind her and her mouth found one of Amanda's nipples. Rachel looked at Alex and motioned to him towards the other nipple and both of them began to lick and nibble at her breasts. He quickly caught on to the game and threw his inhibitions to the winds.

"Oh my God this feels wonderful," she cooed as she squirmed beneath them. She moved her arms around and gently pressed her hands against the back of their heads, pulling them closer to her breasts.

Alex began to work his way down her body trailing kisses as he went. He lowered himself down between her legs and pulled her panties off. Then he sucked and licked her body into submission.

As Alex was sending Amanda into orbit, Rachel slipped off the bed and closer to Alex. She moved her hand over and began to caress his cock. She wiggled around beneath him and took him in her mouth, gently sucking and nibbling on the head.

Alex began to writhe and moan under Rachel's attention, the vibrations of his moans sent Amanda over the moon.

As Amanda came down from her third orgasm she shifted around and pulled Alex up onto the bed. Rachel pulled her mouth off of Alex's cock and helped Amanda maneuver Alex onto his back. As Amanda pushed him over onto his back Rachel moved to kneel above his head. When Amanda straddled him, Rachel removed her panties and began to rub her cock.

As Amanda straddled Alex, she bent over to thrust her tongue in his mouth while reaching above him to stroke Rachel's cock. Then she reached down and lifted Alex's cock away from his body. Amanda lowered herself down and took him inside her in one swift motion. "Oh God," Amanda gasped, "This feels marvelous!"

Rachel watched Amanda ride Alex as she took this opportunity to push her cock into his mouth. Then she leaned forward and began to tongue wrestle with Amanda as the girl rode Alex hard, slamming their bodies against his. In a matter of moments Alex arched his back and shot several loads of his seed into Amanda as Rachel's orgasm overflowed into Alex's mouth. Amanda clenched Alex's cock in a vice like grip throbbing several times until she came down from her orgasm.

They collapsed around Alex panting.

Alex was nearly out of breath. "That was the best! You girls are so beautifully amazing. I'm the luckiest guy on the planet!"

"We all are," whispered Amanda as she leaned over and began to suck on one of Alex's breasts. She nibbled and tongued his nipple then sucked on him hard followed by gentle kisses. Rachel offered similar attention to his other breast. Alex was in nirvana.

He kissed them both on the head and hugged them tightly as the three of them snuggled in Rachel's bed.

"Mmm," Amanda moaned as Alex hugged her. "I need a shower. Can I use your bathroom Rachel?"

"Sure, towels are in the cabinet by the tub. Help yourself, I'll follow in after you."

Alex attempted to get up. "I'll go use mine across the hall."

Rachel pulled him back down into a bear hug. "No you don't," she said with a giggle, "you're not going anywhere, buster. We're all in this together, right Amanda?"

"Absolutely," Amanda chirped as she leaned back out the bathroom door. "Bring him in here. He needs a shave anyway."

"What?"

"Come on, babe, it's time to begin your transformation."

Rachel pulled Alex up and, grabbing his shoulders, she steered him towards the bathroom. Once inside Amanda stood waiting with razors, shaving cream, and a huge grin.

"Stand still sweetie, this will just take a second," Amanda said as she lathered up his legs and balls.

"Here you go," she said handing Rachel another razor. "I'll do the back and you do the front. You have a lot more experience in that area than I do," she added with a sheepish grin.

In no time at all both girls, working in tandem, managed to remove most of Alex's body hair from his legs, butt, chest, and balls. Rachel left a small patch above his cock just to tickle her nose.

Amanda stepped into the shower while Rachel touched up the area around his ass. Once Amanda was done Rachel stepped into the shower and Alex used a spare towel to dry off Amanda. She turned around and threw her arms around him and kissed him passionately.

"You are the most wonderful person I have ever met," she whispered in his ear. "I want you to know that Alex Wells. I'm so happy I met you."

Alex lifted her head from his chest and looked into her glistening eyes.

"Thank you, so are you."

The shower curtain opened briefly and Rachel stepped out. Amanda and Alex both began to towel her dry. She turned around and kissed Alex on the lips then turned him around and swatted his butt as he stepped into the shower. Rachel turned back and wrapped her arms around Amanda.

"Girls can be monsters," she whispered into Amanda's ears, "but Alex was right about you. You're as beautiful on the inside as you are on the outside."

Amanda hugged Rachel as tears began to fall down her cheeks.

Both girls walked out of the bathroom hand in hand and got into Rachel's bed to wait for Alex. A moment later he opened the bathroom door and stepped into the Rachel's bedroom. "Is there room for me?"

"Always," said Rachel.

"Right in the middle where you belong," Amanda replied.

"You know, we three are like stray cats aren't we," he sighed thoughtfully. "We've each wandered through our lives looking for love and tenderness. We are who we are because of what has happened in the past. You both have taught me so much about myself and what it's like to be loved," he said with a sigh. Alex kissed them both. "Thank you."

"We love you too, sweetheart," murmured Amanda as she snuggled up under his arm.

"Yup," murmured Rachel, "now go to sleep."

## =FIVE=

It was Thursday and Alex drove home from his afternoon class.

He walked up to the apartment house and paused before the bottom step. He smiled briefly as he looked up to his third floor window and squinted into the afternoon sun reflecting off the glass. He tried to imagine what was going to happen once he crossed the threshold into the apartment house.

He knew that two beautiful women were about to change his life forever. Hell, they already have changed his life! It's what was going to come next that was making him anxious.

He drew in a big breath then let it out slowly. Then he walked up the front porch stairs and opened the door.

"It is going to be an interesting day," he muttered as stood at the bottom of the three flights of stairs to his apartment. "With those two around there is no telling where things will end up."

Alex started up the stairs towards his third floor apartment when Tom Reilly poked his head out of the manager's apartment.

"Hey Wells," Reilly mumbled his mouth still stuffed with a chicken leg from a late lunch. "You got some time this weekend to help me with the firepit? The city building inspector has a wild hair up his ass and I need to move it further away from the tree."

"Sure, no need to burn down the neighborhood," Alex replied watching Tom pick a piece of chicken meat from a crevice in his teeth. "I should be around Saturday morning before I need to go to work."

"Saturday's no good, do you have time on Friday?"

"I'll look and see," Alex replied as he started to climb the stairs. "I have a paper due online on Saturday. I'll let you know, okay?"

"Sure thing, thanks." Tom ducked back inside and closed his door. Alex could hear a ball game blaring on the television in the background.

As he turned the corner on the third floor landing he looked up to see Amanda and Rachel sitting together at the top of the stairs.

"Uh-Oh, you're both waiting for me aren't you? This can't be good." He grinned and shook his head. "So, what's up?" He stood there trying to look innocent.

"You know full well what's up, babe." Rachel's eyes were shinning with mischief. "Get your little tushy up here now and take a quick shower. We have work to do before we go shopping."

"Aw, do I have too?" There was a mock whine in his voice as he slowly ascended the last flight of stairs.

Amanda stood up as he passed by her and she swatted his butt with a big grin. She shouted, "scoot!"

Alex opened his apartment door and dropped his book bag near his desk. Then he pulled off his coat and shoes and started undressing as he moved towards the bathroom.

"And don't forget to shave babe," Rachel shouted through the bathroom door. "Real close too!"

A couple of minutes later Rachel entered his bathroom and set a robe on the hook on the bathroom door. Alex was lathering up his hair as Rachel peeked behind the shower curtain.

"Hey babe," she said, "I hung a robe on the door. Don't put on anything else, okay?"

"Okay, thanks," Alex said as he leaned forward and kissed Rachel on the cheek. "I'll be out in a minute." Alex paused a moment and thought about what she just said.

"Wait a minute! Why?"

Alex squinted again as he peered around the shower curtain with soap dripping into his eyes. Rachel was already out the door.

When Alex stepped out of his shower Amanda stood waiting with another towel to wrap around his hair. Alex has had long hair since high school when he tried his hand at playing in a rock band.

"What teenager doesn't?" He pleaded with his mom who eventually relented.

It was a short-lived moment; it was mostly because the girl he was infatuated with at the time played the keyboards in a local garage band. But his talent and interest in rock and roll faded along with his interest in the keyboardist.

He did like the long hair though; it made him feel like a rebel, even if he really wasn't one. After that he just sort of stuck with the look.

After Amanda wrapped the towel around his hair she wrapped her arms around his neck and planted a deep kiss on his lips.

"That's because I've been missing you all day today." She smiled impishly. "Now come on, we're going over to Rachel's. That girl has more makeup than Walgreens!"

Amanda took his hand and led him across the hallway into Rachel's apartment. She brought him over to a small stool placed in front of a dressing table and he sat down.

"Here you go Sis, he's all clean and dry." She turned around and started to rummage around in a makeup kit on Rachel's dressing table looking for a foundation that might work on his skin.

Rachel stood behind Alex with a hair dryer combing his hair. Once most of the dampness was gone, she began to pin it back so that it wouldn't get in the way of the makeup Amanda was going to apply. She looked at him in the mirror. "Before we go we have to get you ready, babe." Her eyes were twinkling mischievously.

Alex looked at her quizzically. "What do you mean?"

"Do you want to go shopping and try on girl stuff dressed like a girl or like a guy?" Rachel leaned down and kissed him on the cheek with a wicked grin.

"Oh, I see. A girl, I guess. But won't everyone know?"

"Not when we are through with you they won't,"

Amanda replied. "Now pay attention because there will be a test at the end of the lesson."

Alex blinked a bit shocked.

Amanda had a huge grin on her face and Rachel laughed. Amanda leaned in and kissed him on the cheek. "Just kidding sweetie. But you should pay attention so you'll know how it's done and you can eventually do it yourself."

Rachel reached down and pushed Alex's knees together.

"And don't forget to keep your knees together when you're wearing a skirt."

Amanda looked up from applying Alex's foundation. "Rachel, I don't have a bra that will fit him, do you?"

"I'll look in my dresser but I know the cups will all be too big," Rachel replied. "Maybe I can find a push-up." Rachel's size 'D' plus chest was considerably larger than Alex's 'C' cup but she wanted to look anyway. "Perhaps a demi cup would offer just enough support." She rummaged through her lingerie drawers. "I think I have an old one in here somewhere that just might fit."

While Rachel dug through her dresser, Amanda started on Alex's eyes. A few minutes later, and at the bottom of her bottom drawer, Rachel found a matching set that looked like they might fit him.

She slipped Alex's arms through the straps while Amanda finished with the mascara and eyeliner. After she closed the clasp on the bra Rachel leaned forward and kissed Amanda on the cheek. Then she had Alex bend forward and adjust his breasts into the cups on the bra. Once comfortable Alex leaned up and checked the fit in the mirror.

"You guys make a good team," he remarked watching the two of them working together so closely.

"Yeah, we do," replied Rachel as Amanda smiled sweetly.

While Rachel adjusted the bra straps Amanda finished with his eyes then added a little blush. The bra seemed to fit nicely. Then Rachel walked into her bathroom and returned shortly with a long piece of adhesive tape. She had cut a hole in one end and she split the other end up a little more than halfway.

"Here, could you stand up a second?" She asked Alex. "Sorry Amanda, this will only take a second."

Rachel reached around Alex and tried to slip the head of his cock into the hole on one end of the tape. But he was beginning to grow hard with all this attention and it didn't help that Rachel's mouth was only inches from his crotch.

"I'd love to help you with that babe, but if I do, the rest of the afternoon will be shot." Rachel grinned.

Alex sat down trying to control his heart and his cock from overheating. Amanda stood back and giggled at his predicament.

Eventually, trying to do a series of math problems in his head, things began to calm down. He nodded to Rachel that he was doing better.

"Okay, stand up babe, and let me slip this over the head." Rachel pushed his cock head into the hole she created on the end of the tape.

"Now reach under and push your balls into the hollow in your crotch." She watched him closely to make sure he understood her directions. "Good, now pull the tape underneath and lay your cock against your perineum. Not too tightly, just enough to flatten your front."

As Alex's cock pushed against his balls to hold them in place, Rachel pulled the two pieces of tape snuggly against his ass cheeks, on either side of his crack.

"This will keep you from standing up in the ladies room but it will still allow you to pee. Neat huh?" Rachel grinned as she admired her handiwork then she got up and walked over to her dresser.

"Here babe." Rachel tossed Alex a pair of her high-rise lace panties that matched the bra she selected. "Put these on."

Alex stepped into the panties and looked down at his crotch. The bulge that had been there since he was old enough to notice was gone. It was a bit unnerving at first. He looked up at the girls and smiled awkwardly.

"Now those panties fit you better," she said with a grin and Amanda stood admiring Rachel's handiwork with a smirk.

Alex turned bright crimson as he sat back down. He wiggled a bit to test how well the tape held.

So that was how Rachel managed to hide things. He was amazed at how easy it was. He was glad, for once, that the girls had taken so much care to remove all the hair from his body. Otherwise removing that tape later would have been brutal. He looked up and turned his attention back to Amanda with a sheepish grin.

"Okay sweetie, the trick here is to just put on enough to enhance not embarrass," said Amanda concentrating on her brushwork. "You're not doing a drag show."

Alex glanced over at the mirror and tried to watch what she was doing. Still it was hard to watch every step, especially when the makeup was being applied to his face.

"You already have beautiful features so all I'm doing is giving them a little highlight."

Rachel pulled some of the hairpins out of his hair and, using a hairdryer again, she began to finish drying and straightening his hair. Once that was done she walked back over to her dresser.

Rachel glanced over at Alex then turned back to her dresser. "Where are the shoes that you bought?" She was busy rifling through another drawer looking for clothes that might fit him.

"They're in my closet across the hall." He replied trying to keep an eye on what Amanda was doing with his makeup.

"I'll go get them, I'm almost through with his makeup anyway." Amanda set down a makeup brush and walking towards Rachel's front door.

Alex looked into the mirror and watched Amanda step towards Rachel's front door. "They're in the back on the left behind a box of papers."

"Okay, I'll find them." Amanda walked across the hallway and opened Alex's apartment door.

Rachel pulled a brightly striped scooped-neck tank top out from another drawer and handed it to Alex.

"Here, put this on," she said as she turned back to her dresser.

"Doesn't this reveal too much?" His voice sounded a bit nervous.

"Nope, it'll be just right. Those girls are lovely, babe, you shouldn't hide them. You just want to tease, not advertise. If you know what I mean."

"Do all girls think like this?"

"Not all, but a lot of them do. You've heard the phrase 'if you got them, flaunt them' haven't you?"

Alex nodded as Rachel turned to find him a pair of pants.

"I've got a pair of capris that you can probable fit into but we'll have to use a belt because your waist is narrower than mine, which makes me totally jealous." She opened up her bottom drawer again and dug to the back. "Found them," she said as she pulled out a pair of peach colored capris and handed them to Alex.

By the time Amanda returned with Alex's new heels Rachel was back to Alex's hair. She combed it carefully then pulled it back and up into a high ponytail. She used a curling iron to give the ends a bit of a curl and twist.

"It looks more feminine this way," she said as she brushed his hair and shaped the curl.

Amanda set his new three-inch heels by his feet and dropped a pair of knee-high sheer stockings next to them. Alex reached down and pulled on the knee-high stockings then he stood up to pull on the Capri pants. Next he stepped into his new shoes.

Amanda and Rachel both stood back and watched as Alex slowly turned towards them. He was a bit wobbly at first. But he had a good sense of balance and within minutes he was standing tall in his new heels.

"Whoa," said Amanda, gawking at Alex. "I can't believe it's you, sweetie. Rachel those clothes look great on him. Do you think the heels are too much for shopping?"

"Nah," she replied shaking her head. "Besides, they make his butt even cuter."

Alex blushed brightly and rolled his eyes, which made both women giggle.

"You look good enough to eat, babe," grinned Rachel with a gleam in her eyes. "Your makeup is perfect, nice job, Amanda."

"Thanks, Rachel," she replied. "Now let's go shopping!"

## =SIX=

They all piled into Alex's car and headed out to the local discount strip. Amanda drove, as it was too much to expect Alex to drive in heels for the first time.

"I think Alex needs a new name." Rachel looked across the front seat towards Amanda. "What do you think?"

"I agree," she replied. "Hmmm," she paused a moment in thought. "How about April? It's the month she was born," Amanda replied with a sweet smile.

"I like that, very springy," Rachel nodded her approval as she looked at Alex in the back seat.

"April, we're going to Target first to get all the basic stuff and then we'll head for the mall," said Amanda looking at Alex in the rearview mirror. "This is going to be so much fun!"

"Girls, are you sure about this?" Alex's voice had a bit of a quaver to it. It was easy to hear the tension in his voice. "This isn't some sort of hazing to get into the 'all girls club' is it?" His anxiety levels were continuing to climb.

"April, you'll do fine sweetheart, the only thing anyone will notice is how beautiful you are," cooed Amanda.

"She's right, babe. Come on, we're here," said Rachel, "I call dibs on dressing room assistant."

"Not fair!" Amanda shouted as they scampered arm in arm into the store laughing and giggling all the way to the women's section. Alex followed behind them walking a little less sure of himself with every step.

He blushed slightly as he looked at everyone he passed fully expecting each one of them to point and laugh. But no one seemed to notice. Still, his heart was racing.

As he walked down the main aisle he passed the women's accessory section on the right. Alex glanced over and noticed a woman behind the counter watching him. He smiled at her coyly and she smiled back. Not knowing what else to do, Alex raised his hand and meekly waved at her then he nodded at her at the same time.

Amanda came back over to Alex and grabbed his hand then she leaned up and whispered in his ear.

"What are you doing?"

"Nothing. The woman smiled at me and I smiled back. I think she knows!"

"Knows what?"

"That I'm not a woman!" He whispered through his teeth.

"Oh my God." Amanda replied in a forced whisper. "The way you were looking at her she probably thinks you're a lesbian!"

Alex blanched at the thought.

"Just act like you would if you were wearing jeans and a t-shirt," murmured Amanda. "Now stop being all weird and come on, sweetie."

A moment later they caught up with Rachel in the women's section. She was browsing through the clearance rack and Amanda joined her while Alex stood awkwardly fingering the texture of a blouse.

"Here." Amanda handed Alex a couple of Capri pants and some camisole tops. "Put these into the cart. You can try them on in a minute."

Rachel found a nice cotton sundress and one made out of a jersey knit and dropped them into the cart as well.

"You won't need to try these on because I already know that they'll fit from what you are wearing," Rachel said, already digging through another rack. She found a long black knit dress that dropped daringly low in the back and had a simple scooped neck front. She held it up against Alex to check the fit. Then she tossed it and a similar one in red into the cart.

While the girls continued to rummage through the racks Alex wandered over to the underwear section. He began to sort through the demi-cups for something that might fit.

"Hey sweetie," whispered Amanda, "we're going to Victoria's Secret after this, you don't need anything here."

"I know but this would be for everyday wear," he replied. "Besides, they have cute matched sets."

Amanda's eyes began to sparkle. "That's the spirit!" She helped him pick out a few more sets. Then she tossed his choices into the basket.

"Come on," Amanda said tugging him away from

the bra sets, "let's go to the fitting room."

"April, I've already got you set up in room three." Rachel gestured towards the fitting rooms with a wink towards Amanda.

"You can have Victoria's Secret," she whispered to Amanda as Alex entered the fitting room area. Amanda's eyes began to gleam with anticipation.

Alex glanced at the fitting room employee who stood near the front counter rehanging clothes on a restock rack. He wondered if the girl noticed anything odd about the woman who just walked past her. If she did, she didn't show it. Alex walked quickly back to fitting room three and ducked behind the door.

As Alex slipped off his pants and began to pull on the new ones. Rachel, wearing a wicked grin, couldn't resist the temptation. She reached inside his panties and touched him. Alex squirmed beneath the gentle touch of her fingers.

"Oh God Rachel, you're killing me," he whispered hoarsely. "That strap is a torture device. It works all too well."

"I'll be happy to take care of it once we get home, babe," she replied with a grin as she continued to massage his crotch. "I'm just checking to see if everything is still nice and snug. And it is," she giggled.

"You are a terrible tease!" His whisper was stressed by the tension in his panties.

"Of course," replied Rachel coyly. "But that doesn't mean you can't help me with my problem."

"What problem?"

Alex looked down and saw her cock begin to emerge from beneath her skirt. It tented her skirt as it continued to rise.

"How did you…" Alex whispered frantically.

"I brought the tape."

"But in a dressing room?" Alex listened frantically for any sounds that might suggest that the dressing room attendant was nearby.

"Don't worry babe, it happens all the time in here," Rachel replied nonchalantly.

"It does?"

Rachel kissed him hard on the lips then smirked as she pushed down on Alex's shoulders, lowering him towards her 'problem'.

Alex peeled Rachel's panties down and looked at the cock that was pointed towards his mouth. He parted his lips and kissed the head softly. It was amazing to him that in such a short time the very thought of sucking Rachel's cock has become so natural for him. It seemed to be an act that now felt so completely normal, at least with Rachel.

He could never imagine doing this with anyone else. He wasn't gay. He wasn't even bisexual. He just wanted to be with Rachel and Amanda, to please them as much as he could. Well, maybe he was a little bit bisexual; whatever.

Alex began to run his tongue along the underside of Rachel's rigid cock, licking and sucking her slowly. Then he moved his lips to let her begin to fuck his mouth. She moved her hands behind his head and guided him to take more of her and deeper. She was moving rhythmically in and out of his mouth, feeling him suck and lick her length.

"Ohh, you learn fast, babe," she sighed more a moan than a whisper. "Oh God, I'm close."

Rachel began to pick up the pace, moving quickly

in and out of Alex's mouth. Alex brought his hand up to stroke her base as he concentrated on her cock head.

Suddenly she erupted in his mouth, plunging deeper into him as she squirted down his throat. She held him gently as he hugged her waist tightly feeling her slowly soften in his mouth.

"I'm so glad I met you April," she murmured as her heart rate slowed down. "You and Amanda are simply the best thing that has ever happened to me."

Alex let her fall out of his mouth and he leaned up to kiss her on the small patch of hair above her cock.

"The feeling is mutual Rachel," he said with a sweet smile as he kissed her again. "Now pull your panties up and help me with these bras."

Rachel adjusted herself quickly and helped Alex try on several bras. Then Alex put on one of the dresses that Amanda picked out and looked in the mirror. It was a nice floral print that clung to him in all the right places.

"What do you think?" He asked twisting from side to side to glimpse the back.

"I think it looks great but you'd better show Amanda. She picked it out."

Alex padded softly out of the dressing room and stood in the entryway looking for Amanda. She waved from the shoe section and walked briskly back to the dressing room area.

"Oooh, very nice. Turn around sweetie," she cooed. "Perfect for brunch on Sunday."

"Brunch? Where?"

"At my office downtown. Didn't I mention it to you?" Amanda asked coyly. "It's an annual thing apparently, something to do with when the firm was established. It's business casual. This will be perfect."

"But…"

"Don't worry, Rachel will be there too," Amanda cooed. "Now hurry up and finish we have one more place to go to before we're done."

Alex turned slowly looking a bit overwhelmed. He padded in bare feet back to the dressing room and closed the door softly.

"Did you know about a brunch on Sunday?" he asked looking shocked.

"Amanda did mention something to me about it this afternoon before you came back from class. Why?"

"She…"

"Oh don't worry, you'll do fine," Rachel assured him as she held up a pair of pants to try on. "Here, try these on."

"Rachel," said Alex pointing at the bulge in Rachel's skirt and smirking, "where's your tape?"

Rachel blushed crimson and smiled sheepishly.

"Math problems worked for me," he said with a chuckle.

"I don't know how you do it, Alex Wells, but in only a couple of weeks you've managed to turn me into a blushing school girl." Rachel reached under her crotch and secured her penis with the tape.

Alex smiled and helped her adjust her skirt.

"Thanks," she grinned still blushing. "Here." She handed Alex several pair of pants. "Try these on next."

Rachel helped Alex try on a few more dresses, blouses and skirts. Some of them fit and a few were discarded. By the time they were finished Alex was beginning to amass quite a wardrobe.

"Amanda," he said walking back to his car, "what if I don't want to wear anything like this ever again?"

"The way you went through the bra section sweetheart, I'm not worried," Amanda replied with a big grin, "it's money well spent. Besides, I want you to look good this Sunday."

"Amanda, about this Sunday…"

"I'm sorry April, I should have mentioned it earlier. I guess in the rush to get you ready it just slipped my mind. Would you please join Rachel and me at my office this Sunday? I've told everyone about you and they really want to meet you." Amanda stood in the middle of the Target parking lot with a girlish pout on her face.

"How am I supposed to say no when you ask me like that?"

Amanda squealed and hugged Alex then she kissed him on the cheek. "Come on, Victoria's Secret is calling your name."

Victoria's Secret was truly a different experience altogether. The prices were outrageous and Alex found it difficult to accept Amanda's generosity but she would have none of it. She found three delicious looking nightgowns and an absolutely stunning teddy for Alex to try on plus three different types of bra and panty sets.

"This black lace one is uber-sexy," murmured Amanda as she watched Rachel feel the fine soft lace. "I'm going to enjoy peeling this one off of you," she whispered to Alex and he blushed a deep crimson.

Amanda found two more bras that were totally

decadent and tossed them in a pile near the register.

"My turn to be dressing room assistant," said Amanda melodically. And she wiggled her butt suggestively as she waltzed into the farthest dressing room with Alex in tow.

Once inside Amanda quickly helped Alex pull off his tank top and bra. Then she buried her face between his breasts and inhaled.

"God you smell good," she murmured. She moved her lips over and took a nipple into her mouth. She bit and sucked on the nipple pulling it out and making it swell up. While she worked one breast with her mouth she lifted her hand to the other breast and began to massage it gently then she trailed kissed across his chest and up his neck.

"I am so going to fuck your brains out tonight. God you make me horny," she whispered wantonly into his ear as she continued to fondle his breasts.

All in all Alex was aghast when the final bill was added up.

"Amanda," he whispered, "this is way too much. Please let me pay you back for all of this."

"April darling, you've got it all wrong," replied Amanda as she swiped her credit card in the machine. "I'm paying you back for all you've done for me. Besides," she whispered in his ear, "tonight we get to play dress up and that will more than compensate."

Alex looked up at the store clerk ringing up their sale and blushed as he saw a knowing smirk on the young girl's face.

"Come on. We have one more stop," said Rachel.

Amanda looked surprised. "We do?"

"Yup, the Discount Shoe Warehouse. I'm going to buy you at least one more pair of heels, some sandals, and a pair of flats."

They piled all the bags in the trunk of Alex's car and drove across town to the shoe store.

Alex followed Amanda and Rachel into the store. "I'm glad the shoes I have on aren't that high or I wouldn't have made it this far."

A pimpled-faced clerk stood at the register and watched the girls walk past him towards the back of the store.

"I think he knows," whispered Alex to Rachel.

"Who cares," replied Rachel. "You'll make his day if he ever finds out, but he won't."

"Hey, let's have some fun," Amanda whispered to Rachel.

"What kind of fun?"

"Just follow my lead when we get to checkouts," quipped Amanda with a wicked gleam in her eye.

They wandered down several aisles before Amanda stopped suddenly. "April, look at these. They're just naughty."

And they were; all five inches of those black stiletto heels with a black lace vamp and high ankle straps looked totally dangerous.

"They simply scream 'fuck me'," murmured Amanda with a twinkle in her eye.

Rachel flourished a wallet from her purse. "You got the dresses and the bras, Amanda. I get to buy the shoes and those are definitely on the list. Plus he wears the same size as I do so we can share."

Once they finished roaming the aisles the girls headed back to the front of the store. Alex dropped and armload of shoe boxes on the counter.

Amanda asked the store clerk to help April with her shoes. "She's having such a hard time with the strap," she said coyly.

The clerk walked around the counter towards April. His face was flushed as he knelt down next to April's shoes. He lifted her right leg and checked the fit of the shoe. As she lowered her leg the clerk bent further down and adjusted the ankle straps on each of the shoes.

"I just need to make sure the fit is correct," he muttered as he placed his hands on her ankles. But his movement was less like he was checking the fit and more like he was fondling her ankles. Alex, who now stood several inches taller than before in the five-inch heels, blushed crimson red. The clerk smiled as he made an attempt at a final adjustment then slowly stood up in front of Alex.

"How's the fit?" The clerk asked softly with a squeak and a catch in his throat.

"They feel fine," Alex replied shyly.

"She'll wear them out," said Rachel with a smirk.

The clerk nodded and returned to his register to check them out.

As they walked out of the store Alex leaned close to Amanda. "You are simply too dangerous to shop with," he whispered through clenched teeth. "I was so incredibly embarrassed when that clerk fondled my ankles."

"Oh pooh," Amanda replied with a smirk. "Tell me you didn't enjoy all that attention. You probably made that poor boy's week."

Alex, Amanda, and Rachel walked back to his car for the drive home. They dropped the shoeboxes alongside of the clothing bags in Alex's trunk then

Alex pulled the new set of ballet flats out of one of the boxes and brought them with him as he slipped into the backseat. He handed Amanda the keys to the car and grinned sheepishly. "My feet are killing me."

"You've gotten a lot better at getting into the car without flashing the world," Rachel said watching Alex sit into the backseat. "But it's tougher to do with a short skirt so keep practicing."

They drove out of the parking lot and headed towards their home as Alex took off the new pair of high heels and slipped on a pair of flats.

"Thank you, both of you," Alex said as he leaned forward and wrapped his arms around both girls' shoulders. "You made me feel very special today and I can't tell you both how much this has meant to me."

"You're welcome, April," replied Rachel.

"The same from me," added Amanda.

Alex sat up in the back seat and looked out the window. "Hey, I don't know about you two but I'm starving. There's a place on the corner that's good, let's stop there. And no argument, I'm buying."

The three girls walked into the restaurant and a hostess led them towards a booth by the windows. The hostess continued to glance at Alex as they walked back to their booth. She had a coy smile on her face and after she placed the menus on the table she brushed against Alex's arm and glanced back at him as she left.

Amanda glanced back at the hostess. "Did you see that Rachel?"

Rachel nodded and smirked at Alex.

"That hostess totally stroked April as she left. I think we've created a monster," Amanda glanced at them both with a wicked grin.

"Hush, both of you," Alex whispered blushing bright pink.

A few minutes later their food was ordered and they sat sipping on sodas while they waited.

"This has been quite a day," said Alex with a sigh.

"Hey," whispered Rachel, "don't look yet but those guys over there are totally checking us out."

"Where," asked Amanda looking up at Rachel?

"Don't look," said Rachel quickly. "Three booths down on the opposite side, the redhead is mine I could totally do him," she murmured softly. "Okay, now look."

Amanda and Alex slowly turned around and glanced back several booths to see three guys sitting in a booth all leaning forward and whispering to one another.

"You think they'll come over," asked Amanda?

"God, I hope not," replied Alex quickly turning back to look at Rachel.

About then all three of the young men got up and walked towards the girls. They stopped in the aisle in front of their booth.

"Hey," said the older looking of the three. He was tall and lanky with a shock of unkempt red hair that fell across blue eyes. His eyes sparkled with a mischievous twinkle.

"My name is Ted, this is Bryan, and Taylor," he said pointing to the other two as he named them. "You girls want some company?"

"We'd love to but not tonight, Ted," replied Rachel. "I'm Rachel, and this is April and Amanda. We've just spent the day shopping and we're exhausted. Perhaps some other time?"

"Sure," said Ted holding out a business card to

Rachel, "our numbers are on the back. Call us, okay?" The three boys walked back to the table, turned and waved as they sat in their booth.

"You are one cool chic," murmured Amanda as she waved back to the boys. "You handled that so well. You brushed them off and still gave them hope. You are a goddess."

"You have much to learn, grasshopper," Rachel replied with a grin then she turned to April. "Taylor was totally checking you out, April, I think you could have wrapped him around your little finger if you wanted to."

"Shush," April whispered, blushing again. "He's not my type."

"Oh, and who is your type?" Amanda looked at him with a smirk.

"You two," he replied softly.

After dinner they drove home and walked back in the rear door of the apartment house. As they crossed the foyer and began to climb the stairs Tom Reilly, the landlord, popped his head out of his apartment.

"Hey you guys," he said with a grin, "have you seen Wells?"

Alex began to edge behind Rachel hoping that Reilly wouldn't make any connection. Amanda bit her lip to keep from giggling.

"He promised me that he'd help me this weekend with the firepit in the backyard," Reilly continued. "Something came up and I need to see if he can help me Sunday instead of tomorrow."

"Sorry, Tom," replied Amanda. "But if we see him we'll tell him you're looking for him."

"Thanks," replied Reilly. He stood a moment

and surveyed the three lovely ladies standing before him. "You girls are sure looking foxy today," he growled suggestively with a foolish grin and a double thumbs-up gesture.

"Foxy?" Rachel grinned broadly. "Thanks Tom." She shook her head as she continued to climb the stairs. Amanda and Alex followed her as Tom shrugged his shoulders and closed his apartment door. Alex could hear Tom's television blaring in the background.

"If Nancy ever heard that she'd skin him alive," muttered Alex looking back at the foyer.

"Whose Nancy," Amanda asked?

"Tom's wife," Alex replied with a grin.


Alex collapsed on his couch and the bags he and the girls were carrying were piled around him.

"Damn, I simply don't know how you girls do it," he sighed. "I'm exhausted."

Amanda and Rachel pushed the bags out of the way and flopped down on either side of him.

"That was fun," sighed Amanda. "Thank you for being such a good sport about it. I haven't had a day out shopping like that in ages."

"I have to agree with April," murmured Rachel, "it was exhausting but I loved every minute of it." Rachel stood up and began to empty the contents of all the bags they carried onto Alex. In a matter of moments he was buried in bras, panties and dresses.

"How about we freshen up and meet back up at Rachel's in an hour?" Amanda suggested as she stood up slowly.

"Sounds great," Rachel replied. "I need a shower anyway. April, put on something cute from your new wardrobe when you come over, okay babe?"

"Humm, I can't wait to see what she picks out first," said Amanda with a broad grin.

Amanda and Rachel walked out of Alex's door and left him sitting alone, buried in a pile of new clothes with a silly grin on his face.

After a quick rinse in the shower and touch up of his makeup, Alex decided to go for the black dress that Rachel picked out at Target. He added the black lace bra and matching panties plus the black five-inch stilettos and black stay up hose to complete the look.

He opened his door, paused a moment, then took a breath and slowly let it out. When he was ready he walked out into the hallway. The click of his heels against the aging wood floors echoed along the corridor. It was as if he had discovered a whole new part of himself and that part had now become complete. For the first time in his life he felt...beautiful. It wasn't so much dressing as a woman, but dressing for himself that transformed him. And it felt good. It wasn't going to change who he was, but he was finally going to be true to himself.

He knocked softly on Rachel's door and waited. A moment later the door opened. Rachel and Amanda stood beaming with grins from ear to ear as they looked at Alex standing in the doorway.

"Oh my God, April," squealed Amanda. "You look gorgeous!"

"Come in, come in," repeated Rachel.

As Alex, walked into the center of the room he stopped and turned towards the two girls. He tilted his head in a coquettish manner and smiled coyly.

"You're right Amanda, she looks delicious. Would you like a glass of wine, babe?"

"I would love one, Rachel." He replied and then he turned to Amanda. "Won't you join me?" He extended his hand towards Amanda as they both followed Rachel into her kitchen.

The three of them stood a moment holding their wine glasses aloft.

"I propose a toast," said Alex looking at the two beautiful women standing before him with glistening eyes. "To family."

They clinked their glasses and downed the wine in one gulp then set them on the counter. Alex opened his arms and everyone came together in one big hug.

"Okay babe, I want to see you strut your stuff in that outfit," Rachel growled provocatively.

Alex walked around the counter and paused a moment. He looked back at the two girls and winked. Then he slowly strutted across the living room floor, paused, and then turned to walk back to the center of the room.

"What do you think?"

"I think I want to peel that dress off of you and make love to the gorgeous woman underneath," growled Amanda. "Want to help, Rachel?"

"Let's take this to the bedroom," murmured Rachel as she took Alex's hand and pulled him to the bedroom door.

Rachel and Amanda quickly let their dresses crumple on the floor around their feet as they stepped towards Alex to help him with his dress.

A moment later they all fell into Rachel's bed, kissing and giggling. Alex leaned over and kissed Amanda's nipples while he reached over to fondle Rachel's breasts.

"Oh yesss," Amanda hissed as she writhed under the touch of Alex's mouth.

Alex maneuvered around trailing kisses down her body to lick between Amanda's legs while Rachel began to open Alex up for her to take his cherry. A moment or two later Amanda maneuvered around to sit on Alex's face while she began to lower her mouth onto his swelling cock.

Once Rachel felt he was relaxed enough to take her girth, she opened a condom wrapper and slipped it over the head of her cock. She maneuvered around between Alex's legs and whispered to him. "Are you ready for me babe?"

Alex was pulling gently on Amanda's clit, sending her into orbit and could only moan while he felt Rachel slowly push her cock inside him. Although she managed to open him up quite a bit, he had heard that the first time was always the most intense. And this was certainly intense. Rachel paused so that Alex could adjust to the fullness of her inside him then she slowly began move in and out of his ass.

"Holy mother of God I feel so full with you inside me," Alex moaned as Rachel began to thrust harder.

Alex moved his fingers up to massage Amanda's g-spot while Amanda leaned forward and sucked on Rachel's nipples while stroking Alex's cock. All of this while Rachel continued to thrust in and out of Alex.

Alex drew his fingers across Amanda's g-spot once again and she started to soar as Rachel felt her orgasm build. She reached down and joined her hand with Amanda's to stroke Alex as the three of them climaxed as one.

Later that night Alex walked out of Rachel's bedroom donning one of her silk bathrobes as he crossed the living room floor. He opened the front door and walked across the hallway softly. Inside his apartment he pulled together what he needed to make a pot of coffee and walked back to Rachel's apartment.

Several minutes later, lured by the aroma of freshly brewed coffee, Amanda emerged from the bedroom and joined Alex on Rachel's couch. He got up and poured Amanda a cup then returned to sit next to her as Amanda snuggled up against him.

"Do you think we're going too fast?" she asked softly looking up into his face serenely.

"Maybe, sometimes yes, and sometimes no," Alex replied in a whisper. "I've waited a long time for love to come into my life. A love that could make me feel as complete as you two do."

Rachel, wearing a soft and flowing nightgown, walked softly across the living room floor and knelt down in front of Amanda and Alex. She leaned forward and laid her head into Amanda's lap as Amanda gently brushed Rachel's hair out of her eyes.

"I wish it could always be like this moment," murmured Rachel sweetly.

"So do I love," Amanda whispered, "so do I."

## =SEVEN=

Sunday arrived quietly with the sun peeking through the trees in the front of Tom Reilly's apartment house. Alex opened his eyes and blinked at the sun rudely streaming through his window. It was waking him much earlier than he wanted. Sunrise at six was rude, no matter how anyone looked at it.

Sunrise was coming earlier and earlier as the world drifted towards summer in Wilmington. It also meant that Alex's spring semester was nearly finished and he was facing another round of finals in a couple of weeks. The thought made him sink lower into his pillow. But today he had no time for studying, he promised to devote it all to Amanda.

Today was the day he was going to Amanda's office party with Rachel. It wasn't that he didn't want to go; he did actually. He just wasn't all that confident about going as April, his female counterpart. He'd only been dressing as April for a couple of days now, and he wasn't at all convinced that others would accept him. Besides that, the possibility that he would embarrass Amanda and

Rachel at a big corporate office party was not his idea of a pleasant Sunday afternoon.

Amanda, wearing fluffy pajamas, opened his front door as quietly as she could and slipped inside with a quirky grin. She almost glided across the floor, tiptoeing on bare feet. She slipped under the covers and cuddled up next to Alex.

"Morning, sweetie." She leaned over and kissed his forehead. "Have you decided who's going with me to the party this afternoon?"

"I think it has to be Alex. I'm not confident enough to go out as April. Besides, you've already told them about me as Alex so me showing up as April would be totally awkward."

"That's true, but I so wanted to see you in that new dress," she replied with a pout.

Alex pulled her across his chest and wrapped his arms around her tightly.

"I'll wear it next weekend when I take you and Rachel out to dinner," he replied kissing her neck and nibbling at her earlobe.

"It will just be me, babe," said Rachel softly as she turned to close Alex's door. "We have to take Amanda to the airport on Friday, remember?" She walked across the floor in her nightgown and bare feet to join them on his bed.

"Oh crap, I forgot. What time do you need to be there Amanda?"

"By 6:00 in the morning."

"Ugh, too early." Alex rolled off of his couch that served as his bed and sat at his makeshift desk. He jotted down a reminder so he wouldn't forget again.

"I tell you what, I'll take us to breakfast instead."

He added with a wry grin. "Just us girls."

"Where?" Amanda asked, her eyes sparkling with excitement.

"There's this quaint little Parisian restaurant on Elm Street, Madeline's I think it's called. I stopped in there the other day to check it out. Come on, scoot, I need all the time I can get to not look like a gorilla in drag," he said with a broad grin.

"I'll be back up in a flash to help," Amanda offered.

"Me too," Rachel added.

"Okay, hurry, I want to beat the church crowd," he replied.

Both girls scrambled for the door as Alex walked towards his bathroom.

Thirty minutes later they were both back in his room helping him put on the sundress that Amanda bought. Rachel, wearing flats for a change, quickly blow-dried his hair while Amanda, in sandals and capris, finished up his makeup. She pulled a pair of false lashes from her purse and started to apply them.

"These go on quick, look great, and they're easy to remove," she said as she lightly placed the second lash on his eye. "No mascara to scrub off either."

Meanwhile Alex dabbed a small bit of nail glue on a fingernail then he pressed a false nail in place.

Twenty minutes later he stood up and spun around in his three inch heeled sandals.

"How do I look? Passable?" he asked.

"Heavens yes! Let's go before I mess up your makeup devouring you right there on the spot," Rachel replied with a devilish grin.

"I can't believe I have such beautiful sisters!" Amanda exclaimed.

As the three of them walked down the last flight of stairs and into the front foyer, Tom Reilly poked his head out of his apartment.

"Hey Rachel," he asked squinting and looking a bit haggard in the morning light. "You haven't seen Wells have you?" Tom took a moment and glanced again at Alex standing slightly behind Amanda in a pretty sundress.

Alex looked away hoping that Tom wouldn't make any connections to the missing tenant from the third floor.

"No Tom, he's probably still in bed," Rachel replied with as much sincerity as she could muster given the urge to snicker.

"Thanks." Tom ducked back inside his apartment and closed his door. Alex could hear him muttering to himself even with the door closed.

They turned and walked quickly down the back hallway and out the door towards Alex's car. A French bakery was calling their name.

Madeline's was a quaint little French bakery that served Parisian cuisine for breakfast and lunch. It had an old world charm about it that spoke volumes about taking life at a more leisurely pace. It was always overcrowded by ten in the morning, especially on Sundays. Alex and the girls just managed to make it there before the mid-morning rush so they found a little table in a secluded alcove and sat down to enjoy their brunch.

"We have to do this again real soon," murmured Amanda taking the last bite of her quiche.

"As soon as you get back from Seattle," Rachel replied, "and this time it'll be my treat."

"April, I think you're getting better with being April," Amanda said with an impish smile.

"What do you mean?" asked Alex.

"The way you walk. How you sit. Even the way you eat, it's all becoming a lot more feminine."

"It is kind of fun to watch her bloom," added Rachel. "You're a fast learner, babe."

"Thanks, that's high praise coming from you two, you guys are like drill sergeants you know."

"We have plans," Rachel said with a wicked smile and twisting an invisible moustache.

Amanda laughed and playfully swatted Rachel's shoulder. "How far do you want to go? Would you like to live as a woman full time?"

"I don't think so. Don't misunderstand me, I love moments like this where the three of us can sit here casually and have a conversation, just us girls. These moments are really special to me. But remember that there is still a masculine side to me and that side wants to be here too."

"Are we pushing you too far?" Amanda looked a bit worried.

"No, I don't think so because it's all coming from love."

Alex looked up to see Amanda's eyes twinkle and Rachel's smile.

"I just think I need time to find out who I am, that's all. I think I belong somewhere between April and Alex. I'll get there eventually. I could never have done this without your help, you know. You two have been such wonderful sisters to me.

They giggled and all three held hands.

"Hey, what time is it?" Rachel asked.

"Nearly eleven, crap, we have to go, the party

starts at one," Amanda replied.

An hour later Alex walked across the hallway and knocked on Rachel's door.    He was wearing a nice pair of men's trousers and a light blue dress shirt and tie.

"Can you help me with these?" he asked as Rachel opened her door.   He handed her two diamond stud earrings.   "I'm still new to this and I can't seem to get them to stay."

"Sure babe, come over to the mirror and watch," she replied taking his hand in hers.

Rachel pushed the earrings in place and fastened the backs to them.   Then she looked at him with a smirk and bit her lower lip.

"What?" he asked looking into the mirror a second time. "Oh, yeah, I suppose those should probably go," he added carefully taking the false eyelashes off his eyelids.

Amanda knocked softly and opened Rachel's door.  She stepped into the living room as Rachel and Alex emerged from her bathroom.

"What should I do with these?" Alex asked handing the eyelashes to Amanda.

"Keep them, sweetie, they look good on you," she replied.  "Oh, and I like the earrings too.  Is that a compromise?"

"A little," he replied.   "Nobody at your office really knows me there so I suppose if I go as 'me' then they'll see that these earrings are part of 'me'.

"I like that," Amanda replied with a huge grin.

"So do I," Rachel added.   "What else is a 'part of you'?" she asked with a twinkle in her eye.

"That's a secret waiting for you both to find out

later when we get home," Alex replied with an impish grin.

The elevator chime announced their arrival at the ninth floor of the Ackerman building. As the doors slid open Alex could see a wall of mahogany paneling lining the vestibule. The words 'Dresher, Cummings, and Sanford – Investments and Securities' in bold gold letters were mounted in the middle of the wall opposite the elevators. It was part of the richly appointed hallway that led to Amanda's office.

"Wow, nice place!" exclaimed Alex in a low whisper.

"Yeah, don't let it get to you," Amanda replied. "This is how they like to impress or intimidate their clients, it depends on how you look at it. Don't worry, it's all for show."

"Remember babe, they all put their pants on one leg at a time just like the rest of us," Rachel added in a whisper as they walked towards the reception desk.

"I'll keep that in mind," he responded as they walked past the reception desk and into the commons area of the office. In the commons area a large banquet table was centered in the room. It was filled with all sorts of finger food and fancy delights. The table held a sparkling set of coffee urns, several bottles of champagne and wine, and numerous types of imported beers. It all looked rather festive.

There were about twenty people milling about as they entered. Amanda grabbed Alex and Rachel's arm and began to introduce them to everyone as her boyfriend and her sister.

"I didn't know you had a sister, Amanda," said Margaret Cummings, the firm's chief legal counsel and a senior partner. "Hello, I'm glad to meet you," she said to Rachel.

"Yes," replied Amanda, "she's the best sister in the whole wide world." Amanda gushed and Rachel blushed.

Margaret turned to Alex and smiled. "Hello again. I hope you're feeling better."

"I am thank you," Alex replied with a guarded smile.

Amanda looked a bit shocked. "Alex, how do you know Mrs. Cummings?"

"We had a brief run-in at an intersection a while back. I mentioned it at one of Reilly's backyard parties, remember?"

"He was determined to not let them do a full exam," Margaret added. "No matter what they offered he refused. I was very confused by it all." She held his hand and smiled warmly. "But no matter, it looks like you're doing well in spite of it all."

"Thank you Mrs. Cummings, I appreciate everything you did. Even replacing Tom's beat up bicycle."

"It was the least I could do, young man, you're welcome." She smiled to them all then stepped away towards a new group of guests that had just arrived.

The three of them walked casually over to the refreshments table after finishing their rounds of greeting most of the people in the room. There was quite a spread of canapés and desserts.

"Do you know what all this stuff is?" Alex asked in a whisper to Amanda.

"Not a clue," she replied, "but it looks scrumptious. Let's find out," she added grabbing a plate.

They filled their plates and then found a seat near a window that overlooked a park that hugged a meandering river near the center of downtown.

"Look at that," Rachel said with a chuckle. "You can see Moulin Rouge from here."

"Hmm, yeah," Amanda replied then she turned with a quizzical look on her face. "You don't have to work tonight, do you?"

"Yeah," she replied with a sigh. "I'm on at nine and off at one."

"Me too," Alex added with a frown. "But I'm on at seven. At least I give you a lift home after work if you want, Rachel?"

"That would be lovely," she replied. "Text me when you're on your way."

"No problem," he replied with a smile.

"Well crap, that means I'm alone again tonight. This sucks," Amanda slumped in her seat with a pout.

"Hello Amanda, nice to see you this afternoon," said a tall thin man with beady eyes.

"Hello Mr. Simmons," Amanda replied looking a bit nervous. "This is my boyfriend Alex and my sister Rachel."

"Well so nice to meet you both," Simmons shook their hands without actually looking either of them in the eye. The handshake bothered Alex. It was cold and clammy, like shaking the tail of a dead fish.

Rachel watched Simmons the whole time. He never seemed to take his eyes off of Amanda. And he looked at her as if he was thinking of things to do with her that would be illegal in all fifty states.

She'd seen this slime-ball before but she couldn't quite place where she'd seen him. It wasn't on the tip of her tongue but she'd remember soon enough.

"So Amanda," Simmons continued. He pushed his way in to sit between her and Rachel. "I see that Ballenger account has really taken off with your guidance, nice work, kiddo." Simmons patted her knee as he talked to her.

Amanda began to slide further away from Simmons and up against Alex.

"Thanks," Amanda replied. "I was just telling my boyfriend Alex about that account." Amanda placed an extra emphasis on the word boyfriend. Simmons managed to notice the implication. He glanced over at Alex a moment and watched as Alex glanced down at his hand on Amanda's knee. Then Alex stared coldly at Simmons. Simmons removed his hand from her knee with a smirk.

"Well, I'm looking forward to working a lot closer with you on a couple of new accounts that the firm just acquired. They are very important and the boss doesn't want us to screw them up," Simmons said with a leering grin.

"No problem," Amanda replied, "I'll see you bright and early Monday morning."

Simmons nodded then stood up and turned to saunter off towards one of the clients who just emerged from the elevator.

"That guy gives me the creeps," Alex muttered below his breath as he watched Simmons walk away.

Rachel glanced at Alex briefly then noticed Amanda shivering a little.

"Hey Sis, want to go to the restroom with me?" Rachel asked gently.

"Yeah, I need to wash my hands," Amanda replied a bit shaky and looking to Rachel and Alex for reassurance.

"Go ahead sweetie, I'll wait right here and watch our stuff," Alex said with a warm smile.

Amanda and Rachel turned and walked towards the restroom as Alex sat back down on the bench and gazed out the window.

"Where's the ladies restroom?" asked Rachel.

"We don't have separate restrooms," Amanda replied as they walked through the restroom door. "It's a new trend I guess. Besides, management likes to keep the costs down and if they only have to create one restroom to accommodate the staff then they can make the place nicer. At least that's what I've been told. It's all stalls anyway so I guess it doesn't really matter."

"I think I saw this on 'Allie McBeal'," said Rachel as she looked around the room.

Amanda walked over to the sinks and started washing her hands while Rachel stepped into one of the stalls.

Outside, Alex sat quietly munching on another cracker while gazing out the window. He turned briefly to set his plate down on the bench when he noticed Simmons skulking towards the restroom area. Alex's brow began to knit; it did that when something in the back of his mind told him that things were out of place.

Amanda stood at the sink counter and pulled several paper towels from the dispenser to dry her hands. Rachel was still in her stall when Simmons walked into the restroom.

"Well, Amanda, fancy meeting you here," he said with a leer. The expression on his face was one of expectation rather than surprise.

Amanda wondered if that was the best pick-up line he had as she turned to confront him. She was shocked to see that he was fast approaching her.

Simmons reached around each side of her and placed his hands on the sink counter, trapping her against it. Then he slowly began to move his lips towards Amanda's face.

"What do you think you're doing Mr. Simmons?" Amanda shouted as she pushed back against him.

"Just getting to know you better," he replied sarcastically. "After all, we are going to be working a lot closer together in the future aren't we?"

"Stop it! Get off me!" Amanda shouted as she struggled to push Simmons off.

A moment later a stall door slammed open and Rachel strode across the restroom floor. She planted one foot on the floor and swung her other foot up to firmly place the point of her shoe directly into Simmons' crotch. He crumpled to the floor in pain as Alex burst through the restroom door.

Rachel reached down and pulled Simmons around to face her, her fist was cocking back to slam into Simmons' face as Amanda cowered against the sink counter crying.

"Rachel! What's going on?" Alex demanded as he caught her arm before she could slam it down.

"I finally remembered where I saw this pervert," Rachel spat into Simmons' face. "You used to troll Second Avenue looking for young boys until you nearly got busted for pedophilia, didn't you scum? I suppose campaign contributions got you off the hook. Well not this time! Let go of me Alex, I'm going to smash his face in!"

"I'm sorry, I didn't mean anything by it, I was

just joking around, okay Amanda?" Simmons squeaked out an apology.

"Rachel, don't," Alex spoke softly as he held her tightly. "He's Amanda's boss. As much as I'd like to watch you punch his face in you can't. She could lose her job. It's not right, it never is."

Then he bent down and put his nose inches from Simmons's face.

"But believe me you little fuck, if you ever touch her again I'll find you and fucking kill you," he whispered vehemently, barely audible but loud enough for Rachel and Amanda to hear.

Simmonds opened his mouth as if to protest then he looked again at Rachel then glanced back at Alex. True terror crept into his eyes as he cowered on the floor under their unwavering stares.

Alex stood up and lifted Rachel off of Simmons then he stepped over him to help Amanda stand up. The tears in her eyes were trailing down her face as she shuddered in Alex's embrace. She struggled desperately to fix her dress. Alex looked down and saw that Simmons must have pulled at Amanda's new dress when he fell because one of the straps had torn off. Her bra was exposed in the front and she was trying frantically to hold her dress up while sobbing at the same time.

"Come on sweetheart, let's get you home," he said softly lifting Amanda away from the counter. He held out an arm as they stepped over Simmons and gathered up Rachel on the way out. He kissed her on the cheek as they walked out the door.

"I'm glad I'm on your side beautiful," he said hugging Rachel again.

He picked up his coat and draped it over

Amanda's shoulders as they turned and walked towards the elevators.

"We'll get this fixed next week and it will be as good as new," Rachel said to her as softly as she could. "Or that SOB will pay for a new one," she growled under her breath as they stood near the elevator.

"Rachel, I love you dearly, but that's not how the corporate world works," he said sadly. "No matter how good it would feel to kick his ass right now, in the end she would have to pay for it with her job."

"Not today," announced Margaret boldly as she walked from the reception area with determination. She closed quickly on the three of them standing near the elevator doors. "Amanda, I am so very sorry for what happened in the restroom just now. I promise you that it will never happen again. I was in one of the other stalls and I overheard what happened. Your friends handled everything before I could even open the stall door."

Margaret turned to Alex and shook his hand.

"Thank you young man for keeping your head about you. In the long run it will make what I'm going to do on Monday a whole lot easier."

Margaret turned back to Amanda and smiled warmly.

"Amanda, you're one of our best and brightest analysts and we don't want to lose you or your talents. From now on you'll work directly for me. There are going to be some changes around here come Monday morning, but trust me, you being forced to leave this firm is not going to be one of them."

Margaret extended her hand. She took Amanda's and firmly shook it. A chime sounded and the elevator door opened. Alex, Rachel, and Amanda stepped into the elevator with a look of shock on their faces. As the elevator door began to close Margaret nodded and turned towards the main office.

Amanda, still a bit thunderstruck by what had just happened turned to Rachel and hugged her tightly.

"You truly are my big sister, Rachel," she smiled and hugged her again.

"I just did it because I knew that if Alex saw what he was doing he would have killed the bastard. I hate visiting people in prison," she said with an awkward grin.

Amanda leaned up and kissed Rachel on the cheek. "Thank you, Sis."

Alex wrapped his arms around the both of them and kissed Rachel on the other cheek.

"Thank you love," he added, "for watching over both of us."

Rachel grinned and sighed. "Your welcome, babe."


As they walked towards Alex's car Amanda began to reflect on what had just happened in the restroom on the ninth floor.

Deep down inside she realized that she still hadn't come to grips with the attempted rape that her stepfather tried on her years ago. The trauma of watching someone, especially your father, well, stepfather, try to force themselves on you has left her scarred emotionally. When Simmons tried it she froze rather than trying to defend herself, her self-confidence dissolved.

She couldn't let assholes like Simmons or her

stepfather rule her life. She knew she had to find a way to defend herself. Amanda continued to think about it as Alex drove them back to the apartment house. Along the way she noticed a recreation center with a sign out front announcing upcoming classes in Tae Kwon Do. It was as if karma turned on a light.

"I've decided that I'm going to start taking self-defense classes," Amanda announced to Rachel and Alex. "As soon as I get back from Seattle. I'm sick of being pushed around by assholes like Simmons. And you guys won't always be around to help me out. So I need to do this for myself.

"Sign me up," Rachel agreed. "I'll take them with you."

"Me too," said Alex. "Although Rachel should probably be teaching them!"

Everyone laughed at that remark and the atmosphere in Alex's car became a lot lighter.

"Besides," Alex added, "I could use the exercise, I'm getting flabby."

"Nonsense, you have such a cute tushy," said Rachel coquettishly.

They got back home just in time for Reilly to catch Alex as they walked in the back door.

"Wells!" he shouted. "Finally. I need help with that fire ring, remember?"

"Sure Tom, let me change and I'll be right down."

Amanda opened her apartment door and pulled Rachel in behind her. As she closed her door she glanced up the stairway and caught Alex's eye. He nodded and smiled then disappeared up the next flight of stairs.

Amanda's apartment was larger than Alex's small efficiency but not as large as Rachel's. It was a small three-room apartment with the central room serving as kitchen and living space. There was a bedroom off to the left and through there a small full bath adjoining it.

There was a lovely bay window seat that looked out on a side yard. The window included a lovely view of a huge old maple tree that offered ample shade to that side of the house in the summer. In the short amount of time since Amanda moved into her apartment she managed to make the place seem homey and comfortable. There were a few photographs on the dresser, mostly of her mom and her cousin in Seattle. There were several prints and a few art posters covering the walls. What little furniture she brought with her from Salt Lake City was soon discarded for a much nicer living room set she found at a second-hand store a couple of weeks after she moved in.

"I need a drink, how about you?" Amanda asked opening a bottle of wine and taking out two glasses.

"I'd love one," Rachel replied. She walked over to the couch and flopped down near the window. "What about Alex?"

"He saw us come in here. He'll be in as soon as he's finished playing with Reilly."

She poured two glasses and waked over to sit next to Rachel.

"I wish I didn't have to work tonight," Rachel lamented wrapping an arm around Amanda's shoulders.

"Me too, I really miss you guys when you both have to work late." Amanda paused a moment and smiled at Rachel sweetly. "Rachel…"

"Shush," Rachel interrupted. "We're family, we watch out for each other. That's what families do."

"I was so scared," she murmured softly.

"I know, I was too," Rachel replied softly stroking Amanda's hair.

"All I could think about was my sicko step-dad sneaking onto my bed when I was thirteen. I just froze," she said as she sat closer.

Rachel continued to stoke her hair gently as Amanda leaned against her shoulder and sighed.

Amanda looked up into Rachel's eyes. "Would you hold me?"

"Forever," she said setting down her glass of wine. She held out her arms for Amanda to curl into. In a matter of moments she was sound asleep.

It was nearly five o'clock before Alex was able to finish all the chores that Reilly had on his list. He dusted himself off on the back porch then walked down the hallway towards Amanda's apartment. He opened the door quietly and peeked his head in to see Rachel and Amanda asleep on the couch. As he started to back out of the apartment he saw Rachel open her eyes and motion him over to her.

"She's exhausted," she whispered. "Help me get her to bed, love."

Together they carried Amanda into her bedroom, removed her shoes and her torn dress then laid her gently in her bed. Rachel and Alex both leaned over and kissed Amanda lightly on the cheeks and she snuggled further down into her pillow with a sweet smile on her face.

They tiptoed out the door and closed her

apartment door gently. Then they slowly ascended the three flights of stairs to their apartments. When they arrived on the third floor Alex turned to Rachel and hugged her tightly.

"You are one beautiful woman," he whispered into her ear and she hugged him back. "I've been very remiss in not telling you that often enough."

"Thank you," she whispered her reply, "I love you too."

As they parted to go into each apartment Alex turned and asked, "Do you have your driver's license?"

"Sure, why?"

"Why don't you take the car tonight? You could drop me off and pick me up when you get done. We both get off about the same time don't we? Unless…"

"Oh god, that would be perfect, thank you Alex," she said interrupting. "You have no idea how much I hate the bus. What time do you need to leave?"

"In an hour."

"Come over when you're dressed and I'll fix something light for dinner," she said with a huge smile.

Alex blew her a kiss and smiled as she closed her apartment door.

Ten minutes later Alex opened Rachel's door and peeked his head in. "Hey there, can I come in?"

"Of course." She stood in the kitchen dicing vegetables for a salad. Alex wandered over and sat on a stool at the island counter.

"I like the idea of learning some self-defense," he

said. "Amanda's right, we can't be with her all the time and I've heard that martial arts can build your confidence levels too."

"I know I've always wanted to learn. Everything I know is what I've learned off the street."

"It certainly was effective today," he said with a smirk.

"I hope it hurts that bastard to pee for the next six months," Rachel hissed vehemently.

"It probably will considering the way the point of you shoe connected with his balls," said Alex shaking his head. "I'm surprised you didn't make him a eunuch," he added with a chuckle.

Rachel blushed slightly and gave him a wry grin.

"I like the little crystal flowers," she said coyly. She was referring to the small earring studs that Alex added. "Where did you get them?"

"I saw them in a little shop on Ninth Avenue. I just wanted to add a little accent, nothing flashy," he replied. "Baby steps, you know."

"Of course. They're cute."

"Thanks. Here's the keys to the car," he said pulling a ring of keys from his pocket and tossed them onto the counter. "I hope you're okay with a stick-shift."

"No problem, babe," Rachel replied. "My uncle owns a farm. I learned to drive a tractor when I was ten."

"The image of you on a tractor boggles the mind," he said with a devilish grin.

"I'll boggle your mind," she said swatting his head playfully with a hand towel.

"That'll have to wait till I get back," he replied swinging at her butt and missing.

"Hey, let me see your driver's license," he said with an impish grin.

"Why? Don't you trust that I have one?" she asked digging through her purse and handing him her wallet.

"Of course I do, I just want to see your picture."

"Wait a minute," she wrapped her arms around him and playfully tried to wrestle her wallet out of his hands.

"Oh wow," he said a bit amazed, "even without makeup you look sexy."

"I do not, I look hideous," she said blushing crimson.

"No, you do, especially your eyes. Hmm, your gender is listed as male," he said thoughtfully handing back her wallet.

"Yeah, I know," she said stuffing her wallet back into her purse. "In most states you have to be anatomically female to be listed as a female. It's one of the reasons why I'm extremely careful when I drive. Cops can be pigs sometimes, not all of them, but some."

"Good to know," he replied pulling her close to him and kissing her on the lips.

Rachel giggled a little then her face became more thoughtful.

"What do you think about the three of us getting a house?" she asked suddenly. She tried to act nonchalant about it but it was obvious that she had been thinking about it for quite some time.

Alex paused a moment and considered her question.

"Well, I would love it but I don't see how I could possibly contribute equally to the rent," he replied.

"Every dime I have goes to pay my tuition. I guess I could look for another job."

"We don't see one another enough as it is without you getting another job, babe."

A soft knock and Amanda poked her head in. "Hi, what's cooking?"

"Chicken and a salad," Rachel replied. "I thought you were asleep."

"I was but I missed you two so I came up here before you left for work to kiss you both goodbye," she said with a cute smile. She walked over to Alex and rubbed her hand across his shoulders gently.

"Join us, we were just talking about the possibility of getting a house together. Just the three of us," Rachel said turning back to her salad.

"I absolutely adore that idea!" Amanda exclaimed. "I'll start looking tomorrow."

"Wait, wait," Alex said putting up his hands. "I just told Rachel before you came in that I don't see how I could possibly share the rent equally."

"Don't worry about it, I'm not looking for a 'McMansion'," Amanda replied hugging Alex.

"Exactly, I'm not either," Rachel added.

Amanda nodded in agreement. "We'll find a place that we can all afford."

"I was looking online the other day," Rachel said pulling a bottle of salad dressing from her refrigerator. "There are several neighborhoods nearby where if we look hard enough we can find a place that we can afford. If we combine what we're paying to Reilly we could easily swing the rent on a nice little bungalow."

"With a bedroom large enough for a king-sized bed?" Alex asked with a grin.

Rachel's eyes gleamed.

"You read my mind sweetheart," Amanda giggled.

That night, at nearly one in the morning, Alex stood at the back of the convenience store stocking one of the shelves when several young men dressed like 'gangster-wannabes' walked in the door. From the looks of them they were barely over sixteen but they puffed themselves up and sauntered along trying to look tough.

They wandered up and down the aisles looking more to relieve their boredom than to actually buy something. They pushed past Alex and knocked over a cookie and cracker display in the process.

"Hey, a simple 'excuse me' would be nice," grumbled Alex.

The boys turned around and smirked.

"Fuck you sissy boy," spat the tallest of the three boys. His face was scarred with acne and his lips and nose were pierced with several rings.

"Yeah faggot, shut the fuck up," said another of the boys. His lack of height was quickly compensated by his girth.

"Is there a problem back there?" shouted Inez, Alex's coworker from the front counter.

"Nothing I can't handle, Inez," Alex replied. Then he picked up the packages of cookies and crackers that spilled across the aisle and began to replace them on the display. The three boys snickered maliciously and sauntered away. They stopped at the coolers and looked at the racks of beer on display.

Alex finished cleaning up the mess on the floor. He moved down another aisle and walked into the backroom to pull out another container of product for display. When he came out of the backroom he noticed that the boys were still debating over their choices of beer. He motioned Inez over.

"Look really close at their IDs when they get up front," he whispered. "They're probably fake."

Inez nodded and returned to the register.

Alex smiled at her and glanced at the clock on the wall. It was almost time for his shift to end and he was happy to see it nearly finished. His feet were tired. He went to another display and began to replenish the stock with new product.

A moment later the three boys walked up to the checkout counter. They plunked down a twenty-dollar bill and a six-pack of cheap beer.

"ID please," Inez asked flatly and the boys nervously pulled out their wallets.

The glass doors opened and Rachel walked into the store with a wry smile on her face. The three boys turned slack-jawed and stared at her. Under her coat was a shimmery gown that clung to her breasts and hips provocatively. Her hair was done up in curls and standing in five-inch heels, she towered over the punks at the front counter.

The tallest of the boys looked over at Alex and scoffed.

"What are you gawking at sissy boy? She's hardly interested in a puke like you," he said with a smirk.

"Yeah faggot," said blubber boy, "what are you looking at?"

The third boy started to open his mouth but stopped suddenly. He watched, in shock, as Rachel slapped the chubby boy across the face. The sound of the slap echoed across the store and the force of it sent him flying against the other two boys. They all fell against the counter and nearly collapsed on the floor.

"These IDs are fakes," said Inez flatly. "I'll be confiscating them. If you don't leave this store immediately I'll be calling the cops right now."

The boys slowly stood up and turned to watch in shock as Rachel planted a wet kiss on Alex's lips.

"Evening love," she said with a grin. Rachel turned back to the three boys who stood gaping at her.

"You heard what she said," she snapped. "Get your little dicks out of here and never come back or I'll take a box cutter and cut them off."

The three boys scrambled over each other as they raced for the door. Alex and Rachel laughed as the door hit the third boy in the ass on his way out.

"You have got to find a better way to pay for your tuition, babe," she said with a sigh.

"Inez, this is Rachel. Rachel, Inez," Alex said with a sheepish grin. "One of these days you're going to get into trouble slapping little fat kids like that."

"What? He was trying to molest me," she said with an indignant look and brushing an errant lock of hair behind her ear.

"I saw it too," Inez chirped cheerfully. "It was definitely sexual harassment," she added nodding enthusiastically. "I know what it looks like because I watched a training video on it just last week. So I know for certain."

Alex shook his head and chuckled

"Thank you Inez," she said with a wink in her direction. "Are you about done?" Rachel asked looking at Alex as she dangled the car keys on her finger.

"I just have to clock out," he replied. "Back in a moment."

## =EIGHT=

Monday morning came too soon for Amanda. In spite of what Margaret said at the party, she dreaded having to face Simmons and the rest of the office staff this morning. Even if she would be working for Margaret, she would still have to be in the same building with the weasel. Plus, she knew there would be gossip. In an office there is always gossip.

But dammit, she clenched her fists tightly, she was the victim here not that creep Simmons, and the rest of them can just go to hell for all she cared.

She set her jaw and waited for the elevator to reach the ninth floor. The chime announced her arrival in the hallway vestibule and she turned to see a crowd of her co-workers standing near the reception desk. A second glance proved that most of them were women. One of them turned and started to clap. Soon the rest of them joined in and once again Amanda was dumbfounded.

As she walked into the reception area one of her co-workers, Anna, a receptionist in Acquisitions, leaned over and said, "Thank you so much for standing up to that sleaze ball, Simmons."

"Today is your day Amanda," shouted another of one of the women.

"And lunch is on us!" shouted a third girl from Accounting.

Amanda walked past them with a dazed look on her face. She walked over to her desk and saw a note from Margaret Cummings, CEO of Dresher, Cummings, and Sanford. It asked that she come to her office as soon as she checked in this morning.

Still a bit gun-shy she walked across the commons area towards Margaret's office. A chorus of 'good mornings' and bright smiles greeted her as she passed by. She was not used to this much attention and she was a bit unnerved by it all. She knocked softly on Margaret's office door.

"Come in," came the familiar voice from across the room. "Oh, good, you're here, come in, come in." Margaret stood up and began to come around her desk. "Would you like a cup of coffee?"

"Mrs. Cummings, this is all a bit overwhelming. No wait, I can get the coffee. You sit down, I'll bring it right in. Cream and sugar?"

"Just cream, thank you," Margaret replied returning to her seat.

Amanda glanced around outside of Margaret's office looking for Simmons. No one seemed to be around so she dashed into the copy room and poured two cups of coffee and added cream to both. Then she carried the coffee back into Margaret's office.

"If you're looking for Simmons, he's cooling his heels in the Milwaukee airport right about now. I decided that he needed a little vacation from the fast pace of Wilmington and Milwaukee is just the place for him. Besides, there are only two other employees up there and they're both men over fifty. So Simmons should feel right at home," Margaret said with a grin like the cat that just caught the canary.

"I've been looking for a good excuse to get that asshole out of this office for years. Although I'm sorry it had to happen to you, you provided me with the perfect opportunity. Thank you."

"You're welcome," Amanda replied still in shock.

"And thank your boyfriend again for being so level headed," Margaret added.

"I will," said Amanda meekly.

"Now then," Margaret continued. "Let's get to it." She spread her arms wide across the top of her desk and grinned at Amanda.

"You should be promoted to senior analyst, which is what you deserve, but I can't, at least not yet. I can't have the rest of the staff thinking that I've grown soft. But what I can do is assign you to focus more on several of our senior accounts. And you'll be adequately compensated, of course. The commissions are rather substantial."

Amanda listened a bit wide-eyed as Margaret laid out a detailed plan of what she hoped would be accomplished in the next six months. It was all very complex and a bit overwhelming. Amanda nodded and smiled then pulled a notebook out of her purse and took a battery of notes trying to keep up with her new boss's plans. She was to form a new international section. Margaret wanted her to find people she could trust. And she wanted Amanda to begin implementing her plans as soon as she could orient her team.

"I want you to move out of the commons area and into Simmons' office. Use the empty one next to it for your staff. Have Radcliff…"

Suddenly her phone began to ring and Margaret stopped to answer it.

My god, three months ago she was standing on a bus platform in Salt Lake City thinking she had just been pushed off the edge of the world, and now this. Oh shit, Susan's wedding is this weekend!

Margaret replaced the phone receiver and smiled at Amanda. "That was Donaldson in the Milwaukee office," she said with a chuckle. "Apparently they didn't want Simmons up there either. Now, where were we?"

"Um, I know that this change is important, and I hope this doesn't ruin things but I've got tickets to fly to Seattle this weekend. My cousin is getting married and I know it's probably coming at a bad time and all…"

"Perfect!" Margaret shouted slapping her desk with enthusiasm. "While you're out there you can check in with the Seattle office. Several of the accounts I want you to pick up crossover between the coasts and I want you to make sure that they're doing all they can to keep those clients happy. Add a couple of days to your flight itinerary and ask Carol to look into your flight and book a hotel for you."

"That's okay, I was planning on staying with at my cousins," murmured Amanda.

"Okay, no problem. In that case, add me to the guest register and pick out a nice gift for the bride from me," Margaret replied shuffling through a stack of papers on her desk.

"Oh, and bring me back some cake. I'm a sucker

for wedding cake," she added as she waved Amanda out the door.

She closed the door gently and turned to lean against it. She felt like a tsunami just washed over her in the name of Margaret Cummings. It was all a bit too much to take in one gulp. She straightened her suit jacket and smoothed the front of her skirt then walked with purpose across the office floor. She was trying to think about whom she could put on her team but her head was filled with fluff. Her mind was still reeling from her meeting with Margaret Cummings. All of a sudden she went from part-time lackey to the assistant to the CEO for international accounts. She reached across to pinch herself. She wanted to make sure she wasn't dreaming.

She knew she had to pull herself together. But first, before she could do anything else, she had to call Alex, because inside she was nearly bursting at the seams.

Amanda dashed over to her desk and dropped her coat then turned and walked briskly to an empty conference room. She closed the door and nearly screamed, she was so excited. She pulled out her cellphone and quickly dialed Alex.

"Hey, it's me. I'm sorry to wake you but I have fantastic news. If you have to work tonight cancel it or call in sick or whatever. That goes for Rachel too. We're going out tonight to celebrate, just us girls. So wear something nice because we're going someplace special," she said.

"What's the news?" he asked still a bit groggy. He glanced at the alarm clock and groaned.

"I'll tell you when I get home and we're all together. Ohh, I'm nearly bursting at the seams!" she exclaimed. "Okay, I've got to call Rachel. I love you sweetheart. You are the best! Bye."

Amanda quickly punched more buttons and waited while the connection rang through.

"Tamsen, Willis, and James, this is accounting, Rachel speaking…" Amanda could barely wait through Rachel's greeting before she interrupted.

"Rachel, my lovely sister, I've got great news. If you have plans for this evening, cancel them, we're going out to celebrate, just us girls!"

"What is it?"

"I'll tell you when I get home and we can all be together. I can say that I'm flying first class to Seattle on Friday courtesy of Margaret Cummings." She heard Rachel catch her breath on the other end of the line.

"Yes! Oh god, I'm giggling like a schoolgirl. Okay, I have to pull myself together here." Amanda drew in a big breath and tried to center herself but it was no use, she was flying high.

"I just called Alex and woke him up, poor thing, but I couldn't help it," she added.

"So when do you get home?" asked Rachel.

"Around four, how about you?"

"I'll be there around then too."

"Great, I'll meet you in your apartment at four. Will Alex be there too?" Amanda asked.

"I'm not sure, I know he has a class this afternoon but I'm not sure when it's over," she replied.

They finalized their plans. Amanda said she'd text Alex to make sure he'd be there at the same time as everyone else. Then she sat down in the leather bound chair at the head of the conference table and spun it around to face the world outside a huge wall of windows.

She felt like she was the luckiest girl in the world! She twirled in the seat with a smile and outstretched arms. "Yes!"

"Where do you girls want to go?" Amanda asked nearly bouncing with joy. She had just spent the last fifteen minutes recounting everything that had happened in her office this morning.

"I'll take you to the swankiest restaurant in town, totally my treat!"

Alex walked out of the bathroom and turned off the light. He was dressed in women's slacks and a blouse with dress pumps. He had on the diamond stud earrings that Amanda gave him and the silver necklace from Rachel. He pulled on a women's dress suit jacket and fixed his collar.

"Honestly I'm never impressed by service but always impressed by the quality of the food," Alex said. "I vote we go back to that French restaurant."

"I saw this Indian place on Dexter that looked interesting," Rachel said her eyes gleaming with hope.

"Really? Not some fancy place that charges fifty bucks a plate?" asked Amanda slightly bewildered.

"Alex love, let me fix your hair," Rachel said. She pulled him by the arm back into her bathroom. Amanda followed right behind them.

"Sweetheart, wherever I go with you is fine by me. But don't waste your hard earned money on a pedestrian palate like mine." Alex added kissing her on the cheek.

"Indian, Indian, Indian," chanted Rachel as she brushed Alex's hair.

"Okay, my sweet sister, we're going to the Taj Mahal on Dexter," Amanda replied with a big smile as she touched up Alex's makeup.

Amanda spent most of the dinner outlining Margaret's plans for expansion and reorganization of the firm. She could barely contain her enthusiasm.

The rest of the week flew by in a flash. Before anyone knew it, Amanda's bags were packed for her trip to Seattle and she stood waiting by her door for Alex and Rachel to come down the stairs. Her nerves were all jitters as she checked her makeup in her compact one more time. She could hardly believe it. She was flying first class to Seattle. A trip she made by bus just three months earlier.

Her cousin was getting married and she was a bridesmaid. And she was Margaret Cummings' new assistant for international accounts. She reached over and pinched herself again just to make sure she still wasn't dreaming.

At 7:30 in the morning Amanda's plane roared down the runway and lifted off bound for Seattle by way of Chicago's O'Hare Airport.

She glanced out the window to watch Wilmington quickly recede in the distance. Tonight was the rehearsal dinner and tomorrow will be Susan's wedding. She thought about Susan's wedding for a moment.

She remembered crying in Reilly's backyard when she heard the news that Susan, her cousin and really her only childhood friend, was getting married to her boyfriend of six years. At the time she felt like she wanted to die. A failed marriage and a one-way ticket to 'no-where's-ville' had her thinking that her life was just one big train wreck.

Then along came Alex with his big goofy grin and magical charm. In a dazzling twirl, he spun her around to see how wonderful her life was. She will never forget that moment and how, with just a thought and a smile, he transformed her life.

She tilted her seat back and closed her eyes. She would miss having Alex and Rachel next to her in bed but she smiled blissfully knowing that they were there waiting for her to come home next Sunday.

That night, after Alex's shift ended at the convenience store, Rachel arrived to pick him up. She was dressed in blue jeans and a sweatshirt. She wore her hair up in a ponytail that she pulled through the back strap on a tattered old Boston Red Sox cap. Even with ballet flats she looked totally sexy to Alex. He grinned at her when he saw her standing in the doorway to the backroom of the store. She stood there with a sexy smirk on her face.

"You know, even if you try hard not to, you still look sexy as hell," he said with a wry grin.

They drove to a little park next to the river that meandered through the center of the city. It was the same park that Rachel noticed when she looked out of the window of Amanda's office last Sunday.

Alex looked a bit confused. "I thought you had to work tonight."

"They cancelled my shift at the last minute, it was a slow night anyway."

Rachel parked the car near a set of swings. They got out and walked slowly down along the river's edge.

"I miss her already," she murmured as she picked up a stone and skimmed it along the water until it fell below the surface with a plunk. "With the wedding and the parties, she's probably having the time of her life tonight."

"Maybe," Alex said with a shrug. "But if she was here I bet she'd argue that the real time of her life is right here, with us."

Rachel took his hand and guided him over to sit down on a bench.

"It has been for me." She smiled and leaned her head on his shoulder. The wooden bench they sat on beneath a canopy of trees overlooked the river. She sighed a little and snuggled closer to Alex.

"I never thought I'd be so lucky," Rachel said softly, almost in a whisper. She took his hand in hers and gave it a little squeeze then he wrapped his arm around her shoulders.

"I figured that because of who I am, that the world would only allowed so much happiness for one person. I thought that love and acceptance was just not in the cards for me. Then I met you two, and this cat isn't a stray anymore.

"It's getting chilly out," he said wrapping his coat around her shoulders and pulling her closer to him.

"Another reason to snuggle," she said softly, leaning up to kiss him on the lips.

"Get a room," growled a gravelly voice from beneath a tattered old blanket and padded coat that had seen much better days. "I'm trying to sleep here, assholes."

Alex looked over at the vagrant huddled under the pile of old clothes on the next bench and nodded.

"Come on love, let's go home."

They walked slowly back towards the car arm in arm, Rachel's head nestled against his shoulder. The ride back to the apartment house was quiet and serene.

"Stay with me tonight," she asked softly with a kiss.

"Of course," he replied returning her kiss.

The door closed softly behind them.

"Hey look," Rachel said with a giggle. She came bounding out of the bathroom and bounced across the bed towards Alex. She was clad in her panties and nothing else. She sat next to Alex while she pulled lightly on her right nipple and squeezed her breast. A moment later a small drop of white liquid appeared on her nipple.

"Wow." Alex was amazed. "Is that milk?" He sat up and looked closely at her breast.

"Taste it," she said lifting her breast towards his mouth.

Alex leaned forward and stuck his tongue out to capture the drop as it formed on her nipple.

"It is milk. It tastes sweet."

Rachel glowed with a radiance that looked like she was as happy as she could ever be.

"I can give milk," she whispered.

"I see that! That's wonderful!"

"Yes, it is."

"How is this possible?" he asked.

"Well, since my shift was cancelled, I was doing a little research online this evening looking for more details about reassignment surgeries. And I came across this site that talked about male lactation. At first I didn't believe it but look," she said with a huge grin pressing her left breast and squeezing out a little dribble of milk. "I can give milk. I mean it's not like I can nurse a baby or anything but, my God, I can give milk," she squealed giddy with joy. She hugged Alex and covered his face with kisses.

"Make love to me Rachel," Alex whispered between her kisses. "I really want to feel you inside me tonight."

Rachel stopped a moment and looked into his eyes. Without a single word she kissed him slowly and delicately on the lips. She leaned back and smiled sweetly while she took off his t-shirt. He undid the clip on his bra and his breasts fell free as he pulled the bra straps off his shoulders. She reached out gently and cupped his breast then leaned forward and kissed them tenderly.

She pushed him gently back against the pillows, slid her hands down his narrow waist and took off his panties. His cock was semi-erect and growing with the anticipation of what was happening.

She stood up and removed her panties. Her cock sprung free, aroused by the thought of being inside of him, it stood hard and proud against her stomach. She reached over and pulled out a bottle of lube from the top drawer of her nightstand. She slipped on a condom and lubed her cock slowly, seductively, watching him watch her. She moved her lithe body onto the bed. Her long hair was flowing around her head and shoulders; it shimmered in the moonlight that flooded through her bedroom window.

He moved down the bed and placed a pillow

beneath his butt then he opened his legs to her. She coated his rosebud with lube and slipped one and then another finger inside of him. He clenched momentarily, reacting more to the chill of the lube than her invading fingers. Then he relaxed to her gentle touch.

Alex thought to say something, to tell her how much he loved her, how much he wanted her to make love to him, but the moment had slipped beyond words. He could see in her eyes that she knew everything. He didn't need the stumble of words to break the blissful silence of lovemaking.

She entered him slowly and gently. He could feel every part of her as she moved past his outer ring, every ridge of her cock pulsing and throbbing in tune with her heartbeat. She pushed gently forward until her body pressed against his butt. She rested a moment and then she began to move in and out of him. Gently at first, then her pace began to build as her passion soared.

Suddenly she erupted in him filling the condom inside of him with her seed. He wrapped his legs around her tightly, pulling her deeper inside, forcing her to thrust deeper, to love him deeper. Then they felt something warm and wet spread between their bodies as Alex came. He held her tightly against him, their bodies intertwined in passion and joy.

Alex woke up Saturday morning and stretched. He noticed that Rachel was sitting up in bed and gazing out of the window. Her elbows rested on the windowsill, her chin was cupped in her hands. Alex watched her for a while before he spoke.

He reached over and traced little circles across

her back. "You look lost in thought, love."

"I was remembering the first time I saw you and Amanda together from this window. I sat here watching you two talk during one of Reilly's little backyard parties. You two looked like you were having so much fun. I remember thinking to myself, why can't I do that? Why can't I be as open and carefree as you two were that day in Reilly's backyard?"

"You are now love, you're beautiful. I remember the first time we met too. You were so nervous, so cautious. You told me you thought that every girl was a monster."

"Yeah, I did," she said with a chuckle. "I'm glad you changed my mind."

"I didn't do that," he replied nuzzling her hair and kissing her neck. "It was Amanda who showed you that not all girls are monsters."

"Yes, I suppose she did." She reached back and caressed him as he kissed the nape of her neck.

"Mmm, that feels nice," he murmured.

She leaned back against him then took a big breath and let it out slowly. He wrapped his arms around her and kissed the top of her head.

"You two mean so much to me. I really mean that babe," she said earnestly. "I can't imagine my life without you two."

"So then what's troubling you?" he asked holding her close.

Rachel paused a moment. She knew that she needed to talk to Alex about the thoughts that have been weighing so heavily on her mind. But it was still hard to say the words out loud.

"I…I was thinking about the surgery."

"The reassignment surgery?"

"Yeah."

"Did you schedule it?"

"Not yet. It scares me."

"Because of the pain?"

"That, yes, but there's more to it than that," she replied turning around to face him. "It's the whole mental thing. I thought it was what I wanted, to be a complete woman. But now," she shrugged her shoulders. "I just don't know anymore."

"It's a huge step," he murmured leaning forward to kiss her forehead softly.

"It's not like I can just change my mind and get a refund if things don't work out," she said as she reached up to caress his face. "This is all very scary."

She turned around again and settled against his chest. She pulled his arms around her and held him tightly.

"I love my body," she continued softly, "the way it is, now. I love that I can make love to you and Amanda with my body, the way it is right now. I love that you and Amanda can make love to me the way my body is right now. If I have the surgery will that change everything? I'm scared that I might loose you. I'm not sure I could bare that. "

"Rachel, Amanda and I love you very much. That will never change no matter what you decide. But you have to decide that you want this for yourself and no one else. I wish I could make this easier on you but I can't."

"I know," she said softly as she sat on the edge of the bed a moment before she stood up and padded barefoot to the bathroom.

Alex sighed. He knew she was going through a

lot right now. But there was nothing he could say or do but wait and be supportive no matter what she decided. Deep down inside he knew that last night was a watershed moment for Rachel. What they did together, as innocent and loving as it was, changed everything for her. Perhaps she doesn't know it yet, but his sweet Rachel was becoming more a woman than she ever thought she could be.

The week spun by quickly. Alex and Rachel fell comfortably into a routine with Alex in classes and working at the convenience store at night, and Rachel in her day job and working as a hostess at night. They spent their nights together snuggling in Rachel's bed. When the weather had turned cold outside they spent their free nights lying in bed under a ton of blankets and watching old movies on the television.

The days flew by but the joy and excitement was missing and they both felt it. They were missing Amanda. Neither of them had to say it, but they both knew it. It was like she was the third leg of a stool. Without her, they were not complete.

Finally, it was Sunday afternoon and the sun was dancing along the treetops and teasing with the horizon. Alex and Rachel woke up from a dreamy nap curled around each other in a lover's embrace. He opened a drowsy eye and looked at Rachel's alarm clock.

"Come on honey, we need to get dressed, we have to pick Amanda up at the airport in a couple of hours."

"Shouldn't you go alone," she said in a pout.

"Why?" He stood naked in the middle of the

bedroom wondering where this was coming from.

"Because she loves me like a sister but I know she really only has eyes for you."

"I love you like my sister too, Rachel," he replied. "So what's that got to do with it?"

Rachel looked at Alex with sad eyes then reluctantly she picked her underwear off the floor and slumped back onto the bed.

"Rachel, my sweet Rachel," Alex sighed as he sat down next to her and wrapped his arm across her shoulders. He turned her to face him and kissed her lips gently.

"I love you so very much. More than if you were just my sister. I can't find a word to describe it, I'm not sure one exists in the English language. You are my lover and so is Amanda. You are my sister, and so is Amanda. I couldn't live my life now without you both in it, equally. I know Amanda feels exactly the same way and you have said as much yourself. Now let's go get our sister. You know she'd be very upset if you didn't come with me to pick her up."

Rachel leaned over and kissed him on the cheek then smiling meekly as she slowly padded towards the bathroom.

"I'll follow you into the shower once you're done Sis," he said with a gentle smile.

As small airports go, this one wasn't much to write home about. It's gotten to the point in America that if an airport isn't a hub for a major airline it's dinky. Regardless of how big the city is that it serves. And this one was dinky, pathetically so.

They got there early enough to be able to wait in the lobby for Amanda's plane to arrive. Alex sat thumbing through a city brochure while Rachel checked her voice mail. He glanced over Rachel's shoulder. "Did you find some houses for us to look at next week?"

"I did," she replied putting her phone away. "There is this cute little bungalow that I simply adored but…"

"What?" he asked interrupting.

"Well, it doesn't have off street parking. I know that's one of your must haves. And the master bedroom was kind of small."

"A large bedroom is high on Amanda's list."

"Yeah, I know. But the yard was nice."

"So we'll just keep looking. I'll have some time off soon and I can help."

"We can but I still want you guys to have a look," she continued. "Maybe we can renovate."

"Only if we buy it love," he said looking at his magazine once again.

"Hmmm," she murmured.

A voice on the loudspeaker broke the drumming silence in the cabin of the airplane as it flew into the night. According to the pilot, Delta flight 4723 from Chicago – O'Hare was running a little ahead of schedule due to a favorable tail wind. Amanda glanced out of the window and watched the twinkling lights scattered across the blackness far below. She had fun while she was in Seattle, for the first time in her life she really had fun there. Susan's wedding was small but lovely, the bride was beautiful, and the bridesmaid's dresses were ugly. But that is as it should be, she thought with a huge smile.

When Amanda met Susan at the airport she

could see her beaming with joy, everyone could. Her joy was infectious. For the first time in her life Amanda could share that delight with Susan. She understood what it was like to truly be in love.

That first night, when they could finally be alone, she told Susan all about Alex and Rachel. Well, not everything, but enough for her to understand that Amanda was totally and blissfully in love with two of the most amazing people she had ever met.

It had been a crazy day with an afternoon and evening filled with wedding activities and everybody talking to everybody else and all at the same time. The excitement was contagious. It always is at weddings. So the quiet of a bedroom late at night and a chance to relax and catch up was appealing.

At first Susan didn't understand Amanda's relationship. She told her that perhaps Amanda's brief flirt with life in Salt Lake City had left more of an impression on her than she was willing to admit. But slowly she came to accept that this wasn't something religious but something unique, something beyond a family bound by love and companionship. Well, however it was defined, the life that Amanda now led was perfect for her. Susan told her how happy she was for her.

"If there's ever a chance in the future," Susan said the night they talked till nearly dawn, "I want to meet them. They sound like wonderful people, I'm really happy for you," she added giving Amanda a hug and a kiss on the cheek.

Amanda spent a couple of days at the Seattle office of Dresher, Cummings, and Sanford. They were cordial to her at first, not expecting much out of this 'cutie' from the east coast. They continued to act a bit aloof until the meeting turned to hard numbers and Amanda got busy. She smiled as she remembered the looks on their faces when she finished her report. Apparently they were impressed because the text message she received from Margaret the next day was glowing with support.

All in all, it has been a crazy whirlwind of a week. But through it all, her thoughts were always drawn back to Alex and Rachel. She Skyped them nearly every day and thanked the universe for the magic of a videophone call. She could see them but she missed their touch and caress. She missed the taste of their kisses and she missed their smell. As funny as that sounds when she says it out loud, she missed the way they smell.

The plane dropped down through the clouds that had settled around Wilmington and Amanda could hear the landing gear drop into place with a thud. A moment later the plane was on the ground and moving quickly back to the terminal.

Amanda wiggled in her seat like a schoolgirl barely able to contain her excitement as the airplane taxied to the gate. In her lap was a white box holding a huge slice of wedding cake and a thank you card from Amanda's cousin, Susan. She knew that Alex and Rachel would be standing in the lobby waiting for her. She couldn't wait for the plane to park. The anticipation was overwhelming. A weeks' worth of hugs and kisses were waiting for her.

That night they fell into Amanda's bed. This time the love they shared was slower and sweeter than ever before. They took their time and savored the caress of their bodies intertwined in lovemaking.

Each one touching and being touched.
Each one loving and being loved.
It was as close to bliss as any of them had ever imagined or wanted.

# =NINE =

Ever since the first day they all went shopping for Alex's new wardrobe, he began to add a few feminine items to his daily attire. He added panties and bras – mostly sports bras because they tended to minimize rather than emphasize his bust line. The sports bra added comfort and support without revealing too much. Eventually he added a hint of eye makeup and some concealer to hide a blemish or two.

He would add a subtle change in his clothes here and there as well. He liked to wear the occasional blouse or sometimes a pair of women's flats. None of these things drew much attention to themselves except perhaps for the simple silver necklace and matching diamond stud earrings that he liked to wear occasionally. Partly, he supposed, because the necklace was a gift from Rachel and the earrings were a gift from Amanda and partly because they were so pretty.

At first he felt uncomfortable with the changes to his wardrobe. Gone were most of the flannels and plaids that usually hung off his body, faded and threadbare. Cotton blouses and shimmering poly-cotton tops replaced the faded and well-worn shirts. They shaped his body rather than concealed it. Gone were some of his jeans and chino pants to be replaced by skirts, dresses, and slacks. His wardrobe wasn't totally transformed, he still wore the occasional pair of jeans and faded flannel shirt. He hadn't agreed to live completely like a woman. But there was an obvious shift in the clothing that he wore each day. At first, however, it worried him.

Part of the worry was, he surmised, because of the social taboo of men wearing clothes that were obviously meant for women, something ingrained in him since early childhood. And part of it was because he didn't like to stand out in a crowd.

So many other men came before him who liked to flaunt a garish lifestyle in the name of cross-dressing and flamboyant transvestitism. Because of that and other prejudices, society seemed to turn a jaundiced eye to someone like Alex who was struggling with his own identity. The first few weeks were nerve-wracking for him but eventually he settled down and realized that ultimately, most people just didn't care. He decided to take Rachel's advice and not worry about it. If anyone had a problem with it, it was their issue not his.

Around noon Alex gathered up his notebook and iPad and stuffed them into the backpack that he dropped on a chair by the front door. Usually he would pull his hair into a tight ponytail, wrap it tightly and shove it all under a stocking cap. But today he decided he was tired of looking grungy at school all the time.

He brushed his hair and let it fall gracefully around his shoulders in gentle curls. Then he attached a hair clip to pull it out of his eyes. He was dressed in a pair of skinny jeans and a comfortable cotton blouse that had a nice cowl neck to hide the sports bra beneath.

"Baby steps," he muttered to himself softly.

He wore knee high hose and oxford flats to complete the look. A light dusting of eye makeup and a dash of mascara and he was ready to go. Satisfied with the effect he turned out the bathroom light, grabbed his backpack, and was out the door and down the stairs.

Thirty minutes later Alex walked into Rollins Hall where his afternoon class was held. As he climbed the stairs he glanced from side to side to see most of the people in the hallway didn't pay any attention to him as he passed them by.

As he turned to climb the next flight of stairs to the second floor, Alex was tempted to take the steps two at a time, but that wouldn't be appropriate anymore. Instead he took a more leisurely approach and ascended the staircase slowly.

If Rachel saw him take two at a time she would kick his ass. The thought brought a subtle smile.

Half way up the second flight of stairs he passed by Ray Klein who usually sat next to him in the advanced writing class he was heading for.

"Hey Ray," Alex said calmly waving as he walked by him.

Ray waved back, glancing a second time while attempting to recognize the pretty girl that just walked by.

Alex turned the corner at the top of the stairs and walked down the corridor to room 217. He walked into the room, sat down in his usual seat and gazed out the windows as he waited for Professor Dixon to arrive.

A moment later Ray sat down in the next row over. He cleared his throat then glanced over at Alex with a sheepish grin.

"You know, I always thought you were cute," said Ray casually. "But you always hid yourself under that stocking cap and all. I'm glad you decided to…you know," he mumbled sheepishly, "with the makeup and all."

Alex blushed slightly and glanced back at Ray. He gave him a gentle smile. He knew all too well what it was like to be in Ray's shoes. It wasn't that Ray was asking Alex out on a date or anything, but he could see in his eyes that the question was lurking somewhere in back of his mind. Talking to someone who you were interested in dating had always been traumatic for Alex, so he felt a little sympathy for Ray. But not enough to say yes or anything like that.

"Thanks Ray," Alex replied shyly. "I met someone recently and they sort of like it so I thought, why not?"

Ray nodded his head and sighed the 'damn, too late again' sort of sigh that all men know too well.

About then, Professor Dixon walked in and the room grew quiet. Ray turned around and that was the last time that day that anyone said anything more about it.

For the rest of the afternoon Alex noticed the occasional sideways glances from several of the other men in the room. He expected the glances to be followed by a stifled snicker but in reality, they were all kind of cute in their own sheepish way.

April was finally beginning to blossom.

One afternoon the following week, a fellow female student, Kimberly Crossman, in his English Literature class spotted a bra line beneath his shirt. She leaned forward and mentioned this to him as if she's caught him doing something naughty.

"And your point is?" Alex asked with a wry smile.

"Well, wouldn't you be embarrassed? What if someone else caught you? They'd think you were a cross dresser or something," she whispered.

"You caught me, do I look embarrassed?"

"Well no, not really," she replied blushing slightly.

Alex turned in his seat and smiled at her.

"Kim, do you think I'm a cross-dresser?" He whispered to her conspiratorially.

"Well no, I mean…I don't know, maybe," she replied with a frown turning a deeper shade of crimson. "What if the boys saw it, they might beat you up. Doesn't that worry you?" Her face was suddenly filled with honest concern.

Alex's smile broadened, he was beginning to really like Kim. She was a pretty girl, long straight hair that hugged her face and fell softly past her shoulders. Above the layers of concealer she troweled on her face she had lovely arched eyebrows that framed gentle blue eyes.

But her face was scarred with acne in a few places and she always seemed self-conscious about it. She was a bit heavy handed covering it up with concealer and Alex wondered if that was the reason why she tended to shy away from going out on any dates. Most of the other guys in the room had hit on her once or twice but she seemed to always have an excuse not to go out. It was kind of a sad if that was the case; she's such a sweet girl.

"Nope, we're not in high school anymore, Kim. Maybe they might be embarrassed but that's an issue they have to deal with not me. I don't dress to fit someone else's standards anymore. I've decided to dress for my own comfort."

"Oh... cool. So if I walked in here tomorrow wearing a flannel shirt and no bra you wouldn't say anything?"

"Of course I would! You would look pretty hot in flannel. No pun intended."

She pursed her lips together into a smirk and swatted him on the shoulder.

"You're insane."

"Thank you, I'm glad you noticed," he replied smiling sweetly. "And Kim."

"Yes?"

"Thanks for caring."

She smiled awkwardly and shrugged her shoulders.

Kim caught up with Alex after class was over and invited him to get a cup of coffee across the street in the local bistro.

They sat in silence for several minutes while Kim stirred the cream in her coffee. She was obviously working up the courage to ask him something.

"What did you want to talk about Kim?"

Kim blushed again and looked up into Alex's

face. "What you said in class today, about dressing to suit your own comfort, it really struck a chord with me. I mean about being you and not worrying about what others thought. I thought you were so brave doing that on your own."

Alex studied Kim for a moment then smiled sweetly. "Kim, what do you think of me?"

"I don't know," she murmured softly. She looked down and fiddled with a delicate necklace, she appeared to be surprised by the sudden shift in the conversation. "I thought I understood who you were but recently you've changed so much I don't know anything anymore."

"Do you like the changes you see?"

"Well, yes. You seem so centered now, much more than you ever were before. When I watched you walk over here to meet me just now, you walked with such grace. I've never seen that in you before."

Alex smiled and blushed, silently thanking Rachel and Amanda for their tenacity. "Why don't you go out with anyone in the class? We've been out for drinks several times before and we've always invited you along but you always beg off."

"Promise you won't laugh?" she asked earnestly.

"Of course."

"I'm terrified."

"Of what?"

"Of them, of what other people might think of me," she said, her eyes were tearing up. "Of how I look, how I dress, everything," she whispered with such intensity that Alex was stunned.

"Would you tell this same thing to, uh, Ray for example?" Alex asked gently.

"God no, I'd be mortified."

Alex tilted his head a bit and looked at Kim again. He knew she had a thing for Ray. Alex had seen her glance at him from time to time in class. She blushed crimson then glanced away trying desperately to regain her composure. Alex pulled out his cellphone and punched a few buttons. A moment later Rachel answered. "Hi sweetie, do you think there's room for one more at the dinner table tonight?"

"I think so," Rachel replied casually tossing the last of the vegetables into a salad.

"I'd like to bring a friend from school over to meet you and Amanda," Alex continued watching Kim's reaction. "Would that be all right?"

"Sure, hey Sis, come in here. Alex's is bringing a friend home from school," she yelled.

He could hear them giggling like schoolgirls.

"All right you two, behave. We'll be over in a half hour, bye."

He clipped his phone shut and smiled at Kim. "Oh, if you have any plans tonight, cancel them, we'll probably be going out later too," he added with a grin.

"But I-I can't…" Kim began to stutter.

"Shush Kim, can't, won't and don't are no longer in your vocabulary, at least not tonight," Alex interrupted her. "Come on; we're late for dinner."

He grabbed her hand and pulled her out of her seat. She looked a bit shocked with the sudden turn of events. She paused a moment still holding his hand, then she nodded and they set off towards his car.

Twenty minutes later Alex pulled into the

apartment house parking lot. He walked around and opened Kim's door and she stepped out.

"We're on the third floor," he said a bit sheepishly, "sorry."

Alex glanced up and caught a glimpse of Amanda and Rachel peeking out of the window in his apartment. Once he saw them he could see their faces filled with delight as they quickly closed the blinds. He shook his head as he imagined what was going to happen next. That brought a smile to his face.

"Okay," he said as they started up the second flight of stairs. "I want you to meet the two most important people in my life, Amanda and Rachel. Now I will admit that they can be a handful, but just remember that it all comes from love."

Kim glanced at Alex as they continued up the stairs.

Saying it that way probably only added to her anxiety, he thought ruefully.

Another short flight of stairs and they stood at Rachel's door. Alex leaned forward and knocked gently. A moment later the door opened and both girls stood there with Cheshire cat grins.

"Rachel, Amanda, this is Kim Crossman, a friend from school," he said gesturing to each girl as he named them. "Kim, I like to introduce you to Rachel Thompson, and Amanda Simpson," he finished with a smile.

"Hi," Rachel said as she shook Kim's hand, "welcome to my place, dinner will be ready in a couple of minutes." Kim nodded and smiled as Amanda took her hand next.

"Hi, nice to meet you," Amanda added. "Alex

doesn't bring home any friends from school so we were a bit shocked when he asked us to set another place at the table."

"No more than I was," Kim replied. "I sorry if I've caused any trouble."

"No worries, we'll just take it out on him later on," she said with a devilish grin.

"Oh, don't do that please, he's only trying to help," Kim added apologetically.

"With what?" Rachel asked standing next to Alex in the kitchen.

"Kim has this thing where she worries about what other people think about her," Alex interjected as he carried dishes and flatware from the kitchen. He placed them on a table near the center of the room. "I thought perhaps you girls could help her out with that."

He stood there looking back and forth between Amanda and Rachel with a gleam in his eye.

"What does she know about us?" Amanda asked cautiously.

"Nothing more than you are a terrible tease," he said with a grin.

"Well that's true," quipped Rachel as she carried a salad bowl into the living room.

"What do you want her to know?" Amanda asked still with caution.

Kim watched the exchange between Alex and his girlfriends with intense curiosity.

"Whatever you want to tell her," he replied. "Let me preface this by saying that Kim was concerned about my safety this afternoon. She was worried that I might be assaulted because she thought I was a cross-dresser. Let me add that Kim's a friend and I think I can trust her."

Alex walked over to Amanda and kissed her lightly on the cheek. Then he walked back across the room and kissed Rachel as well.

"Let's eat, I'm starving," said Amanda with an impish grin. "We can talk later."

They gathered around the table and started passing the bowls of food. A moment later any chance of conversation was replaced by murmurs of "this tastes really delicious."

Eventually Amanda shared some gossip going around in her office and Rachel told a funny story about a junior partner getting his tie caught in the copy machine. Kim watched the banter between them with wide-eyed wonder.

As the plates and bowls were cleared Alex started filling the sink with soapy water. It was his turn to do dishes tonight. With the table cleared, they shoved it back into the corner and moved to sit more comfortably on the couch. Rachel found a pillow and collapsed on the floor.

Alex dipped another plate into the soapy water. "Do you have to work tonight Rachel?"

"Yeah, I'm on from eight to eleven tonight."

"I was thinking of introducing Kim to Moulin Rouge tonight, what do you think?" he asked drying a clean pot and placing it on the counter.

"Sounds fine to me if she's up to it, Thursday nights are usually pretty tame," Rachel replied.

"What's Moulin Rouge?" Kim asked.

"It's a club I work at part-time. It's upscale but the drinks aren't too outrageous, just the manager if he's in a snit," she replied with a wry grin.

"Some, but not all of the clientele are gay or

transsexuals," Amanda added. "They have an open door policy, no judgment, just acceptance…of everybody."

Kim blanched a bit but her eyes were bright and curious.

"Alex," Kim said softly after pausing to look between the two girls and then up to him, "who are you?"

Alex wiped the soapsuds off his hands and walked over to sit on the floor next to Rachel.

"Kim, when I was at the DMV last week and filling out one of their forms, there wasn't a box under gender that I could check. It was either male or female, not even other so I checked both."

"I don't understand," Kim said, her face showing signs of concern.

"When you asked me if I was a cross-dresser this afternoon and I told you that I dressed to suit my own comfort, I wasn't trying to be flippant. I was telling the truth. I'm what you might call an intersex person. I'm the person who checks the box 'other'."

Kim was still looking confused. Amanda smiled as she reached over and gave her hand a gentle squeeze.

"Show her the iPad, it worked for me," Amanda quipped with an impish smile.

"Here," he said holding his iPad out for her, "I've Googled it for you."

Kim quickly scanned the page attempting to grasp what he was trying to tell her. She looked up at him still a bit perplexed.

"When this first began to happen I was frightened of everybody and everything. I didn't know what to expect so I expected the worst. I hid in my room and drowned myself in clothing so that no one would suspect that I was different from everybody else. Then I met these two gorgeous women and they changed my life."

"At first," he continued, "I was sure that everyone would point and laugh at me as I began to open up and accept who I am. Eventually, I began to listen to Rachel and Amanda who told me that most people just don't care. They're all too busy with their own issues to be concerned with mine. And they were right."

Kim's eyes began to glisten with tears. Amanda leaned back and retrieved a tissue then she handed it to her.

"It just doesn't matter," he continued earnestly. "Don't throw your life away being afraid of what others might think. Because chances are, they never saw what you fear as an issue."

Rachel got up on her knees and leaned across the coffee table. She took Kim's hands in hers and smiled.

"Come on girl," she said with a gleam in her eye, "what you need is a make-over."

"Absolutely," Amanda exclaimed and the two girls pulled Kim to her feet and pushed her towards Rachel's bedroom.

"Remember what I said Kim," Alex shouted as he watched Amanda and Rachel pull Kim into the bathroom. "Everything they do comes from love. Just go with the flow."

Alex smiled when he glanced in again to see them in Rachel's bathroom scrubbing the heavy makeup off of Kim's face. He returned to the kitchen and the mountain of dishes that waited for him in the sink.

Forty minutes later all three girls walked out of Rachel's bedroom. Kim walked into the center of the room and smiled sheepishly.

"Well Alex, what do you think?" Amanda asked beaming a huge smile.

Alex turned and tossed the hand towel on the counter. He looked across the room at Kim standing in the center of Rachel's apartment.

Gone were the baggy pants and frumpy blouse. Her hair was done up in simple curls and her makeup was gorgeous. Rachel let her borrow one of her dresses. It wasn't one of the more provocative ones that she often wore to work but it did hug her curves and enhanced her silhouette. Kim wore a pair of four-inch heels that shaped her legs and butt nicely as she stood fidgeting with the necklace that fell into her ample cleavage.

"Well Cinderella, all we need to do now is find a pumpkin for your carriage," he said with a foolish grin.

"Is it too much?" Kim asked sheepishly.

"Have you looked at yourself lately? You look gorgeous," he answered enthusiastically.

"Hey," said Amanda, "if we're all going to the club tonight, who's going with us, Alex or April?" she asked with a devilish grin. Alex glanced at Amanda and scrunched his nose.

"Who's April?" Kim looked at Alex with growing curiosity.

"April is me when I'm not Alex," he said with a twinkle in his eyes. "I think that April is going with you all to the club tonight, it'll be just us girls."

Amanda raced around Kim, grabbed Alex's hand,

and pulled him towards the front door.

"Come on sweetheart, let's go get dressed," she said as she pulled him out into the hallway. "Kim, we'll be back in a flash."

"Is she always that energetic?" Kim asked.

"Yes, she is," Rachel replied shaking her head. "Amanda is a goddess, she's so full of life it's hard to deny her anything."

Rachel turned and walked back towards her bedroom then turned back to Kim.

"Are you doing okay?" she asked watching Kim catch a glimpse of herself in the mirror on the back of the bedroom door.

"I think I'm having the time of my life," she replied as she twirled around to watch the hem of her skirt flare out.

"Yeah, that happens a lot around here," Rachel said with a chuckle. "Make yourself comfortable, we won't be too long."

It took almost an hour before April returned to Rachel's apartment. Kim spent the time thumbing through old magazines that were piled on a corner table nearby. As April walked into the apartment Kim looked up amazed at the transformation.

His hair fell in gentle curls around his face and onto his shoulders. His makeup was light but dramatic, enhancing his eyes delightfully. The black dress he wore hugged his body like a glove, and the four-inch heels looked divine. If it weren't for his eyes, Kim would never have recognized him as Alex. She sat stunned for a moment and watched him walk towards her across the room.

"You look beautiful," she whispered.

"Thank you," he replied with a gentle smile then he turned and walked to Rachel's bedroom door. "Hey gorgeous, are you about ready?"

"Out in a minute," Rachel replied. "Where's Amanda?"

"Downstairs waiting for us. I've got a pair of flats with me so that I can drive," he added. He turned to Kim and grinned sheepishly. "I still can't drive in heels," he shrugged.

Thirty minutes later they all piled out of the car and walked into the club. Near the front a tall thin man with a hint of mascara around his eyes and a silk scarf around his neck walked out to greet them.

"What lovely ladies we have joining us tonight," he said with a smile. "Rachel, darling, take them to table seventeen, it's in your section tonight."

Rachel nodded and led the way through the tables that bordered a dance floor and back to more private section of the club. The club was beginning to fill up with guests who glanced at them as they walked by. Amanda could see that Kim was nervous so she reached out and gave her hand a gentle squeeze. Kim smiled; her nerves seemed to settle a bit after that.

Rachel took their drink order and walked across the dance floor towards the bar.

With drinks in hand, the music began to throb and the lights swirled around the club. Kim's eyes began to sparkle with anticipation.

An hour later, Kim and April walked off the dance floor towards their table. Amanda was busy talking to a couple sitting at the table next to her. When they sat down Kim watched the dance floor a moment then she slowly recognized someone who was weaving his way across the floor towards them.

Oh God," she whispered to April trying to duck behind her. "It's Ray. He's coming over here."

"I saw him earlier when he came in with a group of guys from school. I think they're first years I haven't met before," he added nearly shouting in her ear because the music was so loud.

Kim slowly emerged from hiding as Ray approached their table.

"Hi," Ray said to Kim as he stood at their table. "I thought I recognized you out there. You look lovely tonight."

"Thank you," Kim replied meekly.

"Join us," April offered and Ray pulled out a chair to sit.

"I didn't know you came here," Ray shouted over the throbbing music. He glanced at Amanda and then at April. At first it didn't seem like he recognized her then suddenly his eyes grew large and he opened his mouth but no words escaped.

April reached over and gently lifted his chin to close his mouth.

"Hi Ray," he said with an awkward grin.

"Holy shit!" Ray exclaimed. "You're…you're…"

"I'm April, it's nice to see you," she replied. "This is my sister Amanda, and my other sister Rachel is walking over here now," she said gesturing to the statuesque woman striding across the dance floor in five-inch stilettos.

"Nice to meet you," said Amanda brightly. "Are you one of April's friends from school?"

"Y-Yeah, we have Advanced Lit together," Ray stammered a bit shell-shocked.

Rachel walked over to their table and slumped down in a chair next to Ray.

"Trade shoes with me babe, these things are killing me," she said rubbing her feet. She set her heels down on the floor under the table, next to April. She pulled off her shoes and handed them to Rachel.

"We both wear the same sized shoe, thank God," she said to Ray then leaned across the table and gestured to Kim so she could whisper into her ear. "You looked great out there on the floor tonight."

She bent down and buckled April's shoes and then stood. "That's better, thanks babe. I couldn't have made it to eleven with those on my feet. They look better on you anyway." She stepped around Ray then leaned over and kissed April then she looked down at Ray and smiled with a twinkle in her eye. "Can I get you something to drink?"

"Ah, n-no, thank you," Ray stammered looking up at the statuesque beauty leaning down and smiling in his face.

Rachel shrugged and sashayed off across the dance floor moving to the beat of the music.

April slipped on Rachel's stilettos and tied the lacings around her calves. She glanced up to watch Kim and Ray sit awkwardly watching her tie Rachel's shoes. They both seemed too shy to look at one another.

"You know Ray," April shouted as she leaned towards Ray, "Kim here is a wonderful dancer and this place has a great dance floor." Ray's eyes gleamed with anticipation as he glanced at Kim, he was happy for the opening that April provided. He hesitated a moment then he extended his hand and smiled at her.

"Would you like to dance?" he asked a bit awkwardly.

"Kim," April whispered in her ear, "I don't know if you know this but Ray has had a thing for you for ages, at least since the Chaucer and Milton class last year. Take a chance, it might be fun."

Kim blushed crimson and glanced at Ray then she leaned over and whispered to April. "Thank you". With a shy smile she accepted Ray's hand and they walked out onto the dance floor. Rachel passed them by as they walked to the center of the floor.

April stood up and pulled Amanda and Rachel into a big hug.

"I love you two so much," she said holding them tightly. "Thank you for helping Kim tonight."

"We all need a nudge in the right direction once in a while," Amanda replied, her eyes glistening. "That's what friends are for."

"And lovers," Rachel added as both girls kissed April's cheeks.

They turned and watched Kim and Ray glide across the dance floor. They looked so good together. It's all up to them from now on. He wasn't always this good at matchmaking but this one was a 'no-brainer'.

Amanda gathered them both into a huddle as Kim and Ray disappeared among the crowd.

"I think I've found the perfect house," she shouted with a huge smile on her face.

"What?" both April and Rachel asked in unison.

"We've got an appointment to see it on Saturday," she continued with a giggle. "It's perfect. Big yard, a driveway, and a huge master bedroom." Her eyes twinkled in the glittering light from the dance floor.

They pulled each other into a big hug and squealed like schoolgirls.

"We have a house!" they all shouted together.

## =TEN=

"You stupid fucking bitch!  How dare you lead me on like this?"

Standing in the street in front of a large condominium complex, a man grabbed the arm of a woman and shook her violently.

Coming around the corner a half block away, Rachel who was out for a morning bike ride, looked down the street at the couple arguing in the middle of the street.

"A boy?!  Now you tell me!  What the fuck were you thinking?  That it wouldn't matter?  Of course it matters you stupid bitch!"

"Ted, you're hurting me!"

The guy continued to scream obscenities at her. Rachel stopped her bike several yards away then got off and dropped it to the ground.  Something wasn't quite right, she thought.

"Why didn't you tell me this before?  Now everything is fucked!"

"Please Ted, I wanted to tell you before but you always told me how much you loved me and how nothing else really mattered."

"Well, this matters! You're a guy, for Christ's sake, a fucking guy. And you think that doesn't matter? I'm not a homo, maybe you are, but I'm not, you fucking son of a bitch!" Ted pulled his right hand back and punched the woman in the face. She went reeling across the sidewalk and landed against some bushes then slumped to the ground. He walked over, stood above her, and slapped her.

Rachel began to stride purposefully towards Ted.

"We are through Wendy, do you hear me? The wedding is over; it's not going to happen, not with you, never with you! I don't marry dicks!"

"But I don't have a penis, Ted, you know that." Wendy reached up from the ground and tried to touch is arm. "I had an operation before we even met. I'm a woman now, completely. I wanted to tell you when we first met but you were so caustic about 'chicks with dicks' as you called them that I was scared to tell you."

"So now you tell me about this? What if we wanted to have kids? Did they give you a uterus too? Your no woman, you're a fucking freak!" Ted pulled his arm back to hit Wendy again but Rachel stepped between them and pushed Ted back.

"Leave her alone asshole," Rachel spat menacingly.

"Who, the fuck, are you?" Ted asked glaring at Rachel.

"Someone who's going to kick your bigoted ass if you don't get the fuck out of here now," Rachel growled threateningly.

Ted looked at her, looked at her fist ready to strike him, and looked at Wendy lying on the ground with this strange woman between them, then spat at them both.

Rachel swung an upper cut and landed it beneath his jawline. She knocked him to the ground. "That's for that filthy habit, now get the fuck out of here slime ball," Rachel growled taking another step towards Ted.

Ted scrambled to his feet and beat a hasty retreat down the sidewalk. He opened his car door and then turned to look back at Wendy a moment. He shook his head, got into his car, and drove off down the street.

Wendy started crying the moment Ted ran off. The tears began to run down her cheeks like tiny rivers lined with mascara.

"Are you okay?" Rachel asked bending down to look at the scrapes and cuts on Wendy's face. "Hey, he's gone now, everything is okay. You're safe now."

"It's not okay, you don't understand. We were getting married next month. This condo was going to be our new home. Now it's all ruined, ruined, ruined! I've ruined everything!

"Come on, my place is just around the corner," Rachel said as she held out a hand for Wendy to stand up. "Let's get you cleaned up."

As Wendy walked into Rachel's apartment, she found two people standing around an island counter grousing about the real estate market.

"That house on Reynolds was sold right out from underneath us, damn it," Amanda sputtered as she slammed her fist down on the counter. "It was perfect, the lawn, the bedrooms, the driveway, perfect."

"I'm sorry Amanda, we'll start looking again tomorrow," Alex said trying to calm her down.

"What happened?" Rachel asked as she helped Wendy towards the kitchen counter.

"Oh that dumbass, Janet Wheeler, our so-called real estate agent dropped the ball on our offer and someone else got the house, and it was perfect too," Amanda grumbled. Then as if finally realizing that Rachel wasn't alone, "Who's this?"

Rachel steered Wendy to a stool by the sink and sat her down. "This is Wendy. I broke up a fight between her and her boyfriend a little while ago." She pulled out a bottle of hydrogen peroxide and some cotton balls from beneath the sink and began to dab the cuts and scrapes on Wendy's face and arms. "The son of a bitch was going to kill her if I didn't step in."

Alex pulled out his cellphone and began to dial 911. "Where is he now, I'm calling the cops."

"No don't, please. I don't want any more trouble. He's gone now, out of my life for good I hope."

Alex closed his phone and walked around the counter to help Rachel with bandages.

"What happened?" Amanda asked holding Wendy's hand.

"I…"

"They broke up," Rachel interrupted. "It was getting ugly so I stopped it." Rachel finished cleaning her wounds and with Alex's help they added antibiotic and some bandages to all but a few of the scrapes and cuts. "Here," Rachel gestured, "Why don't you rest here on the couch, okay?"

"I'll make some tea," Amanda added as she walked back towards the kitchen.

"Do you live with him? Is there going to be trouble getting your stuff back?" Rachel asked.

"No, I have my own place, we were supposed to move in together once we got married but that's all over now." She began to cry again.

Alex handed her a tissue as Rachel wrapped her arm around her shoulders and gave her a hug.

"I never thought he would have acted like this, he was so open and carefree," Wendy said between sniffles.

"Except for the 'chicks with a dick' comment," Rachel said with a grimace.

Alex and Amanda glanced at one another then at Rachel. She dismissed their unspoken questions with a slight shake of her head.

"I had my surgery two years before we met, he would have never known if I'd kept my big mouth shut but I just couldn't lie to him, I loved him." Wendy quickly glanced up at Alex and then Amanda, she was suddenly frightened about what she just revealed.

"No worries, Wendy, you're among friends," said Alex with a warm smile.

She glanced at Rachel, the old fear still creeping across her face.

"I'm a pre-op transsexual," Rachel replied, "Amanda is a genetic girl, and…"

"I'm a little of both," Alex interrupted, "so you're safe here."

"Welcome to my family," Rachel said with a huge grin.

Wendy let the tension and anxiety drop from her body. She was safe at last.

There's a knock at the front door and Kim

peeked her head around the door. "Hi, anybody home?"

"Hi Kim, come on in," Amanda said getting up to open the door further.

"Ray's here too, we brought pizza," Kim replied as she shoved a large pie into Amanda's arms. "Oh, you have company, I'm sorry."

"No don't worry about it, Wendy's a new friend. She might as well meet the whole gang," Rachel said getting up to retrieve some plates from the kitchen cupboard. "I'll get some plates, set the pizzas on the counter. Wendy, this is Kim and Ray."

"They came over a couple of weeks ago and we haven't been able to get rid of them since," Amanda quipped.

"Ha, ha, very funny, I love you too," Kim replied hugging Amanda.

"Fair warning Wendy, Amanda likes to tease," Ray chimed in with a grin.

Amanda grinned impishly and shrugged at Wendy.

Wendy was surprised at how open and carefree everyone was. Kim and Ray were obviously a straight couple and yet they seemed perfectly at home here with everyone else. "Why can't I have friends like this?" Wendy murmured softly to herself.

Amanda set a plate with a slice of pizza on the coffee table in front of Wendy. "You already do," she whispered back with a gentle smile.

An hour and a couple of empty pizza boxes later everyone sat around laughing at the latest exploits of their favorite landlord Tom Reilly.

"Apparently he got into trouble with his next-door neighbor yesterday when he decided to rent a bobcat and use it in the backyard," Amanda said grinning.

"He was trying to put in a new patio area and he backed the bobcat into the fence," Alex added pulling another slice out of the pizza box.

"Totally shredded the fence," Amanda said laughing. "The neighbor was livid."

"Gotta love Tom, he's always good for entertainment," Rachel added.

"And then, to top it all off, he rolled it on its side and the rental company had to bring in a forklift to sit it up again." By now Amanda was laying in Alex's lap with tears running down her face.

Wendy watched the three of them banter back and forth with a look of wonder. They hugged and kissed then swatted each other playfully while Kim and Ray just sat back and laughed at their antics. The joy was infectious, in no time at all Wendy was feeling like life wasn't as black as it looked just a couple of hours ago.

"Hey, who's on the schedule to work today?" asked Amanda sitting up and wiping her eyes.

"I'm on at five today," Alex muttered, "but at least I'm off tomorrow." He looked at Kim and Ray. "We have three chapters in the Meyer anthology to read by Monday for Dixon and our final draft of that short story is due in Ferguson's class on Wednesday, yuck."

"Damn, I haven't even started," grumbled Ray. Ray and Alex looked at Kim.

"Don't look at me," she giggled, "I didn't take Ferguson this semester for that very reason."

Ray grabbed her and smothered her in kisses

while Alex picked up the plates and carried them into the kitchen. Amanda walked into the kitchen and gave Alex a big hug and a kiss.

"That's for being you," Amanda said with a wry grin.

Rachel wandered back over to sit on the couch with Wendy. "My shift starts at eight again and I'll be late because I have to close."

"Want to take the car?"

"If you don't mind. Can I drop you off and pick you up at the usual time?"

"Sure, thanks," added Alex with a kiss on her cheek.

Wendy was beginning to put people together but for her the math wasn't working out quite right. Obviously Kim and Ray were dating but what about Rachel and Alex, or Amanda and Alex? There were matching rings on their left hands and all but it was still very confusing. Then there were the earrings and the necklace Alex was wearing, was he a boy or a girl?

"You look a bit troubled, Wendy, what's up?" Rachel laid a pillow under her feet on the coffee table.

"Not troubled, just confused," Wendy replied softly.

"About what?"

"About your relationship with Alex and Amanda."

"We're a family, the three of us," Rachel replied.

"Yes, but who's married to who?" she said looking at the wedding rings on their fingers.

"We all are, the three of us," Alex replied. "Not legally because society doesn't recognize our type of relationship so we just say we're a family and leave it at that."

Wendy looked at everybody with a blank look on her face.

"I was totally confused just like you when I first met Alex's sisters," Kim added with a smile. "In my head I wanted their relationship to conform to some sort of 'social norm'. I wanted it to fit neatly into a pigeonhole like everybody else's. But that wasn't going to happen," she said with a laugh. "Once I understood who they were it was clear that the love they have for each other means that society has to catch up with them not the other way around."

"What about the legal stuff?"

"We're working on it," said Amanda from the kitchen. "A friend of mine from work thought it might be good to try to officially create a family but I think, given the legal climate in this country, that a corporation might be a better bet."

"A what?"

"A corporation where we all have equal shares. The corporation owns all the assets so the whole issue of beneficiaries is solved. Legally, we'd be recognized without the hassle of busy-bodies sticking their noses into the bedroom."

"In our eyes, and the eyes of our friends, we're married," said Alex drawing Amanda with him from the kitchen as Rachel stood up to join them. "The corporation idea would be our non-conformist way of conforming. Eventually I want us all to have the same family name, for medical reasons, but there's no rush on that."

"I think it's brilliant," Wendy exclaimed. "But…I guess I'm still a little confused about you, Alex. I hope this doesn't offend you but, are you a boy or a girl?"

"Time for the iPad," Kim and Amanda said in unison and everyone else laughed.

"Huh?" Wendy looked from Kim to Amanda and back to Alex.

Alex blushed a bit then reached for his backpack and pulled out his iPad. "It's becoming the family jest actually. Here, I've Googled it for you. The term is intersex. It's what I am."

Wendy quickly scanned the page and looked up at Alex in wonder.

"Yup, that's me, about halfway down the page," Alex said still blushing slightly and taking his iPad as Wendy handed it back to him. "I'm still trying to get used to this bumpy ride called my life," he pulled Amanda and Rachel into a big hug, "but with these two around the road has gotten a lot smoother."

Wendy shook her head bewildered. "Where were you guys two years ago?"

"Waiting for you to show up today," answered Amanda with a gentle smile as she gathered up empty plates and walked to the kitchen.

Wendy opened her mouth then she closed it, unable to form into words the warmth that surrounded her heart.

"It's called Kismet," Rachel said. "I learned it from Alex."

"Who taught everyone else sitting in here," added Ray.

"Nothing in life is a coincidence Wendy, everything is meant to be," Amanda continued walking back from the kitchen drying her hands on a dishtowel. "We are here for you because you needed us to be. It's that simple."

Wendy began to tear up again and Rachel

grabbed another tissue.

"Oh crap, sorry, we didn't mean to make you cry Wendy," Alex said.

"No, no, these are happy tears. It's been a tough day."

Concerned, Kim looked at Rachel and she whispered, "I'll tell you later."

Kim shrugged her shoulders. "Hey, we got an apartment!" She shouted with glee.

"What?" Alex asked collapsing into a chair near the couch.

"Yup, we signed the lease this afternoon. The pizza was a celebration," Ray added hugging Kim.

"When do you move in?" Amanda asked.

"The first of the month," Ray replied. "My lease was running out this month and Kim's was nearly over so we talked and, well..."

"It was Kismet!" Kim interrupted and everybody laughed again.

"Did I hear you say you're looking for a house Amanda?" Wendy asked between sniffles.

"Yeah, any ideas?"

"Well, I just happen to be a real estate broker so I think I might have a few," she said with a big grin. "Ouch, it's hard to smile when you're still broken."

"A smile is the best medicine," said Kim. "We do a lot of that around here. She glanced at her watch. "Hey, we have to go."

Ray nodded and grinned as well. "Yeah, I have to pack up all my junk, then throw out half because it's just that, junk."

"See you guys," Alex said hugging them both. "Thanks for the pizza and congratulations."

Once they left everyone turned to focus on

Wendy.

"Okay, so when can we see our dream house?" Amanda flopped down on the pillow in front of the couch and leaned her elbows on the coffee table. Her eyes sparkled with excitement.

"Here's my card, how about we meet Monday afternoon and go over what you're looking for."

"Perfect, no wait, we have Tae Kwando Monday afternoon. How about we talk over dinner here?"

"That works for me," Wendy said jotting down a note and slipping it into her purse. "Tae Kwando?"

"Yes, Amanda got us all signed up," Alex replied. "A couple of months ago she had a run in with a former supervisor at her work. Rachel managed to make him a eunuch right before he fled to Milwaukee…"

"Courtesy of my boss," Amanda interrupted with a grin.

"So then we all realized that self-defense classes would be a good investment," finished Alex.

"The name of the school is called 'Karma'. Go figure," Amanda added and everyone laughed.

"Sign me up! I need something like that after the beating I took today," Wendy said pulling out her blackberry and jotting down another note. "If it wasn't for Rachel I might be in the hospital right now."

"Our class starts at three tomorrow afternoon, it's the studio on 28$^{th}$ street near the warehouse district." Amanda scooted over to look at Wendy's cellphone. "I'm sure there's room for at least one more in that session. Yeah, that's the one," she said pointing to the marker on Wendy's GPS. "Master Kwon is cool too, he can be cranky at times…"

"Especially when you don't remember your routines," Alex interrupted.

"But he's got his heart in the right place," Amanda finished scrunching her nose at Alex.

"The more the merrier," chirped Rachel. "Pick me up at work tomorrow and I'll guide you there."

"Where do you work?"

"Tamsen, Willis, and James, I'm in the accounting department."

"I know exactly where you are, my office is in the building across the street." Wendy pulled the three of them into a big hug. "I'm so glad I met you guys. Oh, ouch…still sore."


The following Monday after Alex's classes, he picked up Amanda from her work and drove to the Tae Kwando studio. They were walking to the front entrance as a white BMW Z4 Roadster rolled into the parking lot. Behind the wheel was Wendy and in the passenger seat was a very wind blown Rachel wearing a smile that seemed to hang off her ears. She hopped out and nearly bounced across the parking lot, she was so giddy. "That, girls, is one cool car."

"You're hair is a total mess," Amanda said trying to untangle a few curls.

"That's why I always wear a ball cap when I drive with the top down," Wendy giggled. "I warned her but she was not having any of it."

"Ball caps cramp my style," she replied with a grin and then pointing to Wendy's car. "Someday I will drive one of those."

"Wendy picked me up from work, you should have seen the shocked look on the faces of some of those guys from the office. I wish I had my camera."

"It is a pretty car," Amanda said laughing at Rachel's boisterous charm.

"Come on, let's go, you know how much Master Kwon likes it when we're late," Alex said as he looked Amanda in the eye.

"Pushups are no fun," she muttered.

# =ELEVEN=

Kyle Upton sat on his balcony and sipped his morning cup of coffee. He was stumbling through the email on his iPad without much interest in anything offered until he opened a spam message linking to a new chat space for singles on a site he'd never visited before. He'd lurked on chat room sites, browsed the personals on craigslist, and looked at a few webcam sites but mostly he was too shy to actually open a conversation let alone meet someone offline.

He decided, what the hell, and clicked on the link. The iPad snapped out of his email server and quickly opened up a new browser window. In seconds he was asked to register and login to a site that listed itself as 'open minded'. A few minutes later he was browsing through the thumbnail images of women and men looking to connect with someone. He was about to give up when a new page opened and an image nearly jumped off the screen. It was his neighbor, a woman he'd seen countless times in the lobby of the condominium complex. She was stunning. Her dark brown hair shimmered in the light as it cascaded like a waterfall around a beautiful face near perfect in symmetry.

He looked at the name below the image, Wendy Bingham, hmmm. He scanned her biography below her name. Now he was certain that she was his neighbor. Not only did she live in the same condominium complex but she lived on the same floor and her balcony sat directly across the open space from his. He'd seen her countless times taking her coffee on her balcony on sunny mornings before work.

He smiled subtly and decided to send her a note. 'Hey, I'm sitting outside looking over at your balcony hoping you'd come out so we could chat. Call me.' He left his number and pressed 'send'.

It would be too much like a corny Hollywood movie to expect her to immediately respond but what the heck, it was nice to fantasize a bit anyway. He smiled again, closed his iPad cover, picked up his cup of coffee and walked back inside his house.

Across the way, looking through the sheer drapes that covered her balcony doors, Wendy glanced across to the other wing of the condominiums that faced her side of the building. It was another Saturday, almost like the other Saturdays that have stretched back as far as she could remember except that this Saturday was supposed to have been her wedding day. Her eyes glistened as she thought about what it would have looked like. Her standing in a beautiful white gown, her hair done up in a cascade of curls, and in her hands a beautiful bouquet of flowers. Then the image of Ted's snarling face invaded her dream world. The vision shattered into a million tiny pieces leaving only white sheer drapes to billow in the gentle breeze.

She looked across to the balcony that faced hers. A young man sat sipping coffee and looking at a tablet. He was busy tapping away, oblivious to the fact that across the way a girl's dreams lay shattered at her feet. She sighed and turned towards her bedroom then the phone rang. Without looking at the caller id she opened her phone. "Hello?"

"Hi Wendy, it's me Rachel. What are you doing?"

"Nothing. I was thinking of going back to bed. I'm not much for anything today."

"Come on, we're going to the beach. We'll be over in twenty minutes to pick you up."

"I don't know, Rachel. I'm feeling kind of lousy today. I don't think I'd be very good company."

"Nonsense girl," it was Amanda's voice now. She must have grabbed the phone from Rachel. "We all know what today is and that's exactly why you need to come with us. We'll be there in twenty minutes to drag you out if we have to!" she shouted giggling as Rachel's voice came back on the phone.

"I know my wife, there's no arguing with her. See you in twenty, wear something sexy."

The phone beeped when Rachel disconnected and Wendy sighed. She knew Rachel was right, Amanda is a whirlwind and there is no arguing with her once she has her sails up.

Wendy tossed the phone onto her purse and headed to her bedroom to find a swimsuit.

An hour later they stood on the beach holding

beach towels and sunscreen lotion. Alex was dragging a cooler loaded with drinks and snacks from his car to the beach while Rachel was struggling with a large umbrella.

"Wow, Alex looks good in that one piece," Wendy said softly to Amanda standing nearby.

"You have no idea how hard it was to get her into that let alone convince her to go to the beach today."

"Why? She looks lovely."

"Please tell her that," Amanda replied. "Her confidence is at an all-time low. She's still self-conscious about her body. We can get her to go to the club but anywhere else and she's as nervous as a chased cat." Amanda sighed then hung her arms off Wendy's shoulder. "She wears me out sometimes but she's getting better. Oh, and call her April. That's her name when she's dressed like that."

"That's a pretty name." Wendy watched April and Rachel setup the umbrella as Amanda spread out the towels. This was the first time she had a chance to really look at Alex, er, April's body. She was tall and slender but not skinny. Her breasts were surprisingly full given her slender frame. She filled out the swimming suit nicely. Her golden brown hair fell in gentle curves across her shoulders and it framed a remarkably feminine face with barely a hint of masculinity. She was lucky; some men had to work very hard to achieve any sort of femininity when they went through the 'transition'. Wendy reflected back on her own journey. She thought of the excruciating surgeries, the countless pills, and then the most painful thing of all, the rejection by all of her so-called friends and family. That thought made her wince.

She was still lost in thought as April ran back up the beach towards the umbrella. Amanda and Rachel had been tossing a large ball and playing 'keep-away' with her. April finally gave up and crawled back under the shelter of the umbrella to retrieve a drink from the cooler.

"Those two are too much for me today," she grunted, collapsing on a towel. "I'm still exhausted from work last night. I swear that delivery truck arrives later and later each week."

"Where do you work?" Wendy asked pulled out of her somber reverie.

"The convenience store on Elm near 39$^{th}$."

"I know it, I stop in there from time to time. But I've never seen you in there."

"I usually work night shifts so unless you come in after seven you probably won't see me. I'm glad I don't have to work again tonight, maybe I can get some much needed sleep."

"Have you looked for other work?"

"Not a lot of opportunities for an English major trying to put himself through school. I hope the convenience store is only temporary until I finish."

"When's that?"

"Next spring, I hope." April settled back down and closed her eyes.

Wendy could see that the girls had moved into the ocean with the beach ball. She suddenly felt a bit of jealousy for Rachel.

"Penny for your thoughts," murmured April lying with her arm over her eyes.

"They're actually a little embarrassing."

"What are?"

"My thoughts."

April sat up and looked at Wendy. "Okay, a nickel for your thoughts then." She wore a devilish grin.

Wendy sighed a bit and glanced at her with a subtle smile. "I was just thinking about how jealous I am of Rachel."

April's eyebrows rose as she cocked her head with a curious smile. "She is a beautiful woman."

"I agree but that isn't why I'm jealous." She glanced over at Alex again and saw the quizzical look on her face. "I'm jealous because of you and Amanda. You guys love her and each other so much it makes me jealous. There, I admit it." She hung her head with a girlish pout.

April wrapped her arms around Wendy and gave her a big hug. "Don't be, your turn is coming, I can feel it. Besides you're with us now, part of our extended family."

"Speaking of which, where are Kim and Ray?"

"Ray had to work and Kim is with her uncle helping him get ready for a party he's throwing for her cousin's birthday. They'll probably stop into the club tonight if you want to see them again."

"Which club is that?"

"Moulin Rouge, it's where Rachel works part-time. She's on tonight until midnight, I think. Have you ever been there?"

"I've only heard about it but I've never been there."

"It's kind of a cool place, their policy is open and accepting so a lot of gay and transgendered folks drop by. It can get pretty outlandish some nights but usually it's just a nice place to hang out and unwind."

"I'll check it out." Wendy paused again and

watched Rachel and Amanda playing in the surf, riding the waves as they crashed endlessly onto the shore. "Wait a minute, what do you mean my turn is coming?"

April sat up and smiled winsomely.

"What I mean is that it's just nature's way." She said brushing off the sand from her suit. "You just got out of a really nasty relationship, thankfully; so now Prince Charming is standing in the wings waiting for his cue. It's nature's way of finding balance in the world."

April took Wendy's hands in hers. "The universe wants to work for you Wendy, it has to, but you have to let it happen and not sabotage it in the process. And don't think that you don't deserve it because you do, we all do. It's simple, really. So simple that people sabotage it all the time with negative thoughts. So don't do that. Think of what you need, not what you want. Tell the universe out loud what it is that you need and let it work to make it happen. Oh, and don't attached strings, it slows the process down. So be patient girl, he will be here before you know it."

Wendy looked at April, speechless. Then she grinned and threw her arms around her and pulled her close. She could feel April's breasts press against her chest. They were soft and full. "Thank you April, you're the best."

"What's up?" Amanda asked as she dropped down on a blanket next to April flicking water all over her as she sat.

"Hey, you're getting me all wet," April groaned.

"Well, get in the water lazy butt, it's great out there, the temperature is perfect."

"What about you?" April asked up on her knees.

"I can't, I'm pooped," Amanda replied. "Rachel wore me out."

About then Rachel dropped down on the sand and pulled out a towel to dry her hair. "God, I love days like today. No tourists, peaceful, and the beach isn't too crowded. Who's up for beach volleyball?

"No way, I'm worn out." Amanda collapsed on a towel and groaned.

April got up, kissed Amanda and Rachel, adjusted her suit, and waved to Wendy as she headed towards the surf.

Wendy, waving back, watched her long legs stride gracefully towards the surf. "She's really a lovely girl isn't she?"

Rachel followed her glance towards April. "Yes she is, and I love her dearly." Then she leaned over and tickled Amanda's feet. "Just as much as I love my little munchkin."

Amanda squealed and pulled her feet away. "You have to sleep sometime you Amazonian goddess," Amanda muttered into her towel. "And then I will have my way with you." She leaped up and surrounded Rachel with tiny pokes. Rachel shrieked shouting, "Uncle, uncle." They both fell into each other's arms laughing.

Wendy tried her best to stay out of the middle of the horseplay. "So, how did you two meet April?"

"She lives in the same apartment building." Amanda replied.

"Right across the hall from me," added Rachel. "I first met him as Alex when I was climbing those god awful stairs at two in the morning wearing heels that were, as Alex called them, dangerous on level ground. I have no idea why I bought them. My heel broke and I twisted my ankle. Alex caught me and helped me into my apartment. He was so sweet, he brought me dinner the following night."

"I remember that," Amanda added. "I met him running up the front steps with a large bag of Chinese carry out. He called it 'meals on wheels'."

Rachel pulled a beer from the cooler and opened it. "So we talked and a couple of days later I decided to open up to him. I don't know why but I felt like he was going to be somebody very special, and he was. From there we became friends, then lovers, and now wives."

Wendy glanced over at Amanda who grinned impishly.

"I had just moved into town and all my stuff was just dumped on the front lawn by the movers. Alex was walking up the front steps when he saw me standing there. I probably had the longest face on he'd ever seen. I was miserable. Alex offered to help and within the hour we had all of it neatly stacked in the middle of my new apartment."

Amanda reached over and grabbed a beer out of the cooler. "After that we'd talk occasionally in the hallway or at one of Reilly's backyard parties, then one day he saw me run out of my apartment crying. I went out to the old tree swing in the backyard. It reminded me of the one I had when I was little and living in Vancouver. My Mom had just called to tell me that my cousin Susan was getting married in a month. I was devastated. I thought my life was a total screw-up. Then Alex looked at me with those beautiful blue eyes and told me that I was the luckiest girl in the whole world. He said that I got a do-over."

"A what?" asked Wendy.

"That's what I said. A what?" she laughed. "He said, "It's what happens when the universe deals you a hand that is so terribly wrong that in one fell swoop things are reset and you get to start again fresh." And then he told me "you are truly blessed Amanda Simpson, and that is nothing to be sad about."

"I was dumbfounded. I looked at him for a moment and then I knew he was completely right. In that same moment I realized that I had fallen in love with him," she paused a moment and leaned up to kiss Rachel on the cheek, "and then I met this sweet, beautiful girl and I knew that I'd found my place in the world. Between them and with them."

Wendy's cheeks were wet and her eyes were glistening as she listened to their stories. She took a big breath and let it out slowly. She settled back against her towel to think about where her own life had been and where it might be going. April's words kept repeating in her mind. "Your turns coming; just be patient."

# =TWELVE=

That afternoon after the girls dropped her off at her condo, Wendy flopped down on her couch and picked up her iPad. Work was the last thing she wanted to think about but she knew that she had to check into her email at least once a day to keep up with everything.

Then she saw it. It was the third message down.

It read: Hey, I'm sitting outside looking over at your balcony hoping you'd come out so we could chat. Call me. Beneath his name he left his phone number at the end of the note.

Her face flushed scarlet. Oh my God! He lives in the same complex! Do I know him? How does he know my balcony is…? "Oh Shit." She scrambled off the couch and dashed to the sheer curtains that covered the balcony doors. Directly across from her balcony was an identical one facing it. And sitting on a chair was someone she had only noticed once or twice as she came into the building lobby.

She peeked through the drapes again, and then she grabbed up her iPad and looked at his note again.

He must have seen me sitting on the balcony but I never noticed him sitting there. Does he know about me? Maybe. He has to suspect something if he was looking at that particular website. It's called 'open-minded' for a reason.

What if he's some dumb jock who cruises websites looking for a quick poke? Or maybe he's a stalker, or a rapist? Oh get a grip girl. If my mind keeps going like this I'll end up crazy, old, and alone. I just have to ask. It's that simple. And if he tries to hurt me...

She spun her foot up in a classic roundhouse kick then she settled down and repeated several more forms. "Then I'll just kick his butt," she muttered with a sheepish grin knowing that she'd only been to two lessons so far.

It was late in the afternoon, nearly five o'clock when Kyle heard his cellphone beep. He had stepped inside to freshen up his drink and he got a text message to come out onto his terrace. He stood looking around and then he noticed a girl waving at him from across the way. It was her, the girl he'd seen countless times in the lobby. The girl he saw on that website. His cellphone began to ring.

"Hi" Wendy said waving again timidly.

"Hi back at you."

They stood looking at one another across the open space that separated the two wings of the condominium complex.

"So, do you want to meet someplace where we're not standing so far apart?"

She glanced at the setting sun. "How about dinner?"

"Perfect. Burgers at Rudy's? It's just down the street from here."

"I'll meet you in the lobby in thirty minutes."

"I'll be waiting."

Rudy's was a quaint little 'Ma & Pa' operation that specialized in gourmet burgers and seafood hoagies. The price was reasonable for this side of town and the atmosphere was always warm and welcoming.

Kyle led the way to a seat outside on the terrace away from several others crowded around the television blaring sports news. "Is this okay?"

"It's fine thanks."

"Actually, I've never been here before. I've driven by it enough times to tell myself that I should try it but..." He shrugged and grinned.

Wendy glanced up from the menu and returned his awkward smile. She could see he was nervous. She was nervous too. She took a big breath to settle the butterflies fluttering in her stomach. "I know I'm the same way. But now we're here." She gazed into his twinkling eyes and she could see that Kyle was beginning to relax a bit. "So, you sent me a message."

"And you texted me back."

"Yeah."

They sat looking at one another forgetting that the rest of the world existed, including the waiter who arrived at their table several minutes ago.

"Ahem, can I get you something to drink?"

"Ah, yes, just water for me," Kyle responded.

"Me too."

Wendy watched Kyle take a big breath and let it out with a soft whistle as if he was trying to release some of the tension that was building up inside. She felt the same way only she didn't want to whistle.

"Wendy, I've never been very good at this, meeting beautiful girls and talking to them."

"Well I feel just as awkward as you do so we're even," she said. I tell you what, tell me your most embarrassing moment this week and I'll tell you mine. After that we can't be any more embarrassed than we were then so everything will be just fine."

He smiled sweetly and her heart just melted. "Okay, hmm, oh I know. I was walking out of my office two days ago when I ran into Henderson from accounting. We were both late to a meeting. I was juggling a stack of folders and a glass of water. The water tumbled and I managed to save the folders but not my pants. It went right down the front, splashing all over my crotch. About then the general manager walked out of the conference room. I must have turned fifteen shades of red."

He chuckled as he shook his head and Wendy smiled. "Okay, your turn." He leaned forward and rested his chin on the palms of his hands.

"I'm a real estate broker. I was showing a house to some close friends the other day when we all walked into the main bathroom to see an elderly man standing buck-naked with everything at half mast. I guess he didn't hear us come into the house. I had phoned earlier and left a message but sometimes, try as you might, you manage to see a cock or two when you least expect it."

Kyle laughed out loud. He had such a beautiful smile. His eyes lit up with a sparkle and his cheeks had such cute dimples in them.

"Okay, you win, a cock at half mast always beats

a wet crotch in any poker game I've played." He shook his head and chuckled again. The waiter brought their water and they ordered the house special.

"So, tell me about yourself. You're a real estate broker? That must be interesting."

Wendy sat there a moment and studied Kyle's face then she smiled meekly and sighed. What do I tell him? I will never get into another relationship, even a casual one, without the truth. Wendy hated what happened that day in front of those condos; even more than she feared telling Ted her secret. From now on it's the truth. She took a big breath again and let it out slowly.

Kyle's smile began to fade as she wrestled with what she needed to tell him.

"Today was supposed to be my wedding day."

All of the color dropped out of Kyle's face. "What? What happened?"

"We got into a huge fight a month ago. It was so terrible my friend Rachel had to step in and break it up. If she hadn't, my ex-fiancé, Ted, would have put me in the hospital. I vowed then that I would never allow myself to be in that sort of situation again. So if what I'm about to say bothers you please just leave and we'll never have to speak about it again."

Kyle sat motionless across the table from Wendy. She looked for any hint of resentment or fear. But there was none, his expression was compassionate and sincere.

"I was born James Wendell Bingham the third, into a wealthy family who lived most of their privileged lives in seclusion from the real world. When I was eight I began to have feelings about who

I was and although I didn't understand exactly what I was feeling I did know that I was different from the other boys who I would hang out with or who went to school with me. When I was twelve and starting puberty I found that I liked to do things that my father found distasteful, like playing with dolls and having make-believe tea parties. I can't begin to count the number of times he locked me in my room as punishment for misbehaving like a girl. And there were times he decided that a belt or hairbrush was a better tool of discipline to teach me about manhood than any stern talking too. But where he was persistent I was equally stubborn. I knew what I liked and it wasn't what he considered appropriate boy behavior."

"When I was fourteen, unbeknownst to my father, my mother started me on a hormone therapy. She was struggling to understand what I was going through but she knew that what my father was doing was wrong. She talked to a couple of specialists who referred her to a child psychologist and he told her that her son had issues with gender identity, as he called it."

"The drugs began to reshape my boyish body making it more feminine. In some respects they helped me here as well," she said pointing to her forehead. "The conflicts inside my brain began to diminish and I was starting to see the world from a feminine perspective."

Kyle fiddled with his napkin as he listened earnestly to Wendy's story. When the waiter returned with their meal Wendy paused briefly so that they could finish in silence. Once they were nearly done Wendy continued.

"When I went off to Dartmouth I went dressed as a boy to placate my father but once I left the dorms after my freshman year I got my own apartment. From then on I began to dress completely as a woman. At first I was the subject of ridicule, then it became more sinister. Not from the boys, they were mostly childish and stupid. It was the girls who where sinister. You cannot imagine the ugly pranks they would play on me. Some of it bordered on torture. To this day the thought of being bound to something, anything, by ropes or electrical ties makes me hysterical. I couldn't get through the first half of 'Fifty Shades' without throwing it in the trash." Her cheeks were damp as tears filled her eyes. She lifted a tissue from her purse and dried her eyes.

"The one thing those women kept over my head was the thought that I could never be a woman if I had a penis." Her voice was now barely a whisper. "I yelled back at them in rage. I am a woman in my heart and that's all that matters. They laughed at me. They spat in my face and kicked me in the balls. I screamed at them. "How could a woman still be a woman if cancer has taken her uterus or breasts?" Then someone knocked me unconscious. I was found the next morning by one of the grounds keepers at the college. I decided at that moment that whatever it took I was going to be a woman physically to match who I was here," she pointed to her heart."

"I finished college, I wasn't going to let them beat me. I stood defiantly on the dais, graduating cum laude and told them all, that today was the happiest day of my life because I was leaving them all behind. I smiled graciously, turned and never looked back. Three years later I had my operation." Her face was filled with a ferocity that matched the passion in her heart as she sat back and waited for Kyle's response.

Kyle paused for a moment. His face was almost blank. Wendy couldn't tell what he was thinking and that worried her most of all. Did she go too far, too fast? Does he think she's some sort of lesbian man-hater and that she detests him because of who he is?

Then Kyle leaned forward with a gentle smile. "You are the most courageous person I have ever met."

"What I just said doesn't bother you?"

"I'm having dinner with you, not part of you. I'm sorry about your wedding. Your ex-fiancé is an ass and the rest of your dinner is getting cold." His eyes twinkled with delight as her face lit up.

Hold on girl; let's not jump from the frying pan into the fire. You still don't know anything about him. He could be a serial rapist or something…but I doubt it.

Wendy settled herself into her chair and picked up her burger then paused. "Okay, I guess it's your turn. What do you do when you're not cruising the Internet?"

"I'm a lawyer, yeah I know, here come the lawyer jokes."

"Not from me, I'm in real estate, remember?"

"I work for the Securities and Exchange Commission doing research in the International Trade Division. I spend my day pouring over shipping invoices, bills of lading, goods received and shipped. God, it's boring stuff."

"Are you looking for drugs or smugglers?"

"No that's I.C.E. and the DEA. More

dangerous, less boring."

"Is it your first job out of school?"

"No, I spent some time clerking for a Circuit Court Judge in Colorado before I came here. It was okay but the pay was lousy and I am still swimming in debt from law school. The SEC job gave me a shot at seeing the light at the end of the tunnel so to speak."

"Student loans can be brutal, you can never default on them either."

He nodded. "They sort of have you by the proverbial short hairs."

"Yeah, they do."

"So why did you pick the name Wendy? Is it because of Peter Pan and Neverland?"

"No, but that's a good guess. I heard from a friend that a lot of girls named Wendy come from that reference. My middle name is Wendell and my Mother's name is Dee."

"Got it, Wen Dee, just different spelling."

She tilted her head slightly and smiled at Kyle warmly. He seemed kind and caring. Also honest and open about whom he is and where he's been. "So, my turn for a question. Any girlfriends?"

"Not since six months ago and even then Diane was an on again off again kind of girl. Eventually it became apparent to me that she was looking for someone who could keep her in the lap of luxury that she imagined and I just wasn't that kind of guy."

"Trolling for a big wallet?"

"Yup." Kyle picked up his napkin and wiped his face.

"Why were you on the open-minded website?"

"I don't know, a coincidence maybe? I've been on sites like that one before but that was the first time

I visited that particular site. There was a link to it in my email inbox and I absent-mindedly clicked on it. And now I'm glad I did."

"I have a friend who doesn't believe in coincidence. I'm beginning to believe him," she added taking another bite of her salad.

"Why were you on there?" He asked resting his chin on his palms again. His eyes twinkled mischievously.

"I don't know either, coincidence?"

Kyle laughed out loud again. It was a hearty laugh, open and joyful, she liked that. She liked Kyle too, but in the back of her mind there was still doubt. Ted placed that shadow on her heart. It would take more than a burger and salad with a cute guy to remove it.

A rowdy group of locals came out to the terrace from the restaurant and sat at a table nearby. They were loud and boisterous. The place was starting to get crowded.

"It's Saturday night and it looks like things are starting to pick up," Kyle said trying to talk over the crowd at the next table. "Do you want to go somewhere else?"

"What time is it?"

Kyle checked his watch. "A little after nine o'clock."

"Yes, but I'll drive. Have you ever been to Moulin Rouge?"

"I think I've heard of it but I've never been there."

"Neither have I but tonight seems to be an evening of firsts. Let's go." Wendy scooted her chair back and followed Kyle out of the restaurant.

Outside they walked together down the sidewalk towards the condominium complex. When they came to an intersection Kyle reached over and took her hand in his. Wendy looked up in surprise, blushing slightly. They crossed the street and continued to hold hands until they reached the garage where Wendy parked her car.

"Wow, cool car." Kyle stopped for a moment and admired the sleek lines of the Z4.

"Come on, get in. Should I put the top up?"

"Are you kidding? This is why you buy a convertible!"

She grinned sheepishly and started the car. It roared to life and rumbled softly as she backed the car out of her private parking spot.

"I actually bought it because I like the way it handles." Wendy pulled out of the driveway and the car raced off down the street. "I hope you don't mind, I sort of have a lead foot." The car squealed around a corner and dashed off down the street towards downtown.

Kyle's eyes got rather large but the smile on his face told Wendy he wasn't going to complain.

As Wendy and Kyle walked up to the club entrance it was closer to ten o'clock and there was a sizeable queue lined up on the sidewalk. Wendy looked around for a moment. "Geez, maybe we won't get into the club after all."

"Wendy?" Some one shouted from behind the gated entrance to the club. Wendy turned and walked back towards the head of the line. "Hi Ray."

Ray was standing besides the bouncer who was busy checking IDs. "I just came out for a smoke.

Have you been out here for very long?"

"No, we just got here. The line looks pretty long."

"Wait right here, I'll go get Rachel." Ray dashed back into the club and disappeared behind a beaded curtain.

Wendy turned and motioned to Kyle and he walked up to stand by her. She grabbed his hand and smiled. A moment later Rachel appeared at the doorway. Her hair was up in large curls that cascaded down her back and she wore a rather provocative silver dress that, while barely covering her thighs, it hugged her ample breasts like a well-fitted glove. As she stepped towards them Wendy noticed she was wearing another pair of heels that clearly were in the 'dangerous even on level ground' category.

"Wow, you look amazing!" Wendy shouted over the thump of bass reverberating from the building.

"Thanks. So you decided to check out the club?" Rachel looked down and noticed that Wendy was holding Kyle's hand.

"Yeah, we just finished dinner. It was sort of impromptu. Oh, this is Kyle Upton. He's a friend. I hope we can get in."

"There's a birthday party going on in a private room and that always backs things up. Come on." Rachel nodded to the bouncer and opened the gate for them. "Follow me."

Wendy and Kyle followed Rachel through the doorway and into the club. The music was throbbing and lights were flashing around the room. In the center was a large dance floor that was crowded with people moving to the beat. Wendy looked up to see Rachel glancing sideways at Kyle like an overprotective mother hen.

She was beginning to wonder if she was throwing Kyle to the wolves here. She looked back to see that he appeared to be as dazzled by the place as she was. They followed Rachel back to a table in the corner of the club. As they came closer, Wendy saw some familiar faces. Amanda was talking to Kim and Ray and Alex, apparently now dressed as April from the spectacular gown she was wearing, stood up to greet them.

"Wendy! Great to see you," she leaned forward and gave her a hug. "Who's this?"

"Hi everyone, this is Kyle Upton. We just finished dinner a while ago so we decided to take you up on your offer and check out Moulin Rouge."

"Hello Kyle," everyone shouted back. April stepped around Wendy and offered her hand to Kyle. "Nice to meet you. How do you know Wendy?"

Kyle took April's hand and returned her firm handshake. "We just met today actually, it was quite by accident," he said with a shrug. "We live in the same condominium complex."

Wendy curled her arm around Rachel's and steered her away from the table. "Can I speak to you for a moment?"

"Sure, what's up?" Rachel glanced over Wendy's shoulder and watched Kyle and April talk.

"That."

"What?"

"That helicopter hovering you're doing."

Rachel glanced back at Wendy and blushed.

"Rachel, I'm a big girl. I'm never going to repeat what happened with Ted, never ever. I know you want to protect me like a big sister and I love you for it. But go easy on Kyle. He's kind and considerate and we really hit it off tonight. If you come on too strong you might scare him off and I kind of want to see where this goes."

"Are you sure? Does he know about you?"

"Yes, and yes. We had a long talk, well, mostly I talked and he listened, which is so rare in guys, right? So don't rough him up, okay? Be gentle. I think he's a keeper." She leaned up and kissed Rachel on the cheek and gave her a little hug then she turned and walked back to sit next to Kyle.

After Wendy sat down April leaned over and whispered into her ear. "Prince Charming?"

Wendy face was flush with crimson. She lowered her eyes and smiled demurely then she glanced sideways at April then looked up at Kyle who was busy talking to Amanda. She nodded and whispered back. "I hope so."

"Good." April stood up and leaned over to Wendy and Kyle. "Can I get you anything? I'm heading for the bar."

"A coke for me," Kyle replied.

"Same here," added Wendy. April nodded and started the long weave towards the bar.

Kim and Ray moved over to sit next to Wendy.

"Thanks for helping us Ray," Wendy said reaching over to give his hand a squeeze. "We'd probably still be out there if you hadn't seen us."

"You're more than welcome Wendy," Ray said sipping on his rum and coke.

"How long have you guys know April and her sisters?"

"For me," Ray replied, "I've known Alex for at least two years, we started graduate school together."

"Me too, I met Alex two years ago in the Short Story Composition class. I think it was his first year at the university too," Kim added.

"So how did you guys react when they told you everything?" Wendy asked.

"Oh God, that was crazy that night," Ray replied.

"It was?"

"Yeah, everything changed so quickly."

"Being with those three is like living in a whirlwind," Kim added. "When I first met him, Alex wore mostly faded flannel shirts and worn out jeans."

"He still had long hair but he smashed it down under this ragged stocking cap," Ray chimed in.

Kim nodded and continued. "But lately at school, I noticed that he was beginning to wear more feminine things. I was concerned because boys can be terrible teases so I spoke to him about it. You know sometimes that sort of stuff leads to something more violent."

"Sweetie, boys are nothing compared to girls, but go on," Wendy said emphatically and touching Kim's hand for emphasis.

"Anyway, we got to talking and the next thing I knew he had invited me over to his place to meet his sisters, Rachel and Amanda. They began to explain a little bit about who they were. They did a complete makeover on me. I walked out of Rachel's bedroom a completely different person. When I turned around Alex was walking into the room wearing this stunning black dress and heels. One thing led to another and we were headed here to Moulin Rouge."

"I barely recognized Kim when I saw her that night, she was beautiful," Ray added hugging Kim. "I was here with some friends when I saw her on the dance floor dancing with another girl. When I finally worked up the courage, I walked across the dance floor to talk to her. But not in my wildest dreams did I imagine what would happen next. I sat down to talk to Kim and did a double take when I realized that it was Alex sitting next to me…"

"But now she was April…" Kim added.

"Uh-huh, and we got to talking. Then I met Amanda and this amazing Amazon goddess Rachel. In those five-inch heels she just towered over me. I felt like the woman could squash me."

"She is tall," Wendy mused with a chuckle. "And I've seen her knock a six-foot man to the ground with one punch."

Ray nodded. "So you know what I mean? Anyway we all ended up back at Rachel's apartment. It must have been around two in the morning. We'd had a few drinks at the club and a few more at Rachel's place so once again my courage was fueled by alcohol and I had to ask…"

"Ray's a sweetheart but he can be a knuckle head sometimes."

Ray blushed a bit and shrugged his shoulders. "April got out her iPad and showed me the infamous webpage. Then Rachel told me that she was a pre-op transsexual and Amanda said she was a genetic goddess. The more I know Amanda the more I believe that's true."

"That girl is at the center of the vortex. When she gets going on something she is unstoppable." Kim added.

"Yeah, I found that out," chuckled Wendy. "So are you guys okay with all of this?

"Yeah," Ray responded quickly. "They're

beautiful and besides, if it wasn't for Alex I would never have worked up the nerve to be with this beautiful woman right here," he added hugging Kim tightly and kissing her on the cheek.

"And if it wasn't for all three of them I wouldn't have had the nerve to be with Ray. They're our best friends, I don't know what I would do without them." She kissed Ray lightly on the lips.

Wendy smiled and reached across to squeeze Kim's hand. "Thank you."

"Hey." Kyle rubbed Wendy's shoulders lightly. "You want to dance? It looks like fun."

"I'd love to Kyle but I'm just beat, it's been a long day. Can I take a rain check?"

"Hmmm. A rain check means we'll come back here again doesn't it?"

Wendy nodded and smiled demurely.

"Good, a rain check it is. Do you want to leave?"

"Can we?"

"Of course, you're driving."

"Okay, let me say good night to Rachel, I'll be right back." Wendy stood up and wove her way across the dance floor. She spotted Rachel at a table near the bar.

"Hey, we're going to take off."

"Call me tomorrow, okay?" Rachel shouted over the throbbing music.

"Okay." Wendy turned to make her way back across the floor.

"Wait, I'll walk with you."

They both crossed the floor and made their way to the table in the back. Wendy grabbed her jacket and Rachel reached over to touch Kyle on his shoulder. "Can we have coffee sometime? I'd like to get to know you better."

"Sure, Wendy has your number doesn't she?" Kyle replied while pulling on his coat.

"Yes. Text me when you have some free time." Rachel smiled and glanced behind Kyle to see a warning look from Wendy. Rachel leaned forward and gave Kyle a little hug while mouthing the words "don't worry, I'll be kind" to Wendy.

Wendy pulled her into a hug and whispered in her ear. "I love you Rachel but you'd better behave." Then she kissed her on the cheek.

The elevator door chimed and the doors opened. Kyle and Wendy walked down the long corridor to her condo holding hands in silence. They both wore a subtle smile. Kyle turned when he arrived at her door. "Thanks, it's been a really special evening."

"Yes it has, very special indeed. Thank you for putting up with my whim."

"Whim?" Kyle looked at her with a curious smile.

"Moulin Rouge, I sort of blind sided you a bit on that one."

"You mean introducing me to your friends? Nah, wait until you meet my family, now that will be a crazy time."

"Your family?"

"No expectations, but if it happens you'll have to study up on crazy. I just wanted to warn you in advance."

"Oh, thanks. Well, good night Kyle."

Kyle leaned in and kissed her gently on the lips. It was their first kiss. It was sweet and it set her heart racing. "Good night," he said as he let go of her hands and turned to walk away.

She watched him walk down the corridor with his cellphone in his hand. A moment later her phone beeped. She flipped it open and read the text message. It read: How about dinner and a movie next Saturday night? My treat.

She smiled and opened her door texting: yes.

## =THIRTEEN=

Alex walked into Kim and Ray's new apartment. "Hey, where do you want me to put this box? It's marked K-Bdm. Maybe Kim's bedroom?"

Kim poked her head out of the bathroom door. "That's my stuff. It belongs in the back bedroom. Can you put it along the far wall?" He nodded as he walked through the living room. "Thanks Alex."

Alex carried the box down the hall followed by Rachel and Amanda each carrying boxes and totes. The morning started when everyone showed up at Kim's old apartment. Ray and Kyle picked up the rental truck early in the morning and had already loaded what little he had into it before they arrived at Kim's.

The rest of the morning was filled with packing the last minute items in Kim's apartment, loading the rest of her stuff in the rental truck, and unloading it in the new place. By mid-day the bulk of the move was finished and Ray drove off with the rental truck and to pick up lunch.

Wendy finished folding and setting the linens

into the hall closet. She walked into the kitchen to find Kim and Amanda filling the cabinets with dishes and bowls. "This is a nice little apartment you two found. And the neighborhood is nice too; it's not to far from the condo complex where Kyle and I live. I've sold several condos around here and the people tell me that everyone is friendly and they watch out for one another."

"Thanks Wendy, I know we're going to love it once the dust settles."

Alex and Rachel joined them in the kitchen. "The bed is assembled."

"If you want we'd be happy to put on the sheets and duvet on the bed for you," Rachel added.

"Thanks guys, the linens are in the hall closet."

Wendy walked out into the hallway. "I'll show you." She opened the closet door and pulled out a set of sheets and pillowcases. "I think these all match." Then she smiled and passed them both to walk into the living room. Kyle was busy stuffing Ray's bookshelf with books and magazines. He was surrounded by empty boxes.

"Whew, moving students is almost as bad as moving lawyers." He chuckled as he stuffed another stack of folders in one of the shelves.

Wendy knelt down and wrapped her arms around his neck giving him a big hug and kiss. "Thank you for doing this sweetheart, I know you're busy with work and all, but you've been such a big help."

Kim leaned around the corner into the living room and grinned. "You both have been wonderful, thank you. Everyone, this move has been so easy with all of you."

About then the apartment door flew open and Ray walked in with a stack of pizza boxes. "Lunch break, everyone! Well, maybe a late lunch, there was a line at the check-in counter. Lord they move slow at rental companies."

Amanda walked back into the living room. "I think it's part of their training."

Rachel followed Alex into the living room. She was holding an extra set of pillows. "Kim, do you want me to use these two for the pillow shams?"

Ray dropped the pizza boxes on the coffee table. "What are pillow shams?"

Kyle chuckled still stuffing Ray's bookshelves. "Oh, you have so much to learn, grasshopper." Ray grinned and Kim giggled.

The rest of the afternoon went by quickly; with everyone's help Ray and Kim's move went flawlessly.

Ray walked into the living room to find everyone drinking sodas and laughing about Tom Reilly's latest antics. "Do you guys want to go out for dinner? I'm buying."

Rachel groaned. "Thanks Ray but I can't, I have a late shift tonight at the club."

Alex got up and picked up a few soda cans to take them to the recycling bin in the kitchen. "Me too, I have an early shift at the convenience store otherwise I'd be happy to join you. Can I get a rain check?" He tossed his keys to Rachel with a grin. "You driving as usual?"

"Love to, thanks."

Ray was beginning to look a bit disappointed. "It's okay, rain checks are no problem. Wendy? Kyle? Amanda?"

Amanda chirped up with a grin. "I'm in, but

somebody will have to give me a ride home."

"That sounds great, Ray. There's a little burger joint on the corner we've been to before, not too expensive either, just the thing for a student's budget. Kyle and I will meet you there."

"Great."

# =FOURTEEN=

The emergency room at St. Mary's Regional Hospital was strangely quiet. Triage was working efficiently to move the small amount of waiting patients through the screening process and there didn't seem to be many serious cases to deal with for a change. ~Some minor scrapes and bruises, a broken arm and a few cuts. It looked like it was going to be a quiet night.

Suddenly, the radio dispatch crackled and hissed. Paramedics from engine house four were bringing in a stabbing victim. They shouted his vitals over the radio as the ambulance wove through traffic towards the hospital. Moments later a gurney burst through the outer doors of the emergency room as three paramedics shouted for help from the ER staff.

In a flash Alex Wells was moved through a maze of corridors, up an elevator, and into operating room number three. Standing alone downstairs in the emergency room reception area a frightened Rachel Thompson stood shaking and sobbing. An ER nurse ushered her to the couch in the waiting room.

Several minutes later Amanda rushed through the outer doors. She found Rachel curled up and sobbing on a couch in the waiting room. "Is he all right? Where is he?"

"He's in an operating room right now I think, I don't know anything yet."

"What happened?"

"We were at Moulin Rouge. I was working my usual shift. Alex got off earlier than I did so he took a cab over to meet me. We were just hanging out when a fight broke out across from the bar. I don't know who or what started it but it was getting ugly quick. A guy had one of the waitresses, Susan I think, by the neck and was threatening her with a knife. I shouted at him and he pushed Susan away and lunged at me. But before I could move Alex was between us. The bastard stabbed him three times before he ran off. Girls were screaming, people were scrambling out of the bar; there was blood everywhere. Sydney, the manager, called 911 then Susan and I did what we could to stop the bleeding. Oh God, Amanda, it was like I was watching him die and there was nothing I could do to stop it!"

"Okay sweetheart, okay." She hugged Rachel and held her tight while Rachel sobbed into her shoulder.

Eventually Rachel's tears began to slow and she lifted her head up to kiss Amanda on the cheek. "Thank you, Sis."

"Let me go get some tissues, I'll be right back." Amanda left Rachel sitting on the couch and wiping her eyes as she walked briskly towards the triage desk. She grabbed a box of tissues then glanced at the nurse behind the counter. "Hi, Alex Wells was brought in a while ago; he was stabbed in a club tonight. Can you tell me what's happening with him?"

A triage nurse looked up from her computer screen. "He's in the operating room right now, ma'am. Are you in his family?"

"Yes, I'm his sister."

"Here, I need you to fill out some consent forms. You can bring them back to me when you've finished."

Amanda looked at the clipboard stuffed with medical release forms and sighed. She added the clipboard with the stack of consent forms to the box of tissues and walked back over to Rachel. She handed the tissue box to Rachel and sat down next to her. "He's in the operating room, that's all she could tell me and then she handed me all this stupid paperwork." Amanda sighed again as she began to fill out the forms.

Rachel wiped her eyes and rested her head on Amanda's shoulder. She mumbled softly. "He asked me to stop working there."

"What sweetie?"

"Alex, he asked me to stop working at Moulin Rouge. On the way over in the ambulance, he held my hand and asked me to stop working at the club. He said it was too dangerous. Oh God, Amanda, it's all my fault."

"Now stop that right now, Rachel. If it's anybody's fault it's that bastard who stabbed Alex." She leaned over and kissed Rachel on the forehead. "But honey, you really need to stop working there. It's getting way too dangerous."

"I was working there so that I could afford nice clothes and to help pay for all the HRT drugs I need daily to keep my body in check. My part-time job isn't enough.

"I'll buy you nice clothes Sis, and all the drugs you need. Just stop working there. I worry every night you go off to work...so does Alex. Why do you think he spends so much time there?"

"I never realized..."

"Rachel, my sweet lovely Rachel, you and Alex are the loves of my life, I don't ever want to lose either of you, ever."

A moment later Wendy arrived with Kyle, followed minutes later by Kim and Ray, they all rushed through the waiting room doors. Wendy looked around frantically until she spotted Amanda and Rachel sitting at the far end of the waiting room. "We just heard! How's he doing?"

"He's still in surgery and they haven't told us anything else yet."

Wendy moved to sit beside Rachel and Amanda. "I'm so very sorry, is there anything we can do?"

Amanda hugged her and kissed her cheek. "Just pray it's not serious."

The rest of the family sat close and waited for the emergency team to do their work. An hour or so later, a doctor came through the emergency room doors. His nametag read Dr. Fred Willis. "Amanda Simpson, Rachel Thompson?"

Everyone stood up and clustered around the doctor. "I'm Amanda and this is Rachel."

"He's out of danger and recovering in the ICU. We can't let anyone see him until the anesthesia wears off and he regains consciousness. There was a large loss of blood and several knife wounds but only one was severe. It punctured his kidney on the left side.

We'll have to do some tests to determine if the damage will be long term. He's young and strong so that will improve his chances."

Rachel smiled bleakly. "How long before we can we see him?"

"Not for a while yet, I'll send one of the IC nurses out once he's regained consciousness and moved to a room." The doctor looked at all the concerned faces then recognized a familiar one. "Wendy, what are you doing here?"

"Hi Fred, my good friend Alex is here, we're kind of family. How bad was it?"

"Well, fortunately, the blade didn't do too much serious damage. He'll have a few scars to brag about I suppose. He's in stable condition but like I said, he'll be out of it for a while. After that, I would guess several weeks for full recovery. Wendy, I know you said you're family but do you know about him?"

"What do you mean?"

"About his physical condition, it looks like he's in the middle of a gender change. These scars may disfigure him if he wants to continue with that change."

"Thanks Fred, could you keep his physical condition private please, even with the medical staff. He's very sensitive about it."

"I understand. I'll speak to the duty nurse; she'll keep it under her thumb."

Rachel reached forward and shook the doctor's hand. "Thank you Doctor Willis." Amanda and the rest of the family thanked him as well while Wendy walked over to the far side of the waiting area and made a phone call.

"Don? Hi, it's Wendy Bingham. Yes, thanks,

sorry for calling so late. Look, I need to ask a favor. A friend of mine was just in a pretty severe accident and Fred Willis told me that the scars will be rather disfiguring. Is there anyway you can come in and have a look? He's here at Saint Mary's Regional. Oh, thank you, I appreciate it. I'll call you tomorrow morning when we know more and I'll give you the rest of the details. There are a few things I will need to explain. Yes, the attending is Fred Willis. Okay, I'll ask him to call you. Thanks Don, I'll talk to you tomorrow morning. Say hello to Margaret for me, okay, good night."

For the next half hour Wendy was on her cell phone calling in favors, organizing a surgical team to handle Alex's situation. Amanda and Rachel were amazed at her connections.

Meanwhile Kim was on her phone calling her father, a state's attorney. She told him that Alex's attacker was still at large and she wanted to make sure the cops didn't give it a low priority. All in all, the family was doing what they could to help Alex pull through.

An hour later the ER duty nurse came out into the waiting room and told them that they could see Alex now. "He's on the fourth floor in room 4005. But only for a minute, he's still under the effects of the anesthesia and he'll be rather groggy."

They quietly filed into the elevator, each one holding the other's hands firmly, all with anxious looks on their faces. The elevator chime announced their arrival on the fourth floor. Alex's room was down the corridor and in a cluster of rooms that centered on a nurse's station. The family nodded to the nurses as they filed by to room 4005.

In the room, a variety of tubes and wires were strung from IV bags and monitors and attached all over Alex's body. A nurse was re-checking his IV to make sure it was secure. When she saw the family arrive she smiled and politely ducked out of the way and back to the nurse's station.

"Hey babe, how are you doing?" Rachel gently touched his arm; her eyes were brimming with tears.

Amanda moved to the other side and leaned forward to place a kiss on his cheek. "Hey there sweetheart."

The rest of the family gathered around close and touched him gently as Alex's eyes fluttered open. "Hi." His voice was raspy and soft. "From the looks on your faces it looks like you're here for a funeral."

Rachel kissed his other cheek. "That's not even funny, babe. You're going to be okay, the doctor said you'll be up and around in no time. But for now, no jokes, okay?" He nodded as she kissed him again, her eyes filled with tears.

A few minutes later Dr. Willis reappeared and suggested that they all go home and get a good night sleep. "We're going to give him a sedative to help him sleep so it'll be easier if he doesn't have any distractions."

After Kim and Ray drove off, Wendy told Amanda and Rachel that a Dr. Donald Greeley was going to visit the day after tomorrow. She told them that he was going to do a preliminary examination on Alex.

"Why?"

"He's a plastic surgeon, one of the best in the region. I asked him to take a look at Alex's wounds. Dr. Willis said that they would probably be disfiguring."

Amanda looked a bit shocked. "But our insurance only covers the basics."

"I'll handle it Amanda, it's what families do, right?"

Rachel wrapped her arms around her and kissed her cheek. "Thank you Wendy, you're wonderful."

Amanda's eyes began to tear up again. "Wendy, I-I don't know what to say."

"Amanda, sweetheart, you're welcome. Now let's go home and get some rest, things start early at St. Mary's and I know you want to be there when he wakes up."

Kyle and Wendy got into her car and drove off leaving Amanda and Rachel by Alex's car.

Rachel opened the passenger door and got in. "How did his car get here?"

"After you called, I called Kim and Ray then I called Wendy. I asked Ray to go to the club and bring his car here after he stopped by the apartment house and picked up the spare set of keys."

Amanda slipped in behind the wheel and started the car.

"Can I stay with you tonight?"

Amanda looked at Rachel and smiled sweetly. "I was going to ask you if you didn't ask me."

Rachel watched the blur of streetlights whiz by the passenger window as Amanda drove them back to the apartment house. Even though she was exhausted her mind continued to replay the events that led up to the stabbing. The blood, Alex's blood, was everywhere, the screaming, chairs and tables flying around the room. It was all like a horrible movie that continued to play over and over in her mind. Why didn't she realize that Alex was always there because he was worried about her?

"I'm so stupid," Rachel muttered. "I thought he was there because he liked hanging out at the club."

"You are not stupid my love, you're simply in love like the rest of us. I blame myself for not saying something earlier, and I bet Alex blames himself for not being more direct about his feelings. We love you Rachel, dearly. The club was fun and we loved being there with you but lately it seems a different kind of group has started hanging out there. And the vibe from them is kind of scary. I know you tried to dismiss it but you felt it too, didn't you?"

Rachel nodded, her eyes glistening.

"So it's settled? You're quitting the club?"

"Yes, I'll call Sydney tomorrow."

"And I'm calling our insurance agent tomorrow. I'm going to change our policy to include long-term maintenance meds. That should handle your needs and whatever Alex needs to help him recover."

"Thank you Amanda, you're such a wonderful wife, I don't know what I would do without you."

"I feel the same way sweetheart."

## =FIFTEEN=

It was nearly six in the morning when Alex woke up and the first thing he saw were two beautiful faces smiling down on him.

"I must be in heaven for all I see are angels." He laughed and winced a little. "That was corny wasn't it?"

Rachel leaned forward and kissed him on his forehead. "Total corn ball my love."

Amanda followed Rachel, "yep totally, sweetheart."

Rachel scooted a chair closer and took his hand. "They almost refused to let us in here this morning because we're not your legal family."

Amanda grumbled as she sat next to him on the bed. "We're going to change that starting today. I'm going to ask Kyle to give me a reference for a good family lawyer."

Alex smiled and took their hands. "What name are you guys going to pick for us?"

"You know, I haven't thought about that, what do you think Rachel?"

They watched Rachel consider Amanda's question for a moment. She paused then a broad smile broke out. "I've always been a traditional girl at heart and I've always dreamt of taking my husband's name."

"Me too!" Amanda squealed, her eyes glistening. "When I was a kid I would lay in bed at night and dream about it."

Rachel stood up and leaned over to kiss Alex and Amanda on the lips then she whispered to them both. "Wells."

A half hour later Dr. Willis knocked softly and entered to find all three of them laughing and giggling together. "I didn't know there was a party going on or I'd have dropped in sooner." Someone unfamiliar followed Dr. Willis into the room. Alex, immediately cautious, grabbed his sheets around him in an attempt to hide his body.

Amanda and Rachel smiled brightly. "Good Morning, Dr. Willis."

"Good Morning. This is Dr. Donald Greeley; he's a plastic surgeon and one of Wendy's friends. Alex, Dr. Greeley would like to examine your wounds if that would be okay?"

Alex looked from Dr. Greeley to Dr. Willis as Dr. Greeley stepped around Dr. Willis and offered to shake Alex's hand. "Don't worry Alex, Wendy Bingham already filled me in. You have a very important friend there; she's been pulling in favors all night. Let's see what kind of damage has been done."

Throughout the rest of the day Alex reacted very privately when anyone came into his room. It was obvious to Rachel that he was getting rather annoyed with the parade of nurses and aides coming and going for a variety of what appeared to be insignificant reasons; sometimes checking the same IV drip several times in a row.

Rachel noticed that the female nurses all acted a bit coquettish around Alex. She also noticed how they all seemed to be interested in his chest. It was obvious that Alex's unique condition was a curiosity. They should act like professionals not like a bunch of schoolgirls; Rachel fumed as she stormed out of his room in search of the doctor. Eventually she found Doctor Willis and spoke to him about it. He placed Alex's room on restricted access.

As a result, there was a bit of a stink at the nurses' station. Rachel overheard the commotion outside Alex's door. But it settled down quickly when she walked out in the middle of all the tension to ask the duty nurse if she could have an extra pillow for her "husband."

"You could hear a pin drop after I said that," she told him.

"Thank you."

A minute later one of the night shift nurses, Tiffany, knocked softly and poked her head into the room. "I'm sorry to bother you but I wanted to apologize for my staff's behavior. We weren't acting very professional. I'm sorry. I'm Tiffany Porter and I'm the duty nurse tonight. I wanted to let you know that we heard from Doctor Willis and we understand and will respect your privacy from now on. Again, I'm very sorry."

"Thank you Nurse Porter..."

"Tiffany, please."

"Thank you, Tiffany."

"Can I ask you something?" She came further into his room and softly closed the door.

"Sure."

"Your body, is it natural?"

Alex blushed slightly and pulled his sheets tighter around his neck. "Yes, why?"

"Because, I...I think I'm a little like you."

Alex relaxed a bit as he looked at Tiffany with renewed interest. "Really?"

"Yeah, I heard some of the other nurses hint that there was something different about you and then Doctor Willis told us the room was on restricted access. I was curious so I asked him and he told me that you're intersexed and bothered by all the unnecessary attention. You see, I'm intersexed too, only a little bit different from you, I think. It's called AIS."

"Androgen Insensitivity Syndrome, I know of it."

"Well, I was wondering if we could talk. I don't know anyone else like us."

"Sure, ah, Tiffany, this is my wife Rachel. Would it be alright with you if Rachel stayed?"

"Oh, yes, that would be fine. Are you intersexed too?"

"No Tiffany, I'm a pre-op transsexual."

"You are? I had no idea."

Rachel blushed slightly and nodded to Tiffany. "Thank you."

Tiffany sat down on a chair near Alex's bed and took a big breath. "Have you ever heard of Dr. Leonard Brunner?"

Alex shook his head. "No."

"He came to St. Mary's about five years ago,

fresh out of a residency in Trenton, New Jersey. He's young but he's got a good head on his shoulders. Anyway, his research is focused on the intersex phenomenon. I'm one of his case studies." She blushed slightly then continued. "The rest of his research is from all over the country. He wants to start an institute for the study of intersexed people here in Wilmington. Would you like to meet him?"

Alex glanced to Rachel, looking for some sort of a response but her expression was blank. He turned back to Tiffany and smiled. "I don't know Tiffany, maybe, but not now. I need to think about it. I've been hiding this from the world for a very long time and it's going to take me some time to open up to a stranger. And the parade of curiosity seekers that has been in and out of my room today isn't any help."

"I truly am sorry about that."

"I know, and I understand why you can relate to my situation. So the best I can say is I'll think about it."

"Okay." Tiffany got up and walked over to the door then she turned and returned to Alex's bedside. She handed him a business card. "Here's Dr. Brunner's contact information. Please give him a call when you think you're ready to meet him. I'm sure you'd like him. Thanks Alex. And if you ever just want to talk about stuff, you know 'stuff?'" She glanced up at Rachel and smiled meekly. "My number is on the back, please call."

Tiffany extended her hand to Rachel. "It's nice to have met you; I hope I see you both in the future under better circumstances."

Rachel shook her hand. "Thank you Tiffany, I hope so too."

*><*><*

Three days later, Alex went back into surgery with Dr. Greeley. It was finally time to address some of the scaring where the knife cut into him. After another two more days of convalescing, Alex was released into Amanda and Rachel's care. They wheeled a rather stiff Alex Wells out of the hospital and into a waiting cab to bring him home.

Following another week or so of bed rest, Alex was up and about. He was becoming restless and was half way through getting dressed when Amanda and Rachel walked into his room.

Rachel stamped her foot and Amanda barred the door. "Where do you think you're going?"

"To work, where else?"

Both girls looked at him sternly. "No you're not. You're not going anywhere."

"But, I've got to go to work. If I don't I'm going to go crazy cooped up here all day. Besides, they need me there."

Amanda pushed him gently to his bed. "No they don't. Inez is covering your shifts and your manager said you have a one week paid vacation coming to you anyway."

"I'm part-time, how do I qualify for a vacation?"

Rachel leaned over and kissed him on the lips with a mischievous grin. "I called him and persuaded him to offer it to you."

"How did I ever get by without you two?"

"I don't know." Rachel turned to Amanda with a mischievous grin. "Well Amanda, isn't it time for our patient's daily sponge bath?"

"I do believe you're right."  Both girls began to strip him.

"Wait!  No fair tickling!"

## =SIXTEEN=

"Knock, knock. Reception told me I might find Kyle Upton in here."

Kyle bumped his head under his desk. "Ouch." He peeked over the top of his desk with a big grin. "Hi beautiful, what brings you here?" He ducked back under his desk.

Wendy giggled and sat down in one of Kyle's client chairs. "I was in the neighborhood and thought I'd check out your office. Are you hiding from me?"

"Huh? Oh, no, my keyboard cable came lose and I was trying to reattach it when you came in." He grinned as he stood up and walked around his desk planting a kiss on her forehead as he walked by her to close his office door.

She stood up and fell into his arms as he turned towards her. His kiss was tender and passionate. He wrapped his arms around her and hugged her tightly then leaned back. "Hey, it's nearly lunch, you want to join me somewhere?"

"Hmm, sounds like a great way to start the afternoon." She looked over his shoulder at a group of pictures on one of his bookshelves. "Who are those people in the photographs?"

He released her and followed her as she walked over to his bookshelf to get a closer look. Then he waved his hand across the photograph. "Welcome to my family." He pointed to each person as he named them off. "That's Grandma, Mom and Dad, Uncle Willie, his sons Willie junior, and Hank. That's my sister Annie, and her husband Tom, they live on a dairy farm near Lancaster. Over there is my brother Tommy and, in a rare appearance, my twin sister Candace.

"Rare appearance?"

Yeah, she's the one in the family with a severe case of wanderlust, every family has one I've been told and Candace is our world traveler. That's why it's so rare to catch a glimpse of her standing still, she's always moving. Right now she's up in New York City, at the New School studying filmmaking. She's pretty good at it too. Her last film was a documentary on gender dysphoria. It won a couple of awards on the festival circuit." He laughed out loud. "If you ever meet Grandma be prepared to sit through it at least once, with commentary."

"Gender issues?"

"Yes, something close to her heart. She transitioned when we were twelve, she's my twin. We were identical, now were fraternal." He shrugged sheepishly and Wendy wrapped her arms around him and crushed him in a big hug.

"What was that for?"

"Just for being you."

Kyle leaned in and kissed her. "Then I should be 'me' more often." His stomach rumbled a little and

Wendy giggled. "Sorry, I guess it's lunch time."

"Come on, I'll drive. Rachel told me about this cute little Parisian restaurant on Elm Street, Madeline's I think she called it."

Twenty minutes later Wendy pulled into the parking lot at Madeline's, and ten minutes later they were sitting at a table with a view of a small park nearby.

Kyle peeked over his menu. "How's business? Is the real estate market going strong?"

"Not bad, I think I've found a house for Rachel, Amanda, and Alex. It's not too far from here, we can swing by and take a look after lunch if you have time."

Kyle pulled out his cellphone and dialed his office. "Hi Alice. Can you call Henderson and let him know I'll be a little late for my two o'clock? Thanks." He snapped his phone shut and slipped it back in his pocket. "Sounds like I have time and I'd like to see it." He tapped his menu. "Anything recommended?"

"Alex said everything is great here. I'm going for the salad, a girl has to watch her figure, you know."

Kyle grinned and shook his head. "Wendy Bingham, you must be doing a great job because your figure is stunning and I could watch it for you all day long."

Blushing crimson, Wendy smiled demurely, and then she buried her head in the menu.

"Rachel called me yesterday, she was wondering if I had some time tomorrow to meet her for coffee."

Her nose still buried behind her menu, Wendy tried to sound nonchalant. "Where are you going to meet?"

"I told her I had more time than she did so she suggested a coffee shop on 5th near where she works. A friend of mine owns it so that works out well too."

"I know that shop, the cappuccino is really good." She paused a moment and glanced at Kyle over the top of her menu. "What time did she want to meet you?"

"Around ten, why?"

"No reason, I was hoping you would join me for lunch tomorrow, that's all. Maybe we can meet for dinner instead."

"I'd like that."

About then a waitress arrived at their table with two glasses of water and they ordered lunch.

"Are you worried?"

"About what?"

"My meeting with Rachel. I know she's being a bit of a mother hen but with that run-in you had with your former boyfriend I can understand why she's being a little over-protective."

"I know, and I love her for it, but honestly, you're not like any man I've ever met."

Now it was Kyle's turn to blush. "Thank you."

"Tell me about your sister Candace. You told me the other day that your family was just scrapping by. How can they afford to send your sister to The New School, it's expensive isn't it?"

"Very. Mostly she's there on scholarships, some they offered and some she found on her own. Plus I help her out whenever I can. I've always tried to look out for her when I could. She had a rough time of it after she decided to transition; the girls in high school were especially cruel. There for a while it seemed like I was in a fight every other day pushing off her bullies."

"I know, I lived through it too, but I wish I'd had a twin brother to help me."

"There was a boy she fell in love with in the twelfth grade. He was a jock and popular with all the girls. I told her not to try but she was totally gaga for him."

"What happened?"

Kyle poured some cream in his coffee and stirred it idly with his spoon. "She decided to ask him out. She'd been working up the nerve for a couple of weeks. I snuck along without her knowing. If she had seen me before she asked him she would have beat me up for certain. But I stayed back far enough to not be seen but close enough to hear. The boy's name was Kurt Treadway, he was a real dick but she refused to see it."

"I can see where this is going."

"Yeah, well anyway, Kurt was hanging out with a couple of his buddies from the football team when Candace showed up. She was wearing one of her best dresses and some cute high heels. I mean, if she wasn't my sister I would have totally dated her, she was hot."

Wendy smirked and Kyle blushed a bit then continued. "I couldn't hear everything in the conversation but I got the gist of it. Candace asked him out and he laughed at her.

I heard him shout at her, "I don't do chicks with dicks, freak."

They said a couple more things and then his friends were laughing. She snapped back, "What? You're worried that mine might be bigger than yours?"

"That's when he hit her. He knocked her on the ground and spat on her and I was on him in a flash. Kurt and his buddies proceeded to kick the shit out of me but I got in a few good punches before I blacked out. They must have left shortly after that because when I came to I was lying on a stretcher and being hauled into an ambulance. She stayed with me for the rest of that night telling me how sorry she was. I couldn't say a thing because my jaw was wired shut."

Wendy's eyes glistened as she turned to look out the window at some children playing in a park across the street. What was the big deal anyway? Why couldn't he have just said no? Why is it so hard to treat another human being with respect and kindness even if you're not interested in them? Would he have treated a genetic girl that way? Are they so afraid that being with a transsexual is contagious? Like it's some sort of deadly disease?

She sighed and used her napkin to dry her eyes.

"Hey, it's a beautiful day; let's talk about happy things okay? What about the house you found?"

"It's a cute little bungalow. It has all the amenities they were looking for."

Kyle laughed. "Even a bedroom large enough for a king-sized bed?"

Wendy blushed and nodded. "That too."

The waitress arrived with their lunch. Then half way through his sandwich, Kyle's office called. "Hello? Oh, hi Richard. Uh-huh, I asked Henderson to meet me at two. As soon as I have the final figures from him I can get those estimates to you. Yes, okay, I'll be back shortly. Right, right, okay. Bye." Kyle rolled his eyes. "Sorry, my boss is a poster child for ADHD."

"Do you need to go now?"

"Ha, no. He'll be onto three other things as soon as he hangs up the phone. I'll get the numbers he needs by four when I promised him. He drives Alice the division secretary nuts but at least he's thoughtful and remembers her birthday, his only saving grace."

They finished their lunch and, holding hands, they walked out of the restaurant towards Wendy's car. He nudged her shoulder. "I guess next time it will be my turn to visit your office."

"I can't wait." She was beginning to understand the depth of her feelings for him. That she was in love with Kyle not just in love with the idea of love like she was with her ex-boyfriend, Ted.

"We still have time, do you want to swing by that house you found for the family? At least we can see it from the curb."

"Sure." Then she smiled sweetly and kissed him on the lips. "But you can't tell them anything, I want it to be a surprise."

"I promise."

## =SEVENTEEN=

Kyle walked into Robbie's coffee house on Fifth Street a few minutes after ten in the morning. He glanced around a moment looking for Rachel. The place was filled with customers, laughter and coffee. The hiss from the espresso machine filled the air with the rich aroma of a dark roasted Parisian blend. It smelled heavenly.

Rachel saw Kyle first and waved him back towards a booth near the back. "Hi, thanks for choosing this place so close to my work."

"Well, like I said, you have less time than I do and anyway, I like this place, Rob makes his own blend of coffee, it's not bitter like the name brand stuff."

"You know the owner?"

"Sure, we went to undergraduate school together. I left for law school and he went to South America in search of the perfect coffee bean." Kyle lifted his cup to his lips with a wink. "I think he found it."

Rachel glanced at Kyle. "Yes, he did. I suppose you know why I asked you to meet me?"

"Hmmm. You want to know if I'm a rogue and a scoundrel and only after Wendy's vast fortune, is that it?"

Rachel opened and closed her mouth then frowned and looked away. It was clear to anyone watching the couple interact that she was upset. Apparently Kyle's attempt at levity wasn't scoring him any points.

"Okay, ask me your questions, no more flippant responses, I promise." He crossed his heart and held up his right hand.

"You're a bit of a smart-ass aren't you?"

"Only when I'm nervous, which is why I never was any good as a litigator, I couldn't deal with the nerves." Kyle glanced at Rachel's cup. "Would you like some more coffee?"

"No, I'm fine. Kyle, Wendy didn't want me to meet with you, she's afraid that I'll scare you off. But somehow, I don't think that's going to happen. Not just from that last remark you made but from the way you two are together. Still, I want you to understand that I really respect her and care for her. And I don't want anything to happen to her that would make her cry."

"Neither do I, although she came pretty close when Alex got stabbed."

"Yeah, that was a rough night for everybody." Rachel paused a moment and sipped her coffee. She glanced over at a couple sitting nearby and holding hands. "Have you ever known a girl like Wendy before?"

Kyle took a big breath and let it out slowly. "I've mostly dated regular girls in the past, albeit not many of them because I've always been a bit awkward around them, sort of like I am around you now. And because my family is a bit eccentric for lack of a better description, that sort of put off my chances for dates in the past too. They still live with grandma outside of Philadelphia, except for my sister Candace. She's studying filmmaking in New York at the New School."

"Do you come from a big family?"

"Not really, a brother, a sister, and a twin. The rest are uncles, aunts, and cousins."

"You have a twin?"

"Yeah, Candace, we used to be identical, now were fraternal."

"Huh?"

"She was born a boy and she transitioned when we were twelve. My family has always been supportive, God bless them, but her school life sucked. She's tough though, we're all really proud of her."

Rachel paused a moment, Kyle continued to amaze her. "I've heard of the New School, it's private isn't it?"

"Yeah, and expensive too. My family has always been trying to make ends meet but they also wanted to help her with her dreams. When the scholarship came through, she worked doubly hard to find more financial aide. She pieced it all together and I help her out whenever I can but she's stubborn about it. She knows I have huge student loans to pay off as well."

The back of the booth that Rachel and Kyle sat in had rather high backs which made it feel private but at the same time difficult to see the front of the store. It also made it difficult for Rachel to notice a cute brunette in sunglasses and a big floppy hat sit down in the booth next to them. The woman leaned back and quietly listened to the conversation going on in the next booth.

Kyle stirred the cream in his coffee slowly. "It's been a blessing to know Wendy. There aren't a lot of people I know who would understand my twin sister like she does. Hopefully, she'll get to meet her sometime."

Rachel sighed and gazed out the window at people passing by the coffee shop on the sidewalk outside. "Wendy is a lucky girl."

"So are you. The rest of us should be so lucky to find the deep love you have for Alex and Amanda."

"Is it that obvious?"

"It only takes a glance, Rachel. I've only known you for what, a couple of weeks? And yet the first day I met you I knew. Everybody knows if they take the time to look. And you also have this mother hen thing going but it's cool, I can tell you really care for Wendy and I'm fine with that."

Rachel blushed and looked away. Then she glanced sideways at him. "Who are you Kyle Upton?"

"Just a guy who has blissfully stumbled upon a group of friends who are kind to one another, and who care for and love one another. I think I'm the luckiest guy in the world. Oh, what time is it? I was supposed to text Wendy about this." He pulled out his cell phone and began to punch buttons.

"About what?"

"About this meeting between you and me, she wanted to know how it's going."

Rachel looked askance at him. "And, how do you think it's going?"

Kyle grinned at her. "And send. I think we had a bumpy start but right now I'd say we're doing great."

In the next booth the woman in the floppy hat and sunglasses frantically scrambled to find her cell phone before it beeped and gave her away. Too late, the distinctive chime rang out loud and clear.

Kyle looked at Rachel then smiled a knowing smile. He stood up and peered around the booth to find his new girlfriend dumping the contents of her purse on the table. "Hi there."

Wendy looked up and grinned sheepishly. "Hi."

"Do you want to join us? We were just talking about you."

"I know." She looked around the edge of the booth to see a frown on Rachel's face.

Wendy shoveled the pile of stuff on the table back into her purse and scooted out of the booth. As soon as she stood she saw Rachel giving her 'the look'. She quickly mouthed the word 'sorry' to her and then took a seat next to Kyle.

Rachel twisted her mouth into a wry grin. "Hello Wendy."

"Hi."

"Excuse me ladies, I need to get a refill." Wendy stood up for Kyle and then she sat down next to Rachel.

Kyle slipped back out of the booth and disappeared around the corner. He suspected that they wanted to talk in private and getting a refill of coffee was a convenient reason to give them some privacy.

Rachel wore a stern expression. "Wendy Bingham, I'm hurt that you don't trust me."

"I'm sorry Rachel, but I really like him, and..."

Rachel pulled her into a hug. "Oh, forget about it. I'd have done the same thing or worse if it was Alex."

"Speaking of Alex, how's he doing?"

"Better, thank you. He went back to work last night and his last semester of classes start next week. But don't think changing the subject will get you off the hook."

"I did apologize."

"I know, so maybe buying us all dinner this weekend will set things right."

Wendy grinned and hugged Rachel as Kyle rounded the corner to slip back into the booth.

"What did I miss?"

Wendy let go of Rachel and smiled sweetly at Kyle. "An apology, and a promise to never doubt her again."

"Rachel, Wendy and I have a date tonight, you're more than welcome to chaperone."

"We do?"

Rachel blushed brightly and swatted Kyle on the arm. "And what would you say if I said yes?"

"I'd say you'd get to drive because we'd be in the back seat."

Rachel laughed. "No thanks, I'm hanging up my mother hen wings, my little girl is all grown up and she's found a wonderful guy to be with."

"Thank you Rachel." Wendy turned to Kyle with a huge smile. "Where are we going?"

"The symphony, Brahms and Schubert tonight."

"Ooo." Wendy's eyes sparkled with delight.

"On second thought, maybe I do need to chaperone you two." Rachel winked at Kyle with a smirk.

Wendy turned surprised. "Don't you have to work tonight?"

"Nope, I'm through with Moulin Rouge, I promised Alex and Amanda."

"Good," Kyle and Wendy said in unison.

## =EIGHTEEN=

Kyle and Wendy found their seats the third row back on the Mezzanine level of Orchestra Hall. After a moment Wendy leaned over and whispered in his ear. "How did you know I love the symphony?"

He smirked. "Lucky guess?"

"Fat chance, spill it."

"Okay, I called your secretary and she told me you had season tickets last year."

"I'm going to have to speak to Rebecca about divulging all my secrets."

"Good luck, I paid her off in chocolates."

The concertmaster walked out on the stage to applause. He bowed to the audience, turned to the orchestra, and raised his violin for the final tuning.

An hour and a half later Wendy entwined her arm around Kyle's as they walked to his car in the parking lot. "I simply love Brahms, especially his first symphony, it has such a sweet melody."

After the symphony, Kyle drove them back to their condominiums. Wendy snuggled next to him and rested her head on his shoulder.

As he parked his car she leaned over and kissed him on the cheek. "Would you like to come up to my place for a glass of wine?"

Kyle's eyes shone with excitement. "Yes, I'd like that very much."

Kyle followed Wendy down the corridor to her apartment. He waited while she opened her door and flipped on a few lights. She walked into the kitchen and pulled a bottle of pinot noir from the wine chiller under her counter and proceeded to open it up. Kyle walked up behind her and wrapped his arms around her waist then nuzzled his nose against the back of her neck.

"You should know that drives me wild, sweetheart."

Kyle continued to kiss her neck and nibble at her earlobe. "Good, after the tranquility of Brahms I think a wild night might be fun."

Wendy left the half opened bottle of wine and turned to pull him into a passionate kiss. "You like playing with fire do you?"

Kyle trailed kisses down her neck to the cleavage between her beautiful breasts. "Yes, fireworks are always exciting."

"Oh my God Kyle." Wendy grabbed his hand and pulled him out of the kitchen and down the hallway.

Near her bedroom she squealed with delight as he swept her up into his arms and carried her into her bedroom. She wrapped her arms around his neck as he released her. Her feet barely touched the ground as she covered his face with kisses.

He reached behind her and lowered the zipper on her dress as she struggled to unbutton his shirt.

She giggled as they tried to undress each other at the same time. "I think we need to do this one at a time."

Kyle leaned forward and kissed her. "I agree my love, ladies first." He finished with her zipper and her dress crumpled to the floor around her feet. Now she stood there in bra and panties with stay-up hose and heels.

She reached behind her back and undid her bra, allowing it to slowly reveal her ample breasts. They were full and pouty with dark brown areolas and nipples that stood out proudly, begging to be sucked. Kyle leaned forward to lick them and she wagged her finger in his face.

"Uh, uh, uh, not yet my sweet, next my hose and heels then it's my turn to undress you." She sat on the edge of the bed as Kyle grinned sheepishly then knelt to roll down her hose and remove her heels. He lifted each foot and kissed a dozen kisses up each leg as she moaned softly running her fingers through his hair.

He stood up slowly, his shirt hung off his slender frame half unbuttoned. She sat up from the sensuous assault on her legs and pulled open the buckle on his pants, slipping them off his hips to fall like her dress and crumple on the floor by his feet. His shirt quickly followed. She reached down to remove his socks and delicately moved her hands up his legs trailing her fingernails along his thighs. He shivered with excitement.

She hooked her fingers into the waistband of his boxers and, looking up into his seductive eyes, she slowly lowered them to fall like his pants at his feet. His cock sprung free from the confines of his boxers and stood rigid against his stomach. She leaned forward and nuzzled against it. Reaching out with her tongue she licked the underside of his shaft. She moved up to the mushroom head and planted a kiss on the tip. He moaned softly feeling the velvet touch of her tongue.

He looked down at her with a lusty smile. "My turn," he whispered and he pushed her gently onto her back on the bed. He fell beside her and his mouth quickly sought her breasts, sucking and nibbling, he sent her soaring. Then he moved to her collarbone, then to the small of her elbow and then he moved to finish sucking gently on each fingertip.

She was writhing in pleasure as his tongue assaulted all the pleasure points on her body. He moved back to her shoulders while his fingers began to move gently over the soft wet folds of her pussy. He found her clitoris, swollen from passion, and began to gently rub it as he trailed kisses from her neck to her waist and below. He grabbed a bottle of lube on her nightstand and coated his fingers liberally.

Soon his tongue found her clitoris. He nibbled and sucked the swollen nub as she her body undulated in submission to his tongue. His lubricated fingers slipped gently into her vagina. He moved them around searching for her g-spot. Suddenly he touched it and she was rocketing off into outer space screaming his name and wrapping her legs around him.

"NOW! God, oh God, NOW! I need you now!"

Kyle opened the bottle of lube again and squirted some in her hands. She coated his cock with the lube and pulled him down to her vagina, urging him to enter. He slipped inside her, feeling every little muscle contract around his penis as he pushed deeper.

She spread her fingers across the cheeks of his ass and turned her nails to bite into his flesh, urging him to go deeper, to thrust harder, and faster.

She was soaring now, higher than she had ever flown before. He was like a magician; his touch was like an elixir for her soul. Each thrust brought her closer to the edge; each lunge brought her closer to oblivion. She felt him swell inside her, she knew he was close. His thrusts became stronger, more demanding. She wrapped her legs around him and locked her ankles as if she would never let him go.

Suddenly he tensed and she could feel his seed coat her vagina. There was so much it began to spill back out and trail down her perineum to drip onto her ass.

She was in ecstasy. She hugged him tightly and held her breath, as if breathing now, or ever again, would break the spell of pure bliss.

Eventually she came back to earth. She rubbed and caressed his body, holding him tight as she covered his face with kisses. "My God, I thought I knew what sex was like for a woman. You are amazing. Where did you learn to make love like that?"

Kyle just beamed. "It helps when you have such a beautiful and receptive partner."

She pulled him into another hug. "Oooo, you make me feel wonderful!"

He shifted his position so that she could feel that he was still rock hard against her stomach. "Want to go again?"

This time they went slower. But with the slower pace she was able to soar even higher. She knew what sex was, she had slept many times with Ted her ex-fiancé. But this wasn't just sex, this was making love. This was pure, unadulterated joy."

Later, in the afterglow, Kyle asked Wendy about her transition. "What was it like for you to go from a male to a complete female?"

Wendy sighed a bit then gently stroked his hair as he nuzzled her breasts. "The operation felt like it lasted for weeks but that was the easy part."

"How do you mean?"

She pointed to her head and her heart. "It's what happens here and here that is the toughest part."

He looked at her earnestly, his eyes urging her to continue, to tell him everything. His fingers traced tiny circles around her breasts as he listened to her.

"It's funny, now as I look back on it, what I thought was going to be the toughest part was the easiest. I remember standing in line at the DMV. It was six weeks after my final operation and I held a doctor's certificate that finally identified me as female. I was mortified thinking that all the clerks behind the counter would laugh and point but they didn't. They just stamped the form and issued me a driver's license with the letter 'F' under gender. You can't imagine how much joy that gave me. Finally, my body was correct; I was a woman, a complete woman. No one would ever take that from me again."

"And the hardest part?"

"Telling my family. I expected that they wouldn't accept me, and they didn't. But I had to try to make them understand anyway. My father wouldn't even acknowledge my presence in the room. All my mother did was cry and the rest of them snickered and walked out. But then, I didn't expect that it would be any different than it was. I just hoped it would be less humiliating and it wasn't."

Kyle shifted his attention from her breasts to brushing back a lock of her hair behind her ears. "So what other changes did you experience?"

"Oh, changes still seem to be happening to me. Little things happened to my body over time."

He looked out the bedroom window as if he was lost in thought. Then he glanced back at her.

She could see that he was working through something. Even though she was afraid to ask, she knew she must. "What are you thinking about my love?"

He leaned up and kissed her lightly on the lips. Then he took a big breath and slowly let it out. "Have you ever thought about adoption? My Aunt Susan was adopted and I always thought it was like offering a child a gift of a lifetime."

Wendy squealed and threw her arms around Kyle's neck and hugged him tightly. "Yes," she whispered, "yes."

## =NINETEEN=

"Knock, knock, anybody home?" Wendy opened Rachel's apartment door and peeked her head in. Sitting around the kitchen counter, Alex, Rachel, and Amanda huddled over a fresh brewed cup of coffee. They responded with a groan. "Well, I can see you three aren't morning people."

Amanda pointed to Rachel and grinned. "We're not, but this one over here just got in this morning after he finished his two a.m. night shift at the convenience store."

Wendy gathered them into a big hug. "Hmm, I love you guys!"

Rachel looked sideways at Wendy. "Okay, what happened?"

"Nothing, I just had the most wonderful night of my life last night with Kyle."

Amanda squealed glee. "Oooo, details, details."

"Nope, not a word, but I will tell you that he knows exactly how to make a girl feel loved, over and over and over again." They all laughed and clapped for joy. "But that's not why I'm here. Come on, get dressed, I have a surprise for you."

Alex sat down his coffee cup. "You've found us a house."

"Yes! It's a beautiful little bungalow in a quiet neighborhood. It's just perfect. Now come on, I can't wait to show you." Wendy was almost dancing, she was so excited.

Alex and Amanda raced out of Rachel's apartment to get showers and get dressed as Rachel set a cup of coffee in front of Wendy and did the same. A half hour later they were all dressed and dancing with excitement in the apartment house foyer.

Wendy opened the front door with a flourish. "Alex, you're going to have to drive, my car is a bit small to fit all of us."

They all crammed into Alex's car and twenty minutes later they were standing in front of a cute little home built in the craftsman style that looked out on a quiet street just a few blocks from where Kim and Ray rented their apartment.

"It's a little on the high side of your price range but with some creative financing I think you can swing the mortgage."

Alex snapped his head around. "What? This isn't a rental?"

Amanda and Rachel's eyes sparkled with anticipation.

"No, I thought you told him Amanda." Wendy arched her eyebrow as she glanced at Amanda.

"I was going to, then the whole incident at the club and well..." She walked over to hug Alex. "I forgot sweetie, please forgive me but Rachel and I talked it over and we both thought if we could find a house we could afford we should just buy it rather than pay off somebody else's mortgage."

Alex looked at her and then he turned to Rachel. Both girls smiled hopefully. Then he turned to Wendy. "Well, let's at least take a look inside."

Amanda and Rachel squealed and gave Alex a big hug. The three of them followed Wendy through every room and peeked into every closet and cupboard. Before the hour was up they were back standing on the front porch and looking out on the neighborhood.

Wendy put the key back into the lockbox then she turned to join them. "Well, what do you think?"

"The numbers you quoted, are they accurate?"

"I think the market rates are falling Amanda, so my quote may be a bit higher than reality once you lock in your rates. But I think they're pretty close."

Amanda looked at Rachel and Alex. "What do you guys think?"

Alex wrapped his arms around both girls' shoulders. "You two are better with numbers than I am but if you want my opinion, and if we can afford it, then I think we should hug our little sister Wendy for finding us such a great place to call home."

# =TWENTY=

"I feel like I've finally found my home." Wendy lifted her glass to meet Amanda's and the rest of the table followed.

"To family!" They shouted in unison and others around the restaurant applauded.

April downed the last of her wine and set her glass on the table. Her eyes sparkled as she smiled at Wendy. "Thank you, for finding us such a beautiful home, little sister." Then she gestured to everyone at the table. "There will always be a place for all of you at our table."

Wendy smiled serenely, her eyes were glistening, and Kyle wrapped his arm around her shoulders and gave her a big hug. She mouthed the words "thank you" and kissed Kyle on the cheek.

Ray leaned forward towards Rachel and Amanda. "So when do you guys close on the house?"

Amanda jabbed her thumb towards Wendy. "I don't know, she's the expert."

Wendy laughed and playfully swatted Amanda on her arm. "Hopefully next month, if we're lucky. The offer was made and accepted, the paperwork signed and delivered. Now all that's left is to wait on the bank approval. Residential loans move at a snail's pace and commercial ones take even longer. This one's tricky because a corporation is buying the property and we have a few more hoops to jump through. It'll be fine. I know the loan officer, he assured me that the loan would pass with flying colors."

Several waiters arrived with the main course and the table was quickly filled with laughter and idle conversation while everyone enjoyed the meal.

Amanda dabbed her mouth with her napkin. "Wendy, what are you and Kyle up to next week?"

"Kyle promised me a trip to the Poconos. He has Friday off so we're leaving Thursday afternoon and driving up."

"Where?"

Kyle set his fork down and took a sip from a glass of water. "The Pocono mountains, they're in upstate Pennsylvania. It's where my folks live."

Amanda giggled. "Ooooh, going to meet the parents. Things are getting serious." Her voice had a lyrical quality to add to her teasing.

Wendy and Kyle both blushed. Kim nudged Amanda's shoulder. "Oh don't tease them, it's a big step, Amanda. I haven't met Ray's folks yet but we're supposed to go to their place for Thanksgiving. I'm a nervous wreck."

"Don't be sweetheart," Ray whispered softly. "They are going to love you."

Kyle nodded knowingly. "I just hope Wendy isn't disappointed, my family can be a lot to handle sometimes. Eccentric is a word that comes to mind often."

Amanda giggled. "Eccentric is a good thing, it keeps life interesting."

April leaned over and kissed Amanda on the cheek. "That it does!" She blushed and kissed her back then the waiters arrived with dessert.

Later that evening Rachel and April, stood at the foot of the stairs that led to their apartments three flights up. April sighed. "God I hate having to climb these stairs in heels."

Rachel wrapped her arm around her shoulders and gave her a hug. "No more than me, babe."

Amanda turned from unlocking her apartment door. "You know, I think it's my turn to host the late night party. Why don't you girls stay with me tonight."

Rachel smiled. "That sounds interesting, a slumber party?"

April nodded. "Can we bring anything?"

Amanda stood in her doorway and wore a mischievous grin. She walked over to the two girls standing near the stairs and whispered. "Just your luscious bodies cause I'm all worked up and I want to play."

April slipped off her heels and started up the stairs. She glanced back at Rachel with a grin. "Race ya."

They scampered up the three flights trying not to giggle. A minute or two later, and slightly winded, they opened their apartments and dashed in to change.

Ten minutes after that they both emerged onto the third floor landing wrapped in warm fuzzy robes and wearing slippers. Rachel pulled April into a hug. "God I love you, babe. Meeting you was the luckiest day of my life." She pressed her lips against April's and she tasted cherry-flavored lipstick as she slipped her tongue between her lips. "Mmm, you taste good."

"So do you." April leaned back from her embrace. "But we had better head back down before Amanda accuses us of starting without her." April could feel Rachel's cock press against her thigh through the thickness of her terrycloth robe.

Rachel pulled her close and moaned into her ear. "I'm so going to have my way with you tonight, my love. All I thought about during dinner tonight was how much I wanted to be in bed with you and my little munchkin."

April giggled. "Me too, and Amanda kept squeezing my thigh. There must have been something in the water."

Rachel stepped away and offered her hand to April. They both walked back down the three flights of stairs silently in slippers. A couple of minutes later they knocked softly on Amanda's door then slowly opened it.

Inside, the room was mostly dark, except for a dozen or so flickering candles sending dancing shadows across the room. Standing near her bedroom door with her hands covering her crotch, Amanda posed coquettishly wearing a sheer pink baby doll negligée. Her feet were adorned with five-inch pink stilettos heels fastened with a tiny ankle strap. Her hair was pulled up and curls cascaded around her face. She'd added sultry false eyelashes and some dark, sexy makeup. The total ensemble made her look dangerous.

April's mouth dropped open. "My God girl, you look hot."

Rachel stared into her eyes as she shut Amanda's door. "Totally. I don't ever remember seeing you look this hot, Amanda."

"That's because tonight I have a special surprise for both of you." Amanda removed her hands from her crotch and a large pink strap-on dildo dropped into view. "Tonight is my turn to top and I'm going to have my way with both of you." She leaned against her bedroom door and it opened behind her as she stepped back.

Inside, her bedroom was filled with more candlelight. The window shades were drawn closed and the bed covers were pulled off. Amanda sashayed across the room; her long pink phallus bobbed and weaved with every step. She turned and looked at both girls standing in the doorway. Then she lifted her hands and gestured for both of them to join her.

Amanda knelt down on her bed as Rachel and April removed their robes and slippers. They held each other's hands as they walked towards Amanda and stood at the foot of her bed, now wearing only their negligées. Their eyes were gleaming with passion.

Amanda pulled gently on the string that held her skimpy nightgown in place. It quickly released and the sheer fabric floated off her body. With a simple gesture, the silky fabric floated across her arm then spilled off the bed and onto the floor. She raised her arms and both girls fell into her embrace. "I love you two so much," was all she could say before she was smothered in their kisses.

Rachel sat up and pulled on the drawstring of her negligee. She leaned over the edge of the bed and let it fall on top of Amanda's. She reached over to the nightstand and opened a drawer. She pulled out a bottle of lubricant and a condom as April pushed Amanda down on her back and began to lick and suck on her nipples.

Amanda cooed under the delicate touch of April's tongue and she squirmed beneath April's caress of her clitoris while she watched Rachel open the bottle of lubricant and slipped the condom over her silicone cock.

Rachel rubbed a thick coat of lube on Amanda's strap-on cock with a devilish gleam in her eyes. She lifted her leg and straddled the dildo, slowly impaling her body as April reached over to switch on the vibrating phallus.

Watching Rachel slowly engulf Amanda's cock, April untied her negligée and let it fall off the bed as well. Then she pulled her stiff cock out of the confines of her panties. As she did so, Amanda's hand quickly began to stroke her penis, gripping it tightly while Rachel continued to move slowly up and down Amanda's silicone shaft.

The vibrations sent shivers up and down Rachel's spine as she felt the dildo fill her. She leaned forward and Amanda's hungry mouth sought her nipples. Rachel murmured her delight. "My God you fill me up my sweet sister, I could do this all night."

"Mmm, that was my plan, Sis, all night long." Amanda replied between kisses. "I've been waiting to do this forever."

April looked down at Amanda with a gleam in her eyes. "When did you buy that?"

"About a month ago." Amanda bit down on one of Rachel's nipples making her moan in ecstasy. "I was just waiting for the right moment to show it to you both." Amanda lunged upward and sent her silicone phallus deep inside of Rachel.

"Oh my God, this feels amazing. Deeper, Amanda, deeper."

April moved around behind Rachel and reached between the two girls to stroke Rachel's rigid cock while she used her other hand to push two fingers between Amanda's harness straps and into her dripping wet pussy.

As April stroked Rachel's beautiful cock she twisted her fingers around in search of Amanda's g-spot. The moment Amanda arched her back April knew she'd found what she was looking for. She pressed harder against the sensitive patch and Amanda screamed as she pushed her dildo deeper into Rachel.

Rachel was beginning to pant as her ass was reamed by Amanda's dildo and her own throbbing cock was swelling beneath April's tight grip. A moment later they both climaxed as Rachel sent her cum streaming across Amanda's chest to fall on her chin while Amanda squeezed and pushed April's fingers out of her pulsating pussy as her body rocked to a magnificent orgasm. They both collapsed on the bed, panting.

After a few minutes to catch their breath, they recovered enough to pull April down on her back. While Rachel shoved a pillow beneath April's butt Amanda pulled open a condom wrapper and slipped it on her silicone cock. Rachel picked up the bottle of lube and dribbled the slippery liquid onto Amanda's dildo and then on her own growing cock.

Amanda slipped between April's legs and slowly pushed the dildo into her ass as Rachel waited a moment until Amanda was settled before pushing her cock into Amanda's pussy.

They writhed in passion, Amanda's vibrating cock made April nipples tingle as Rachel pushed harder into Amanda. In a moment, Amanda could feel Rachel's cock swell then she felt her seed gush deep inside Amanda's vagina.

As Rachel softened she fell out of Amanda's pussy. She slipped off her and watched Amanda continue to thrust into April's ass.

Suddenly, Rachel watched a thought play across Amanda's face as she pulled her dildo out of April and unclipped the strap-on harness. She straddled April then she reached down to lift April's rigid cock and impaled herself on the rigid shaft. Her muscles tightened around April's cock and she began to milk her, coaxing her seed from her balls.

April's cock began to swell. She arched her back as she sent rope after rope of her cum deep inside of Amanda's vagina. Amanda, totally spent, collapsed between April and Rachel. She crossed her legs and clamped her pussy lips together tightly not wanting to loose a drop of the precious seed trapped deep within her vagina.

Rachel glanced across to the exhausted April trying to catch her breath. She leaned up on an elbow and gazed at Amanda's blissful expression. Then a curious thought occurred to her. "You're off the pill aren't you?"

Amanda blushed as she smiled sweetly and nodded. "I want your babies. I want a part of both of you to grow inside of me."

Rachel glanced across to April. The shocked expression on April's face grew into a wondrous smile as tears began to fall across her cheeks.

Huge tears began to fill Amanda's eyes as well. "I want to have your children, is that okay?"

Rachel looked down at Amanda and then to April whose face was glowing, her eyes glistened in the candlelight. She looked back to Amanda and nodded whispering, "Yes, thank you."

They kissed. They hugged. And they all fell asleep, blissfully entwined in love.

## =TWENTY-ONE=

Kim walked into Rachel's apartment the following Saturday to see all three of her friends standing around the island counter pulling on their coats. "Hi, I just got off work. Where's everybody going?"

Amanda dashed into the bathroom as Alex slipped on a pair of women's flats. "Shopping, want to join us?"

"Sure, what are you looking for?"

Amanda poked her head out of the bathroom with a toothbrush sticking out of her mouth. She pulled the toothbrush out and grinned. "For a new bed, one big enough for the three of us to romp and play. Ours just won't do anymore, its too small."

Kim's face flushed crimson and she shook her head with a grin. She was getting more accustomed to Amanda's teasing ways but the girl still shocked her sometimes. The thought of the three of them lying in a king-sized bed entwined together in passion was quite the mental image.

Rachel chuckled as she wrapped a scarf around Alex's neck. "Where are we going to store this mattress, Amanda? We haven't closed on the house yet and it will be too big to make into one of our apartments."

"I called the mattress store and they said they could store it for us until we close on the house. I told them it'd probably be a couple of weeks and they said okay. Come on, let's go." Amanda wrapped a scarf around Rachel's neck. "Bundle up sweetie, it's cold outside." Then she gave her a peck on the cheek.

Kim pulled her coat back on. "Those earrings are cute Alex, where'd you get them?"

Alex pulled on a smartly tailored camel hair women's coat he found at the Salvation Army Thrift Store. "I saw them at a little shop on Forest Avenue. It's a quaint little place and I love going there. They have a nice selection and I don't get weird stares from other women like I do at the big box stores."

"They look cute on you, take me there sometime. I like supporting small stores if I can.

Alex smiled and opened the door for them all. "Thanks Kim, maybe we can go there after class on Wednesday."

"Great."

They all filed out of Rachel's apartment and headed down the stairs to the foyer. As they reached the last step Tom Reilly poked his head out of his apartment door. "Hey girls, what's up?"

Alex managed to partially duck behind Rachel as they walked across the foyer towards the back door and the apartment parking lot.

Rachel turned and grinned at Tom. "Not much Tom. How's Nancy?"

"She's fine. Hey, can I talk to everyone for a

minute?"

They all stopped and turned towards Tom as Kim stepped aside. "Sure."

"I know you three are planning on moving out soon and I know you're all on month to month now. So, could you give me at least a month's notice on when you plan on vacating? I need to get an ad in Craigslist. There aren't too many students looking for something this time of year, and I want to be at the top of the list of those who are."

Alex buttoned up his coat and pulled the scarf up around his ears. "Sure Tom, we'll be happy to give you as much notice as we get from the bank."

"Thanks." Tom offered an awkward grin and closed his door softly as everyone else turned towards the back door and the apartment house parking lot.

The mattress store was on 21$^{st}$ street along with a collection of restaurants, antique shops and a few boutique stores. It was a trendy shopping area away from downtown without looking too suburban.

Twenty minutes after entering the store Amanda and Rachel fell onto a king-sized bed with a soft pillow top and sighed.

Kim glanced over to Alex and grinned. "I think they have found the one you're going to buy."

Amanda sat up and gestured towards him. "Come on sweetie, join us. Let's see if we all fit."

Alex climbed onto the bed and settled in between Amanda and Rachel.

Rachel reached over and pulled Amanda towards her squishing Alex between them. "Kim take a picture."

Kim snapped a few photos on her cellphone then Amanda got up and ran around to grab her.

Kim squealed with laughter as Amanda pushed her onto the bed between Alex and Rachel announcing, "see girls, there's plenty of room," as she flounced down beside them.

Kim sat up, her cheeks flushed with crimson. "Amanda my dear, Ray is already too much for me to handle so…"

Rachel leaned up on one elbow and swatted Amanda's shoulder playfully. "Stop teasing the poor girl Sis, she's turned three shades of red already. One of these days Kim is going to totally shock you Amanda and I only hope I'm around when it happens."

Alex laughed as he wrapped her arms around his sisters. "Me too, I'm sure it'll be spectacular."

A salesman walked over to stand near the foot of the bed and watch the girls with a smirk as he held out his hand. "Which card shall I put this on?"

## =TWENTY-TWO=

There was a light dusting of snow on the foothills that led up to the Pocono Mountains in western Pennsylvania. The roads were clear, as it wasn't quite cold enough for snow to stick for very long.

Wendy snuggled up to Kyle as he navigated his way along familiar roads. "It's so pretty up here sweetheart, I want to come back in the spring when everything is new."

Kyle flipped on his turn signal as he slowed to turn off the main road and onto a state highway. "It's really beautiful in May when the azaleas and dogwood are in bloom."

"Next time we'll take the roadster. Country roads are made for convertibles."

Kyle smiled blissfully as he glanced over to watch this beautiful woman take in the beauty of the country. He was glad Wendy liked the outdoors. A lot of city girls are just not cut out for a life beyond condos and upscale restaurants. Wendy seemed so at peace in this world. She seemed to relax the moment they left the freeway.

"I suppose I should brief you a little about what you can expect after we arrive. My family is probably one of the reasons I never had too many girlfriends from my hometown. They are a bit, well, for lack of a better word, eccentric as I've said before. They can be a handful sometimes."

He turned off the main highway onto a paved county road.

"Norma is my mother. She lives with my uncle, Willie, along with his two sons, Henry, we call him Hank and he's a cop, and Willie Jr., who works as a mechanic at a body shop in town."

"My mom had four children. Twins, me and Candace, who was born Kenny, Annie who married Tom Andrews, a dairy farmer, they live near Lancaster, and finally Tommy who's just finishing high school this year and plans to go into the Army this coming July."

"Everybody sort of just gets along, no great aspirations, just a desire to live happy and healthy I suppose. My uncle Willie is a handy-man-carpenter, odd jobs sort of guy. There probably isn't a home for fifty miles that he hasn't fixed something in it one time or another."

"Norma, my mom, is a nurse at the community hospital in Mount Pocono. She's been there for nearly twenty years. I keep asking when she's going to retire but since Dad died three years ago she just shrugs her shoulders and smiles. I think she likes it too much."

Wendy gazed out the passenger window watching the world whiz by. "So just you and Candace were the ones with the wanderlust?"

"I suppose so, although from the sounds of it,

some of it rubbed off on Tommy."

Wendy leaned over and kissed him on the cheek then she rested her head on his shoulder as he drove up the twisted little highway further into the mountains. She fell blissfully asleep.

A half hour later Kyle pulled into a gravel driveway that led up to a simple two-story home that had a country farmhouse appeal to it. He nudged Wendy and she sat up wiping the sleep from her eyes.

"Hey sleepyhead, we're here."

As they approached the house they could hear arguing inside. They climbed the porch stairs and stood outside the screen door. Kyle whispered to Wendy as he pointed to the two standing in the center of the living room. "That's my uncle Willie and his niece, my cousin, Martha Johnson.

Martha stood in the middle of the room with her hands on her hips, a defiant scowl on her face. "What do you mean that's not crazy? Who teaches their boys to pee on trees in public? In the school yard no less?!"

A pleasant faced woman with wisps of grey hair swirling around her face turned to see two people walk in through her front door. "That's all right Martha, we won't say anything more about it. Hello Kyle, is this your girlfriend Wendy?"

Kyle ushered Wendy through the foyer and into the living room. "Yes, Wendy, Mom, Mom, Wendy."

Wendy shook the hand that was extended and smiled sweetly. "Hello Mrs. Upton, I glad to meet you."

Norma patted her hand. "No ceremony here dearie, call me Norma."

Kyle dropped their bags near the hallway stairs.

"Hi Martha, Uncle Willie." He turned and whispered to his mother. "What did Uncle Willie do now?"

Willie turned to Kyle; his voice was filled with bluff and bluster. "I only told her boy Rodney, that no matter where you are in this world, you have to have a whizzing tree, what's wrong with that?"

"My son is not a bear in the woods, Willie, my side of the family does not condone public urination in Philadelphia."

"This isn't Philadelphia Martha, it's Swiftwater, and it is in the woods."

"Aargh! Stay away from my Rodney, Willie, or next time I am calling the cops."

"All right Martha." He pulled out a small notepad and scribbled a note. "Here's Henry's number if you need to call him." Willie turned to Wendy and winked. "My boy's the duty sergeant tonight and he could use an excuse to visit. It gets pretty boring most nights down at the police station."

Martha flipped the note over her shoulder and stormed off slamming the screen door on her way out. Kyle could hear her muttering about old coots with no sense of decency.

Uncle Willie turned to Wendy. "Don't worry, Martha's my sister's girl. She gets a bee in her bum about something and you just have to wait it out until the ride is over." He stepped closer and leaned in to take a closer look. "So you're Wendy. It's nice to meet you."

At that moment a woman strode out from the back bedrooms dressed in a bra, pajama bottoms, and snow boots. She was carrying an ax as she walked through the living room towards the kitchen. Everyone paused as the woman strode across the room. "Denise, this is Wendy, Kyle's new girlfriend."

Denise waved the ax over her head as a welcome gesture without breaking her stride. Wendy watched her go through the kitchen and out the back door. The screen door slammed shut with a whack. "Where's she going?"

"To chop wood. Winter is nearly around the corner." Willie chuckled as he sat back down in a recliner and picked up the remote.

"She's on a mission. Denise is sort of my wife, although it's not official. We've been together now for nearly twenty years. I promised her a couple of year's back that we'd go to Las Vegas and make it official. She said we should dress up like Elvis and Priscilla and ride in the back of a limousine. I thought that sounded like fun."

He scooted around in the recliner and craned his head up towards Wendy. "Have you ever been to Vegas?"

"No, I never have been there."

"I think I've got enough saved up now so plan on it. They say you have to bring your own witnesses. Kyle, you up for a trip to Vegas?"

Kyle walked back out of the kitchen. "When would that be Uncle Willie?"

"Christmas...maybe."

"I'll check my calendar."

The television started blaring the roaring sound of racing cars. "Oh good, NASCAR's back on. One of these days we'll get our own cable so I don't have to keep borrowing it from my neighbor."

That night Wendy was in the guest bathroom while Kyle was downstairs talking to his mom. He walked into their bedroom to hear her whimpering in the bathroom as if she was in pain. Suddenly, "Shit, fuck, oh shit that hurts." This was followed by another whimper.

Kyle knocked softly on the bathroom door. "Wendy? What's going on? Are you in pain?"

"Don't come in here Kyle."

"Okay, I won't, but are you all right?"

"Yes, I'm just doing something that I hate to do and it hurts like a bitch sometimes. I'll be okay, just stay out please."

Kyle walked over to sit on the bed.

A moment later Wendy walked out of the bathroom carrying a small cloth bag. She blushed as she glanced into Kyle's eyes then she sat next to him on the bed. "I'm okay sweetie, it's just something I have to do everyday and sometimes it can be painful."

"Can you tell me what it is?"

"It's so embarrassing." She opened the small bag. Inside were several long cylinders that were shaped like dildos of various sizes. Only the cylinders were smooth and without the all the details that are common on silicone dildos. "I have to use these twice a day to keep me open and the larger ones really hurt sometimes. I've had to do this since my surgery."

Kyle looked at the small bag and then up into her eyes. "Why?"

"The doctor told me that if I don't my vagina will collapse. I know of a girl who had to have reconstructive surgery because she didn't do it and her vagina collapsed down to a little less than two inches. She couldn't have vaginal sex."

"Holy shit, is there something I can do to help?"

"No sweetie, just love me."

"That's easy, I already do." Kyle leaned over and kissed her lips gently. "So is this a permanent thing? Do you have to do this for the rest of your life?"

"Maybe, at least for a couple more years until everything settles down there." She stood up and put her small dilation bag back into her suitcase. "I've been doing some research and I discovered a procedure that allows for a permanent solution to my problem."

"You should do it then, I don't like to hear my girl in pain."

She curled her fingers and tickled his ears. "It'll mean a couple of months without sex, even masturbation."

He grinned sheepishly. "There's other things we can do while we wait."

She nudged his shoulder and pushed him back into the bed then she climbed on top and straddled his chest. "Hmmm, I'm willing to explore if you are."

The next morning sunlight filtered through the curtains in the guest bedroom and Wendy stretched as she woke up. That was undoubtedly the best night's sleep she had had in years. It was so peaceful up here in the woods. She looked around the room. The bathroom door was standing open so Kyle was probably downstairs.

She grabbed her robe and busied herself in the bathroom. She fixed her hair and dabbed on a little bit of makeup. As she got closer to the top of the stairs she could hear laughter and the clatter of dishes coming from the kitchen below.

Kyle appeared at the bottom of the stairs.

"Good morning beautiful, I was just about to come up and give you a wake up kiss."

Wendy began to step down the stairs towards Kyle. "How about I meet you half way?"

They met in the middle and Kyle wrapped his arms around her. "Good morning beautiful. Sleep well?"

"Like a baby, it's so peaceful here. I love it."

Kyle kissed her cheek again. "Then you wouldn't mind coming back for Tommy's graduation?"

"I wouldn't miss it." They turned and walked arm in arm down the rest of the stairs.

"Great! How about breakfast?"

"I'd love some, I'm famished."

In a quiet moment, while doing the breakfast dishes, Wendy managed to ask Norma what she thought about her daughter Candace?

"Oh she's terrific. She's working for a production company up in Albany right now. I heard they're working on one of those vampire TV shows. I forget which one. They're all the same to me. She's having the time of her life."

"I meant, what did you think when she told you she wanted to become a woman?"

"Oh, well, I was worried at first, we all were. People can be so cruel you know. But she has so many good friends here and in New York that we didn't worry too much, beyond what any mother worries for a daughter in the big city. So Kyle told you about her?"

"Yes he did." Wendy turned and leaned against the counter. "You see I've gone through a similar transition myself."

"You have? Goodness, I wouldn't have known if

you hadn't told me. You're quite lovely my dear."

"Thank you, Norma." Wendy dried a large platter and set it on the counter near a stack of plates. "And the family? Did they accept her decision?"

"Of course, once they understood it. We all did. But we kind of saw it coming so it wasn't a big surprise. Kenny, that was her name before she became Candace, was always awkward as a boy. And Kyle was always there to protect him. School children can be so cruel sometimes."

Wendy nodded sadly as Norma handed her another skillet to dry. "But when she transitioned she just blossomed. It was wonderful to watch her grow. Of course she had a few hard knocks in high school."

"I know, Kyle told me about one of them."

"You mean the one with that football player Kurt and his buddies?"

Wendy nodded.

"That was one of the worst that happened. Kyle was her protector in high school, he took a lot of abuse because of his twin sister but through it all he never uttered a word of complaint."

Norma lifted a large pot out of the soapy water. "You know, in a way, a change like that really tells a person who their true friends are, doesn't it? People who will stick with you because they like you for who you are not what you are, they are the ones you can count on."

Wendy nodded. "Yes, I think you're right." She glanced out of the kitchen window and watched Kyle help his Aunt Denise chop and stack wood.

Kyle's car wove down the narrow country highway, heading away from the Upton family home.

Wendy leaned her seat back and gazed languidly out the passenger window at the forest as it whisked by. On the radio, Aaron Copeland's "Appalachian Spring" filled the car with melodic tones that made the ride through the forest seem magical.

She glanced over and looked at Kyle as he maneuvered through a narrow country one-lane bridge. What an amazing man he was. Since she'd met him and her sisters Rachel, Amanda and April, her life had taken a complete turnaround.

April was right, my turn was coming and my Prince Charming was indeed waiting in the wings. She took a big breath and let it out slowly, closing her eyes to relish the sensation of just being with someone who really, truly loved her. Her eyes began to glisten. She dabbed the tears away and tried to settle her emotions.

"Do you think there might be a cabin up here we could rent for a week or two sometime in the spring or summer?"

"Of course, my cousin has a few cabins she rents out every summer to people. I could ask her."

Wendy smiled serenely as she returned her gaze to the passenger window. "Thank you, I'd like that."

"You know we have a standing offer to come back to my mom's place anytime we want."

"I know, but this would be just the two of us."

Kyle smiled and blushed slightly. "I'd like that," he whispered. He stopped at a stop sign and waited for a logging truck to rumble by.

Wendy reached over and squeezed his hand gently as he looked down the road for other traffic. Once the road was clear he turned onto the highway heading south and back to Wilmington.

She snuggled under a blanket she found in the backseat and smiled sweetly. Life was good. She finally understood that slogan.

## =TWENTY-THREE=

Amanda's legs were spread wide as Dr. Julian Rogers, her OB-GYN, hovered around. The first baby was nearly crowning as Amanda pushed again. Dr. Rogers sat down between Amanda's legs and lifted the sheet back. Several nurses stood by waiting for the first delivery.

"Oh fuck this hurts!" Amanda screamed, grabbing onto Alex's hand and squeezing tightly.

"One more push, Mrs. Wells, the first one is crowning, almost here," said Dr. Rogers.

Outside in the waiting area, Kyle and Wendy burst through the entry doors to find Kim and Ray sitting quietly in a corner.

"We just got back from Vegas an hour ago," said Kyle, breathless. It was a long overdue wedding adventure that Wendy and Kyle promised to witness for his Uncle Willie and his wife Denise.

Kim jumped up, followed by Ray, and they both hugged Wendy then Kyle. "Welcome home," Kim said with a big grin. "How was it?"

"It was a crazy ride," Wendy replied. "How's

Amanda?"

"Still in labor as far as we know. She went into the delivery room about four hours ago."

"Alex will let us know as soon as possible," Ray said gesturing for them to all sit down. "So…how was the wedding?"

Kyle laughed out loud and Wendy just beamed. "Picture a sixty year old man with a scraggly beard and a bad Elvis wig standing next to a woman who looks like she could chop down a tree with one swing of an axe. She was wearing a pink ball gown and a plastic Priscilla Presley wig. They were both leaning out of the moon roof of a solid gold Cadillac limousine screaming their heads off." Wendy shook her head in wonder. "It was priceless."

"Gotta love family," Kyle grinned.

"We're glad you're back," Kim added with another hug for Wendy.


As Amanda strained to push the first baby out there was a brief pause between contractions. She looked over to Alex sitting nearby. He was holding her hand, and coaching her to breathe. Her mind flashed to everything that had led up to this moment, from the look on his face as her stuff was dumped on the front lawn of Reilly's apartment house to the moment she pulled him into her to conceive this child.

Tears began to fall as she thought of Alex standing in the middle of Tom Reilly's backyard with his arms spread wide and a huge grin on his face. "I think you live a very charmed life, Amanda Simpson, you got a 'do-over'. It's what happens when the universe deals you a hand that is so terribly wrong that in one fell swoop things are reset and you get to start again fresh. You are very blessed Amanda, and that is nothing to be sad about." He finished his announcement with a flourish and a bow.

That moment faded into an image of Alex leaning into her old boss Simmons's face and hissing, "Believe me you little fuck, if you touch her I'll find you and fucking kill you," he whispered those words vehemently, barely audible, but loud enough for her to hear.

The impulse to push came once again and she squeezed his hand; then, as if to let her catch her breath, her contractions paused, albeit briefly.

She saw Alex dressed as April walking out of a shoe store in four-inch stilettos, her face flushed crimson. "You are simply too dangerous to shop with," April whispered through clenched teeth. "I was so incredibly embarrassed when that clerk fondled my ankles."

"Oh pooh," she remembered replying with a smirk. "Tell me you didn't enjoy all that attention. You probably made that poor boy's week."

She closed her eyes and screamed as the baby pushed harder against her vaginal wall. "Ffffuuuuuuuucccccckkkkk!"

"Hold on Amanda, sweetheart, you're almost there," Alex said using his free hand to dab her forehead with a damp cloth.

She looked up at him and smiled always wanting to remember this moment as she pushed harder. "Oooohhh Mmmmyyy Goddd!" And then release. The baby slipped free of her womb and into the waiting hands of her doctor.

The first child was born.

"It's a girl," Mrs. Wells," said Dr. Rogers and the delivery room was filled with the wailing of a newborn child. "And she's a screamer!"

"That girl has a healthy set of lungs," said a nurse holding the remains of the umbilical cord.

"Do you want to cut the cord, Mr. Wells? It's customary these days," Dr. Rogers said offering Alex a pair of surgical scissors.

Alex moved over closer to his daughter held gently on her mother's belly as she screamed her head off. He took the scissors from Dr. Rogers and snipped the umbilical cord where the nurse indicated while the doctor quickly tied it off. Then the baby was passed to a second delivery nurse to be wrapped in swaddling and wait for her sibling.

"It looks like it's time for number two," said the nurse.

"The second one is nearly here, Mrs. Wells," the doctor said taking up her position in front of Amanda. "I can see the crown."

Amanda looked across to Rachel. She reached out to hold her hand as she pushed again. She remembered the first moment when Rachel marched across Alex's room and shoved Amanda's hand into her crotch. "Still want to be my friend?" Rachel demanded. She remembered the piercing glare from her eyes that suddenly glistened as Amanda grinned and said, "yes, I do."

She remembered watching Rachel, wearing a soft and flowing nightgown, walk softly across the living room floor of her apartment to kneel down in front of Amanda and Alex. Rachel leaned forward and laid her head into Amanda's lap as Amanda gently brushed Rachel's hair out of her eyes.

"I wish it could always be like this moment," murmured Rachel sweetly.

"So do I love," she whispered. "So do I."

She thought of Rachel bawling her eyes out when Alex got stabbed and hovering like a mother hen when Wendy brought Kyle to meet the family. Finally, she remembered the moment of recognition when Rachel understood what Amanda had done the night the three of them made love nine months ago.

Rachel glanced across to an exhausted April trying to catch her breath after such intense lovemaking. She leaned up on an elbow and gazed at Amanda's blissful expression. Then a curious thought played across her face. "You're off the pill aren't you?"

Amanda remembered blushing as she smiled sweetly and nodded. "I want your babies. I want a part of both of you to grow inside of me."

Rachel glanced across to April. Amanda could see the shocked expression on April's face grow from surprise into a wondrous smile as tears began to fall across her cheeks.

Huge tears began to fill Amanda's eyes as well. "I want to have your children, is that okay?"

Rachel looked down at Amanda and then to April whose face was glowing, her eyes glistened in the candlelight. She looked back to Amanda and nodded whispering, "Yes, thank you." How her eyes glistened the moment she understood the enormity of the gift that Amanda wanted to give to her and Alex.

"Holy Mother Of Goooooodddddd!!!!"

The second child slipped from her mother's womb and landed gracefully into the waiting arms of Amanda's doctor.

"It was another girl," Dr. Rogers announced gleefully.

"And another screamer," added a nurse nearby with a wide grin

"It apparently runs in the family," Alex said laughing as he watched the doctor place the second child on her mother's belly.

"Time to cut the cord, Mr. Wells," said Dr. Rogers.

Alex glanced over to Rachel and smiled. "I think it's Rachel's turn."

After the cord was cut the babies were wrapped in swaddling and the nurses took both babies to the weighing station to run a series of tests. "Both girls are nearly seven pounds, which is good. Responses are positive, everything checks out well," said the delivery nurse.

Shortly after that, Amanda was moved to her hospital room to recover.

"Rachel, would you stay with Amanda while I stop outside for a minute to let the rest of the family know what's going on?"

Rachel nodded and looked down at her sleeping wife. "She's going to be a beautiful mother, isn't she?"

"Our children are blessed," he said as he slipped quietly out of the room.

Alex walked through a set of double doors into the waiting area to find everyone sitting quietly.

As he entered the waiting area Wendy was the first to rush up and hug him. "Well Dad, what's the news?" Kyle, Kim and Ray joined her standing around Alex.

"Two beautiful girls, both healthy and real screamers, according to the nurses," Alex said with a chuckle. "They're both nearly seven pounds which is good, and their mother is recovering in her room. The doctor said it would be a little bit before she's ready for guests, but it shouldn't be too long. I'll let you know as soon as she's ready."

"Congratulations! We can't wait to give her a hug," Kim and Wendy replied almost in unison.

Amanda opened her eyes and saw Rachel sitting in a chair nearby. She was nodding off, trying to stay awake. It had been a long night of labor and delivery. Then she looked up to see Alex come back into the room.

"Hi sweetie, how's the mother of my children doing?"

"I'm exhausted beyond description, but blissfully so," Amanda replied softly.

Rachel, roused from her slumber, reached forward to caress Amanda's forehead, pushing back a damp strand of hair. "Are you okay, hon? Can I get you something?"

Amanda sighed and shook her head. "Just stay with me that's all I have ever wanted."

"Forever, Sis, forever."

Alex pulled a chair over and sat down. "The delivery nurse just asked me for the names of the girls. I know we talked the other night but..." Then Alex shrugged.

Amanda smiled then she looked over at Rachel, took her hand and gave it a squeeze. "I thought a lot about it after our discussion the other night. If I ever have a choice," she began slowly, "I'd like to name my first born girl Ella, after my grandmother." She turned to Rachel. "Rachel?"

Rachel glanced at Amanda then to Alex who nodded with a smile. "If I have a choice I'd like to name a girl Abigail, after my aunt who took me in and cared for me like I was her own when I was kicked out of my home."

"Those are both beautiful names," Alex said as he leaned back in his chair. "Then, shall I tell the delivery nurse that Ella and Abby would love to see their mother as soon as they're able?"

"Thank you," Amanda and Rachel whispered, their eyes glistening with tears.

Two weeks after Amanda returned from the hospital they had a baby shower and Rachel, Amanda, and Alex invited all their friends over for a big backyard bash in the Tom Reilly style of backyard bashes. Of course that included Tom and his wife, Nancy, Wendy and Kyle, Margaret and her husband Carl, some people from Amanda's job, some folks from Rachel's job, a couple of students from school, Kim and Ray of course, and Inez from the convenience store.

Amanda chuckled about their new neighborhood. She met several of the neighbors and there seemed to be a bit of confusion on their part. "The neighbors can't figure out if three girls live here or two girls and a boy or three girls and a boy."

"Every neighborhood has at least one or two old snoops. My neighborhood has at least a half dozen!" Amanda exclaimed coming into the house one day. "It's like we live on Wisteria Lane for God's sake.

The party was in full swing. Alex had installed a

fire ring, like the one Tom Reilly had in his backyard, but learning from Tom, he set it far enough away from the deck so as not to catch anything on fire. Kim and Ray sat tending the bonfire and several of Kim's friends from the college joined them. Alex hadn't met them before as they were mostly first years.

Tom Reilly commandeered the grill, flipping burgers and hotdogs like a master chef. Nancy, his wife was helping Amanda and a couple of her friends from her office with the salads as Alex brought out another cooler filled with iced down beer. It was looking to be a great party.

The phone began to ring. "I'll get it," Rachel shouted as she dashed into the kitchen and grabbed the house phone off the cradle.

Rachel stood in stunned silence as the person on the phone spoke to her. Alex glanced at Amanda and gestured to take his hand then he led her into the kitchen to stand next to Rachel.

"Yes, thank you doctor, I understand," murmured Rachel. She held the receiver a moment then replaced it in the cradle on the counter. "That was Doctor Barnes, my mom's doctor in Springfield." Alex took Rachel's hand and led her to a chair at the kitchen table. Rachel sat dejected.

"The doctor said that my mom had fallen again and that she was in the hospital with a fractured hip."

Amanda pulled another chair up and sat down to hug Rachel.

"He said she couldn't be on her own anymore. She has moments of disorientation that may lead to blackouts. It hasn't happened yet, but it could." Rachel looked into Alex's eyes then she hugged

Amanda. "I don't know what we are going to do. She can't afford assisted living and she's too active for a nursing home. Even that would be a stretch on our income."

Alex ran his hand across her shoulders as she began to cry softly. "I have no choice. I'm going to have to move to Springfield and back in with my mom. This sucks!" She shouted then buried her face in Amanda's shoulder.

"It's okay, everything will work out, okay?" Amanda softly stroked Rachel's hair. "This will always be your home, my love, even when you're living far away."

Rachel glanced up at Amanda then at Alex. "But what about the mortgage?"

"It's not an issue love, I'll cover your share until you come back," Amanda said.

"I don't know when I'll be back, it could be years!"

"It's okay, sweetheart, we're in this together, right? We're a family, that's what families do, they help each other," Amanda murmured as Alex nodded.

The rest of the evening was much more somber, there were still moments of merriment but overall; the spirit of the evening was dampened by Rachel's news. Before the evening was over Alex and Amanda decided privately to follow Rachel up to Springfield next Friday and see what they could do to help.

The next morning Alex and Amanda drove Rachel to the airport. At the security gate they both gave Rachel a big hug. Wendy and Kyle were watching the twins.

"Don't forget to call us the minute you get to the

hospital. We both want to know what's going on," Alex said giving her another kiss on the cheek. "Promise?

Rachel nodded. "I'm going to miss our twins!" She kissed Amanda again then she turned to enter the security area. A moment later she disappeared down the concourse and was gone.

The following Friday, Amanda and Alex traveled to Springfield to visit with Rachel and her mother Rhea. The twins were nestled in car seats strapped securely in the back.

Amanda glanced over to Alex as he drove up the freeway towards Springfield. "Did Rachel say anything to the law firm about leaving or quitting or anything?"

"I don't think so, it all happened too fast. I think she's taking some vacation time this week. She might be planning on turning in her notice next week." Amanda gestured off to the right. "I think that's the exit."

In fact, Rachel hadn't quit her job yet, and Alex was right, she was on vacation time at the moment. It was her plan to give the law firm two weeks notice after she flew back down at the end of the following week. Meanwhile she was in the middle of making arrangements for her mother to have weekly in-home care when Alex and Amanda arrived.

"I'm sorry," Rachel said to the receptionist on the phone, "someone's at the door. Can I call you back in a few minutes? Thanks." She hung up the phone and walked to the front door. As she opened the door she was greeted with a huge hug from the Alex as Amanda shoved one of the twins into her arms and hugged her as well.

"What are you guys doing here?"

"What do you think, dummy," said Amanda strolling into the living room like she lived there. "We're here to help out. Now where's your mom? We'd like to finally meet her."

"Mom, we have company," Rachel shouted as she led Alex and Amanda through the hallway to the back bedroom.

What they found was a spry old woman who was full of spunk but her body was failing her. Her eyes still had the glow of someone full of life while her hip was the only thing holding her back, but only for the moment.

As Alex walked into her bedroom it dawned on him that Rhea should return with them to Wilmington and live in the family home until they can find an assisted living facility to fit her budget.

"You know," he said, "There are a lot of new programs that offer assistance to the elderly on fixed incomes. "

"Besides," said Rhea, nodding, "I want to see more of my grandkids!"

"Excellent idea," Amanda said as tears began to stream down Rachel's face. "I'll start on the arrangements this afternoon. We can look into selling this home as soon as your mother is settled into ours."

Two weeks later, with Rhea comfortably ensconced in the former guest room, Amanda woke up from a much-needed nap. She walked out into the hallway and looked around. The house was way too quiet. By now, the twins should be screaming their heads off needing to nurse. She wondered where Alex and Rachel were? She remembered that she mentioned something about having to supplement the twin's feeding with formula; although she hated the idea. Maybe they went out to buy some.

She walked down the hallway that led to the nursery and quietly opened the door. Inside, Alex and Rachel sat rocking, each with a twin nursing at their breasts.

She tiptoed into the room and whispered softly. "How did this happen?"

Alex smiled as he looked down at baby Ella nursing on his breast. "Two weeks ago I just started producing milk," he said as he glanced over to Rachel. "She always has had some milk but about a week ago her breasts began to really produce. So, we thought, since you were exhausted we should help out. I hope you don't mind."

"Mind? This is brilliant!" Amanda raced over and hugged them both. "I was afraid that I wouldn't have enough and we'd have to go on formula. Oh, this is perfect!" She knelt next to Rachel and brushed a tiny curl out of Abby's face. She leaned forward and kissed her on the cheek as Abby nursed contentedly from Rachel's breast.

Amanda glanced over to Ella quietly suckling from Alex's breast and smiled. "Our children are truly blessed."

"We can't let you have all the fun," Rachel said, her eyes twinkling.

Amanda's cellphone began to ring. "Hi Margaret," she whispered. She turned to Alex with a grin. "I'll just take this outside, you guys are marvelous." She stepped to the door and opened it quietly. Then shut it behind her as she walked into the living room and stood in the middle of the room.

"Okay, what's up? Late afternoon calls on a Sunday are pretty rare."

"Carl and I are moving."

"What?"

"Several of the senior staff members in Seattle are retiring and we need to move part of our operation to Seattle. At first I thought we could send you out as a senior analyst but Carl had a better idea."

Amanda staggered a bit as she sat down on the couch.

"Carl thought it a better idea if I were to spearhead the Seattle office and leave you in charge of our fifteen employees here in Wilmington. We can shift our focus to international sales on the east coast as well. Plus, there's no need to be in New York when it's only an hour away by train and everything is done electronically anyway."

"But…" Amanda stuttered, struggling with the curve that Margaret just threw her.

"Everybody loves you here, they already work more for you than they do for me."

"That's not true!" She protested as Rachel and Alex walked into the living room, an expression of concern on their faces.

"Yes it is and you know it. This is perfect! Carl has been after me to move to the west coast for decades but I always resisted it because of my job here. You, my wonderful protégé, are my ticket to martial bliss and a larger share of the market! Besides, most of your clients are on this coast."

"But…"

"No buts dear, I'll send you an email this afternoon with more details. Kiss your babies for me." The phone clicked silent when she hung up.

Amanda looked shell shocked.

Alex sat down on the couch next to her, Abigail on his shoulder ready to be burped. "What happened?"

Amanda looked at Rachel then at Alex. "I think I've just been promoted to partner."

Rachel shifted Emma to her shoulder. "What?"

"In two weeks Margaret and Carl are moving to Seattle to head up the west coast operation leaving me to handle things here in Wilmington. You were so right Alex; I do lead a charmed life. You two, now four, are the best thing that could ever have happened to me."

Rachel and Alex grinned and the twins burped.

# =EPILOGUE=

Life goes on for the Wells' family. The twins are growing stronger and taller every day, Alex now writes feature articles for the Wilmington Times and Rachel still handles the accounts at the law firm. Amanda has moved into the corner office, her staff couldn't be happier. The international accounts have soared on the stock exchange and most of the firm's clients are ecstatic. Several curmudgeons complain that it's not like it was in the old days. Amanda shook her head. Well, you can't have everything.

Kim and Ray finished up their studies and Kim now teaches at the local community college while Ray stays at home with their new baby (yes, their bundle of joy arrived last month and the family is overjoyed. He is working on his first novel).

Rhea volunteers at the community center, and Wendy is finally planning that wedding she always wanted, only this time with Kyle.

As Alex once said in Riley's backyard so many years ago: our life is blessed, we all got a fantastic do-over.

\* \* \*

It's been three years and the family is gathered on the front steps of their home on a sunny day in June. It's a birthday party. Everyone is there. Wendy and Kyle brought their two adopted children, Jin Lee and Lilly, two sisters from China, Ray and Kim are there (Kim is pregnant with a boy, their second), and Alex/April, Rachel, and Amanda with the two twin birthday girls, Ella (after Amanda's grandmother), and Abigail (after Rachel's aunt).

They are gathered for a family photograph on the front steps of their home. It's a beautiful day, a snapshot of life.

Alex, in addition to doing print advertising for Amanda's firm and working at the Wilmington Times, got his first novel, *"Stray Cats"*, published with a small publisher who focuses on books and anthologies dealing with gender issues. Rachel's mother moved to an assisted living facility nearby so she could still be close to her grandkids. Rachel opened the doors on her own accounting firm two months ago. She still handles the books for Amanda's firm but in addition she has several new clients.

Kim and Ray graduated two years ago. Ray is still working on his first novel while watching the kids and Kim teaches part-time while writing feature articles for a local online community based e-magazine.

The children are beautiful, and love is abundant.


Life is good.

Stray Cats

## A NOTE TO THE READER:

This story is a work of fiction. All of the characters, their names and the places that they visit, are purely from the imagination of the author. Any resemblance to persons, places, or things is not intentional and purely coincidental.

If you believe in coincidence I'm happy for you. However, if you read my other works you know that I do not, but the lawyers like to see that word in there anyway.

Thank you for reading my work, I hope you enjoyed it. If this is the first time you've read one of my stories, welcome. I hope you take a look at the rest of the work that I've published on Amazon and at other online sites like Smashwords.com. If you are a returning reader, welcome back, it's nice to see old friends.

If you liked what you've read please leave a review. It helps support my work as an author.

# ABOUT THE AUTHOR:

GUY WINTERS is a writer, playwright, and artist, who spends his days working in Virginia, and his evenings writing.

**If you're into paranormal romance, checkout these newly release novels,**
### Vampire Rain
After his wife died, Alex thought his life was permanently on hold until he met a girl considering suicide as she sat in the rain. Emma forever changed his life. She was the beautiful Vampire Halfling he met that night. From the mundane world of academia, he's thrust into a violent struggle for survival in a battle between vampire and dhampir. PG-13 for language and violence.

*Vampire Rain* is a story about vampires, and it's a story about trust.

But most of all, It's a story about love.

or
### Vampire+Love
Ian McIntyre thought his vampire romance book was just a lark, a romantic adventure with a twist. He knew that vampires were a myth. He brushed off would be admirers with a scoff, "Vampires are just a figment of our imagination." And that's what he thought, until he met one.

Dangerous and beautiful, Naomi is an intoxicating combination that even he couldn't resist, and she needs his help. PG-13 for language and violence.

**They are available at Smashwords.com and other fine eBook distributors.**

**Other erotic novels by GUY WINTERS include:**
*Once Upon A Bite So Sweet,*
Enjoy this adult romp of a vampire tale with a quirky twist. Forget the myths, they're all wrong. The vampires are more human; the sexual tension between Alicia and Jacob is electric; and Jacob's worldview has just taken a quantum leap. Vampires with a moral imperative! Go figure!

An adult novella with explicit sex and language.

Not intended for readers under 18 years of age.

### *Sleeping on the Terrace*

What started out as a hot day to be without an air conditioner ended in romance for Jason even if he got his toenails painted red by his new neighbor. This is a new adult romantic comedy from the desk of Guy Winters that contains adult situations and language not suitable for readers under the age of 18.

### *Dark Places*

A romantic story of a college professor who doesn't quite know how lonely his life has become, searching for a transgendered women to interview for his thesis project. Suddenly running into someone who makes him understand just what kind of a job he's bitten off. She propels him into far darker places than he was really ready to be taken.

An adult novel with explicit sex and language, not intended for readers under 18 years of age.

**They are available at Smashwords.com and other fine eBook distributors.**